THE FLEET STREET MURDERS

Christmas 1866, and the amateur sleuth Charles Lenox, recently engaged to Lady Jane Grey, is happily celebrating the holiday. Across London, however, two journalists have just met with violent deaths – one shot, one throttled. Lenox soon involves himself in the strange case, which proves more complicated as he digs deeper. However, he must leave it behind to go north to Stirrington, to fulfil a lifetime dream: running for a Parliamentary seat. Once there, he gets a further shock when Lady Jane sends him a letter whose contents might threaten their nuptials. Lenox must negotiate the complexities of crime and politics, not to mention his imperiled engagement.

THE FLEET STREET MURDERS

by

Charles Finch

Magna Large Print Books
Long Preston, North Yorkshire,
BD23 4ND, England.

British Library Cataloguing in Publication Data.

Finch, Charles
    The Fleet Street murders.

    A catalogue record of this book is
    available from the British Library

    ISBN   978-0-7505-3884-8

Published in Large Print 2014 by arrangement with
Little Brown Book Group Ltd.

Magna Large Print is an imprint of Library Magna Books Ltd.

Printed and bound in Great Britain by
T.J. (International) Ltd., Cornwall, PL28 8RW

To my father

ACKNOWLEDGMENTS

First thanks must go as always to my agent, Kate Lee, and my editors, Charlie Spicer and Yaniv Soha. All three of them are supportive and discerning, and this would be a lesser book without their aid.

Supplementing their work were two people I must thank: my mother, who can navigate the trickiest plot points and seems to understand my characters better than I do, and Emily Popp, who time and again tied together loose strings to tighten the structure and prose of this book. I'm so grateful to both of them.

A few notes: Berry Brothers and Rudd and Ye Old Cheshire Cheese are still in business. I highly recommend visiting both. The description of the London Mint is accurate, but I changed some of its internal architecture to suit the exigencies of the story. And lastly, while Stirrington is a fictional town, it has many real counterparts in Durham, and the events that occur there are, I hope, entirely authentic in their nature.

PROLOGUE

It was late in the evening, and a thin winter rain beat down over London's low buildings and high steeples, collecting in sallow pools beneath the streetlights and insinuating its way inside the clothes of the miserable few whom fate had kept outside. Inside Charles Lenox's house, however, tucked on a short lane just off of Grosvenor Square, all was warm and merry. It was Christmas and only a few short days from 1867. There had been a long, hearty meal, a delicious pudding, and more than a few glasses of wine, and now just two people, the amateur detective and his older brother, Sir Edmund Lenox, sat up, sipping short glasses of a digestive anise and reminiscing about holidays past, as men of their age, just on either side of forty, often will at Christmas. Animated disagreements and frequent peals of laughter filled the long, narrow dining room, as a fire died behind them. Midnight had long passed, and Edmund's wife and two sons were asleep upstairs. It was an hour since Lenox had walked his betrothed, Lady Jane Grey, back to her own house next door.

They looked alike, these two men. Both had brown hair, slightly curly, and handsome, kind faces. Edmund, who preferred rural to city life, possessed a haler and ruddier aspect, while Charles, who spent so much of his life pondering the enigmatic, seemed more thoughtful and more

11

introspective. Since the death of their parents, the two brothers had spent their holidays at Lenox House, their family's ancestral home in Sussex. This year, though, Edmund, who was the Liberal Member of Parliament for Markethouse, had been held in London by pressing political matters, and Charles had suggested they might alter their tradition and gather under his roof. He was especially happy that they did so because it was a kind of consecration of his very recent engagement to Jane, one of the oldest friends of both brothers. In all the happy hours since she had assented to his proposal, seeing her smiling face ranged among his family's at the candlelit supper table was the happiest. As he sat with Edmund now his heart felt full, his life blessed. It was wonderful.

Not very far away, however, was a different, unhappier scene. Near Savile Row a solitary man was sitting in a small but sumptuous apartment, decorated with gold clocks and hunting prints and bearing all the signs of bachelorhood that long tenancy can bestow on a set of rooms. A pair of mended trousers sat next to a half-full wineglass on the table before Winston Carruthers, writer and London editor of the conservative newspaper the *Daily Telegraph*. He was a short, fat, red man, wheezy and ill looking. Ignoring his landlady, who came in to rake the coals and shot him a look of hatred as she departed – a look not unusual for her countenance but more intense than usual, perhaps because it was Christmas Day – Carruthers wrote furiously on a large sheet of paper, turning and folding it again and again to fit all he had to say.

They would be the final words the journalist wrote.

'...iniquity not seen in this age or several since,' he scrawled and then with a great gesture of finality laid down his pen, blotted the paper, and leaned back in his chair to read it. He held the document very close to his face and several times just pulled it back in time to avoid covering it with his wet cough.

'Damn draft,' he said, looking about dis- agreeably. 'Martha? Is that you?'

There was no reply to his question, however, and he went back to reading, occasionally paus- ing to sip the hot negus that had gone lukewarm as he worked. Nearing the end of the sheet he began a short addendum.

It was as he wrote this that he heard a footstep behind him, and before he could turn he felt a sharp, rending pierce in the back of his neck. Futilely he clutched his throat. In an instant he had fallen to the floor.

Behind him a man moved quickly to look through the papers in the apartment, leaving noth- ing out of its place but nothing unchecked. At last he gently plucked from the still warm hand the broad sheet of paper Carruthers had been writing on.

In an aristocratic voice, the murderer said, without pity in his voice, 'Stupid sot. I hope you burn in hell.'

He put the paper back and fled to the open window, the one from whence the draft that had irritated Carruthers in the final moments of his life had come. The man unrolled a rope ladder and climbed down quickly. The apartment was only on the second floor.

After he was gone Martha came in, ignoring the body and the long knife protruding from its back, and went to the window, took the rope ladder back up, and after raking the coals again began the slow process of burning it, as downstairs her children slept.

At the same time about a mile across London, Simon Pierce was sitting at his desk in an austere-looking home office that seemed deliberately antithetical to the extravagant gold and mahogany of the rooms of Winston Carruthers. There were plain oak walls, ringed with a series of severe family portraits, and a very quiet sort of fire burning in front of two empty armchairs.

Technically Pierce was married, but he rarely saw his wife above once a fortnight. She was a fat woman of limitless vanity, who rather than minimizing her bulk by dressing plainly seemed more by the day to resemble a very loud floral-patterned sofa. Most of her evenings were spent at her father's house in Lamborn (which in simple honesty she wished she had never left, to make the obscure middle-aged marriage that was all her family's long lineage had been able to buy her). Pierce, on the other hand, often slept on the long cot in his office at the *Daily News*. There, unlike in his own home, he was a man of importance, the international editor and a frequent columnist on the editorial page. The couple had a daughter neither much cared for. At eighteen she had married and fled to India. They received twelve punctual and polite letters a year from her. The most recent had wished them a Happy Christmas, and given Pierce an unexpected and genuine pang for her. The softness of age, he figured. Simon Pierce was not far from his fifty-fifth birthday.

In looks he was tall, thin, and gray, with bifocals that forced him at all times to lean slightly forward. These made him particularly unpleasant to talk to at parties, where one felt inspected and analyzed at every conversational turn. The excellent free education at his school in Norfolk had paved his way to Oxford, and from there he went straight to London, full of ambition and a belief in hard work that had quickly been borne out by his career's trajectory. The *Daily News* was a liberal, if not radical, paper, in line with the views of its founder – Charles Dickens. Pierce had molded himself to the paper's beliefs, rather than the other way around. He was a powerful man now.

Unlike Carruthers, he was not writing on that Christmas evening but reading. The Bible was in his hands. Pierce was, unusually, a Roman Catholic. Even on Christmas he would probably have preferred the office to his home, but he had instead endured a long supper with his wife, who was full of her father's stories. After she had gone to bed he had come into his study restless. He took no wine and felt clearheaded.

Just as he turned to the first page of the Book of Matthew, Simon heard a soft knock at the front door of the house. The servants were asleep, and with a weary sigh he rose to his feet and made his way along the corridor between his office and the door. It was a sign of disrespect, he felt, that there

15

was no scurry of foot audible below stairs. It didn't occur to him to wonder why the visitor had knocked, which was sure to raise the notice only of someone nearby, rather than rung the bell, which would have sounded directly in the servants' quarters. Simon Pierce rarely felt entirely comfortable anywhere other than the office or church, and it was with anxiety that he approached the front hall.

He opened the door.

'Yes?' he said. Before him stood a squat, strong man. 'You'll find no alms here. Seek work.'

The swish of falling rain muffled their words.

'Don't need any,' said a distinctly unaristocratic voice. 'Have some.'

'How may I help you, then?'

'Mr. Simon Pierce?'

'Yes,' said Pierce with mounting worry. 'Who on earth are you?'

The man turned and looked up and down the street. One house was lit, its windows glimmering orange, but it was a hundred yards off. He took a gun from his belt and, just as Pierce stumbled backward in panic, rushed forward and shot him in the heart. The rain and a well-placed handkerchief stifled the sound of the bullet to some degree. Still, it was louder than he had expected. The squat man staggered down the steps and turned down an alley while Pierce was still on his knees, struggling vainly against death.

Half an hour later the murderer was in a different alley, in an altogether more refined part of town. He met a tall, blond, hearty-looking man, with an upper-class accent.

'It's done, then?'

16

'Yes, sir.'

'Here. Your payment. In addition to the debt – that's gone, as I promised,' he said, 'but only as long as you keep quiet. Do you understand?'

He thrust a purse jangling with coins into the squat man's hand and turned to leave without a word.

'And a merry bleedin' Christmas,' the shooter muttered, counting the money. His hands were still shaking.

Simon Pierce was the first man he had ever killed.

CHAPTER ONE

Lenox woke up with a morning head, and as soon as he could bear to open his eyes, he gulped half the cup of coffee that his valet, butler, and trusted friend, Graham, had produced at Lenox's first stirring.

'What are Edmund and Molly doing?' he asked Graham.

'Lady Lenox and her sons have gone to the park, sir. It's a fine morning.'

'Depends what you mean by fine,' said Lenox. He looked at his window and winced from the sun. 'It seems awfully bright. My brother's in as much pain as I am, I hope?'

'I fear so, sir.'

'Well, there is justice in the world, then,' Lenox reflected.

'Would you like me to close your curtains, sir?'

'Thanks, yes. And can you bring me some food, for the love of all that's good?'

'It should arrive momentarily, sir. Mary will be bringing it.'

'Cheers, Graham. Happy Boxing Day.'

'Thank you, sir. Happy Boxing Day, Mr. Lenox.'

'The staff got their presents?'

'Yes, sir. They were most gratified. Ellie in particular expressed her thanks for the set of–'

'Well, there's a present for you in the wardrobe if you care to fetch it,' said Lenox.

'Sir?'

'I would do it myself, but I doubt I could lift a fork in my present state.'

Graham went to the wardrobe and found the broad, thin parcel, wrapped in plain brown paper and tied with brown rope.

'Thank you, sir,' he said.

'By all means.'

Graham carefully untied the rope and set about unwrapping the paper.

'Oh, just tear it,' said Lenox irritably.

Nevertheless, Graham stubbornly and methodically continued at the same pace. At last he uncovered the present. It was a broad charcoal drawing of Moscow, which he and Lenox had once visited. Both of them looked back on it as the adventure of their lives.

'I hardly know how to thank you,' said Graham, tilting it toward the light. He was a man with sandy hair and an earnest, honest mien, but now a rare smile dawned on his face.

'I had it commissioned – from one of those

sketches you drew us, you know.'

'But far surpassing it in size and skill, sir.'

'Well – size anyway.'

'Thank you, sir,' said Graham.

'Well, go on, find out about breakfast, won't you? If I waste away and die you'll be out of a job,' said Lenox. 'The papers, too.'

'Of course, sir.'

'And Merry Christmas.'

'Merry Christmas, Mr. Lenox.'

Soon breakfast came, and with it a stack of several newspapers. These Lenox ignored until he had eaten a few bites of egg and bacon and finished a second cup of coffee. Feeling more human, he glanced at the *Times* and then, seeing its subdued but intriguing headline, flipped through the rest of the stack. The more populist papers positively screamed the news. Two of the giants of Fleet Street were dead, their last breaths exhaled within minutes of each other, according to household members and confirmed by doctors. Both the victims of murder.

Lenox picked up one of the papers at random. It happened to be the cheapest of the weekly Sunday papers, the threepenny *News of the Day*, a purveyor of shocking crime news and scurrilous society rumor, which had come into existence a few decades before and instantly vaulted to popularity among the London multitudes. Most men of Lenox's class would have considered it a degradation to even touch the cheap newsprint the *News* came on, but it was the detective's bread and butter. He had often found stories in the *News of the Day* that no other paper printed, about

19

domestic skirmishes in Cheapside, anonymous dark-skinned corpses down among the docks, strange maladies that spread through the slums. The paper had recently played a crucial role in reporting the case of James Barry. A famous surgeon who had performed the first successful cesarean section in all of Africa, he had died – and after his death was discovered to have in fact been, of all things, a woman. Margaret Ann, by birth. It had been for a time the story on every pair of lips in London and was still often spoken of.

SHOCK CHRISTMAS MURDER OF FLEET STREET DUO, the headline on the front page shouted. Eagerly, Lenox read the article.

The SHOCK MURDER of two of London journalism's finest practitioners has shocked London this morning. 'Winsome' Winston Carruthers, London editor of the Daily Telegraph, *and the CATHOLIC Simon Pierce of the* Daily News *died within minutes of each other on CHRISTMAS NIGHT. An unknown assailant shot Pierce in the heart at Pierce's South London home, waking his entire household and throwing his wife into fits of HYSTERIA, at approximately 1:07 A.M. this morning. No witnesses have contacted the Metropolitan Police: COME FORTH IF YOU SAW ANYTHING, readers.*

Not FIVE MINUTES before, according to police reports, scarcely an hour into Boxing Day, Winston Carruthers was STABBED in his Oxford Street apartments. Police found Carruthers STILL WARM after a resident of Oxford Street reported seeing a tall, disguised man climbing down a rope ladder!

Exclusively, the NOTD has learned that Car-

ruthers's landlady and housekeeper, a Belgian woman, was on the scene and cooperated with the police officers – *ONLY TO VANISH THIS MORNING*, leaving her apartments and their contents behind save for several small bags. Her two children left with her. Word has been sent to the ports of England with a description of the housekeeper. She is fat, with a prominent nose and a shriveled left hand. *IF YOU SEE HER*, readers, contact the police, or the NOTD's editorial offices.

According to *INSPECTOR EXETER*, reliable and much decorated officer of Scotland Yard, the housekeeper (name withheld at our discretion) is *NOT* a suspect: At the same brief moments of the murder and the murderer's absconding, she was witnessed by a few dozen people along Oxford Street visiting a local alehouse. *HOWEVER*, readers, she *MAY STILL BE AN ACCOMPLICE TO MURDER!* If you see her, contact the police.

CARRUTHERS, forty-nine, was a native of our fair city, a childless bachelor who leaves behind a sister in Surrey. *PIERCE*, fifty-four, leaves behind a wife, *BESS*, and a daughter, *ELIZA*, who is stationed with her husband in *BOMBAY*. The NEWS sends its sympathy to all of the bereaved.

ADDED FOR SECOND PRINTING: INSPECTOR EXETER has already cracked the case, according to a reliable source, and found a definite link between the two men *BESIDES* their profession. *WATCH THIS SPACE* for more.

Below this piece of sensationalism were two lengthier profiles of the men. Turning to the other papers, Lenox found much the same stories, with minor variances of biography. A shooting and a

21

stabbing, five minutes apart. He wondered what the 'definite link' between Carruthers and Pierce might be. Straightaway he thought it must be some story they had both covered. Perhaps he would try through covert means to discover what it was. A fascinating case, certainly – but did he have time to try to help solve it?

It was a busy period in Lenox's life. Recently he had solved one of his most difficult cases, a murder in Oxford, and been shot for his efforts. Only grazed, but still. After a long life of solitude, too, he was engaged to be married. Most pressing of all, soon he was to participate in a by-election for Parliament in Stirrington, near the city of Durham. His brother and several other Members of the Liberal Party had approached him to ask him to run. Though he loved his work as a detective and bravely embraced the low esteem in which the members of his class held his profession, to be in Parliament was the dream of his lifetime.

Still – these murders would be the great story of the day, and Lenox felt a longing to be involved in their solution. One of his few friends at Scotland Yard was a bright young inspector named Jenkins, and to him Lenox wrote a short query, entrusting it to Mary's care when the maid came to fetch the remains of his breakfast. He felt better for having eaten. A third cup of coffee sat on his bedside table, and he reached for it.

Just then Edmund knocked on the door and came in. He looked green around the gills.

'Hullo, brother,' said Charles. 'Feeling badly?'

'Awful.'

'Did eating help?'

'Don't even mention food, I beg of you,' said Edmund. 'I would rather face Attila the Hun than a plate of toast.'

Charles laughed. 'I'm sorry to hear it.'

'Molly had the heart to take the boys out earlier. Not even a word of reproach. What a treasure she is.' A sentimental look came into Edmund's eyes.

'Do you have meetings today?'

'Not until five o'clock or so. The Prime Minister has remained in town.'

'You said last night.'

'I need to sharpen up before then, to be sure. Perhaps I'll go back to sleep.'

'The wisest course,' Charles assured him,

'Then I'll have a bath and try to put myself into some decent shape. At the moment I feel like the offspring of a human being and a puddle on the floor.'

'Have you seen the papers, by the way?'

'What happened?'

'Two journalists were murdered last night – opposite sides of town within just a few minutes of each other.'

'Oh yes? Well, you've other things to concentrate on at the moment.'

'I do, I know,' said Charles rather glumly. 'I wrote Jenkins, though.'

Edmund stopped pacing, and his face took on a stern aspect. 'Many people are counting on you, Charles,' he said. 'Not to mention your country.'

'Yes.'

'You should spend this month before you go up to Stirrington meeting with politicians, granting interviews, strategizing with James Hilary.' Hilary was a bright young star in the firmament of Liberal politics and a friend of Charles's, one of those who had entreated him to stand for Parliament. 'This time can be quite as productive as any you spend in Durham.'

'I thought you were sick.'

'This is crucial, Charles.'

'You never did any of that,' the younger brother answered.

'Father had my seat. And his father. And his father. World without end.'

'I know, I know. I simply feel irresponsible if I stay out of things, I suppose. My meddling ways.'

'Just think of all the good we'll do when you're in the House,' said Edmund.

'Especially if we don't stay up late drinking.'

Edmund sighed. 'Yes. Especially then, I grant you.'

'See you downstairs.'

'Don't let them wake me up before I'm ready.'

'I won't. Unless it's nearing five.'

'Cheers,' said Edmund and left the room.

CHAPTER TWO

That afternoon Inspector Jenkins answered Lenox's note by visiting in person. Lenox was sitting in the long, book-filled room he used as library and study. Just down the front hall of the house, it had comfortable sofas and armchairs and a long desk, as well as a broad, high row of windows that looked out over Hampden Lane. The rain of the evening before had gone but left in its place a low, rolling fog that thickened over the streets of London. Lamplighters were out early, trying to provide the city with visibility.

Jenkins was young and clever. He wore glasses on his earnest face and had an unruly crop of light brown hair.

'How do you do, Lenox?' he asked and accepted a cup of tea. 'Exeter's not letting me near the case, so I thought I'd come by.'

'I know how he can be.'

'Oh, of course, of course.'

Inspector Exeter, a powerful man in the police force whose blunt tactics and lack of perception had both alienated him from the amateur detective and pushed him up through the ranks, was famously territorial about his cases and particularly disliked Lenox's occasional interference. Despite that, Exeter had had occasion to call on Lenox's skills and might not entirely reject his help if the case of the two journalists reached an impasse.

'What details did you keep out of the papers?'

'The Belgian housekeeper?'

'Yes?'

'Martha Claes, she's called. Apparently she had bragged to one or two of her friends that she was coming into a bit of money. We think the murderer paid her enough that she could leave.'

'That tells us something about the criminal, then.'

'What?'

'Well – that he would rather use money than violence. Not many criminals are that way, in my experience. Not many criminals have enough money to send three marginally genteel people out of London, leaving all their possessions behind. No robbery from Carruthers's rooms, I presume?'

'That's correct, actually, yes.'

'Probably he knew the household well enough to approach Mrs. Claes as an acquaintance.'

'You think the criminal had visited Carruthers?'

'Wouldn't he have had to? Simply approaching the man's housekeeper on the street would have been extremely foolhardy.'

'Yes, of course.'

'It seems more likely that he was visiting upstairs than downstairs, given that he offered Mrs. Claes money.'

'Of course assuming she didn't actually inherit it.'

'A lone foreigner in this country, without a husband? Then, too, if she had come by the money honestly, why run?'

'Fear?'

Lenox shook his head. 'I doubt it. The murderer is either very rich or willing to spend his last farthing to murder these two men. More likely the first than the second, I would wager.'

Jenkins took a note of this. 'Yes,' he said. 'We hadn't thought that through.'

'How is Exeter handling the matter?' asked Lenox.

'As he usually does,' said Jenkins without inflection, his loyalty in this instance to the Yard rather than his superior.

'With all the tact of an angry bull, then?'

Jenkins laughed. 'If you choose to say so, Mr. Lenox. He's roused every able-bodied stable boy and driver on the street to accuse them of the crime.'

Lenox snorted. 'A clever stable boy, to use a rope ladder rather than risk getting caught by servants who walk between houses every day.'

'Indeed,' said Jenkins. 'Though it backfired in the end, that cleverness – we found the ladder, after all.'

'What else?'

'One other thing about Carruthers.'

'Yes?'

'There were a pen and blotter on his supper table, both freshly used, and ink on his hands.'

'But no paper in evidence, I suppose you'll tell me. So the murderer was partly there to steal a damaging document.'

'He might have filed it away,' Inspector Exeter argued.

'Yes, yes, or brought it from his newspaper's office, or given it to a dove to fly to Noah's Ark with. I'm familiar with the inane pattern of thought Exeter might employ.'

'Well.'

Lenox sighed. 'I'm sorry. I oughtn't to talk like that.'

'No, perhaps not.'

'What about Pierce?'

'That's altogether more mysterious, actually. Nobody saw or heard a thing, other than the shot.'

'Nothing missing from his house?'

'No, nothing.'

'Do you read the *News of the Day*?' asked Lenox.

'Since you recommended I do so, Lenox, yes.'

'What was the "definite link" between Carruthers and Pierce?'

'Excuse me?'

'Ah – you must have gotten up early to get the first edition.'

'Yes, I've been up all night, trying to help.'

'According to the second edition of the *News* Exeter had discovered a solid link between the two men, aside from their careers.'

Jenkins looked uneasy. 'Oh, yes – that.'

'What was it?'

'It's sensitive information, in fact. I fear I must exact the traditional promise from you.'

'Nothing you say will leave this room,' promised Lenox gravely.

'According to Exeter, Pierce and Carruthers were two of the three journalists who gave testimony against Jonathan Poole at his trial.'

Lenox inhaled sharply.

The British government had executed Poole six years before for high treason. During the Crimean War, Poole, born an aristocrat but with a grandmother from the Baltic region, had spied on England for Russia. Poole's subordinate, an anonymous navy officer called Rolk, had written to three newspapers in England when he started to suspect his superior of treason. Before the letters made it home Rolk was dead – accidentally drowned, or so it appeared. By then Poole was already making plans to defect to Russia, but the British navy had apprehended him at the last moment. The trial had been a celebrated one, titillating both because of the high-ranking personages who spoke on behalf of Poole's character and the perceived heroism of poor Rolk. Three journalists had testified behind closed doors to receiving Rolk's letters. Apparently two of them were Carruthers and Pierce.

'Yes,' said Jenkins, as if to confirm Lenox's surprise.

'Have you looked out for the third journalist?'

'He died four years ago.'

'How?'

'Naturally, from all we could gather this morning. His widow didn't appreciate our questions. According to the coroner it was an entirely average death. In his sleep.'

'Still – Poole has been dead for years! I doubt most people have thought of him since it all ended.'

'Well – yes,' said Jenkins in a measured tone.

'What is it?'

'I'm not sure I should say before we've gathered all of the information we need.'

Lenox understood. 'Yes, of course.'

Jenkins stood up. 'At any rate, you'll know before anybody else.'

'Thanks so much for coming by. Let me know if you need help.'

'Any initial thoughts?' said Jenkins, walking to the door.

'Wait,' said Lenox. There was a pause.

'What is it?' asked Jenkins.

Lenox thought for a moment. 'I've got it.'

'Yes?'

'He had a son, didn't he? Poole?'

Jenkins stopped in his tracks. 'Oh?'

'I just remembered. Poole's son, he's back. He'd be nineteen, twenty, thereabouts, wouldn't he? His grandparents took him to the Continent, but there was a small item in several of the papers about his return. Living by St. James's Park.'

Jenkins sighed. 'What a prodigious memory you have.'

'Thanks.'

'We have no evidence whatsoever to link him to Pierce or Carruthers, though,'

'Christ. I wonder if he could have done it.'

'Inspector Exeter has sent out a canvass to find him.'

Lenox shook his head. 'Asinine. If you're to find him you must do it subtly.'

'I agree,' said Jenkins, shrugging.

'Well – good luck at any rate. Keep me informed, won't you?'

'I shall.'

'Good-bye.'

The inspector left, and Lenox sat in an armchair thinking. What puzzled him was the second murderer – for there must have been one, if the murders were so close together in time. How could Poole's son, who had been out of the country, know anybody in London well enough to enlist them in such a plot?

CHAPTER THREE

Two days later a mild late December sun set over Hampden Lane. Lenox sat with Lady Jane Grey on the sofa in her rose-colored sitting room – a chamber famous for the exclusivity of the evening gatherings it hosted and for its inaccessibility to all but Jane's favorite people – fixing his cuff links. She was telling him about the dinner party they were to attend that night.

Lady Jane was a lovely woman, with fine skin that in the sunless winter had gone quite pale, though her lips were ruby red. Her eyes were lively and gray, often amused but never cynical, with the generous cast of someone more accustomed to listening than speaking. Her intelligence shone out of them. A dark corona of hair was piled atop her head, precariously designed for the dinner party. Lenox liked it best when it shook down in curls across her shoulders, however. She dressed plainly and well; the widow of James Grey, Lord Deere, she had lived these fifteen years next door to Lenox, his closest friend in the world. Only recently, however, had he found the courage to declare his love – and found to his ongoing elation that she returned it.

Far more so than Lenox, she was a member of London's very highest society. In that caste there were two types of ruling women: those who campaigned, gossiped, and mocked, and those who through natural grace and intelligence gradually became arbiters of taste. Lady Jane belonged definitely to the second group. Her closest friends were Toto McConnell and the Duchess of Marchmain, and the three of them formed a triumvirate of power and taste. Their houses often hosted the defining parties of a season or the most select evening salons. Yet it was typical of Lady Jane that she was going to marry a man who would much rather be searching for clues in the alleyway of a slum than having supper in one of the palaces of Grosvenor Square. She never let her place in society determine her actions or thoughts. Perhaps that was the secret of having her place there to begin with.

This was the woman Lenox was to marry, whose counsel he valued above any other, and who was to his spirit both sun and moon, midnight and noon.

'Shall we take anything to supper?'

'Oh – yes – they asked me to bring wine, didn't they? Bother, I forgot.'

Lenox perked up. 'Let's go by Berry's,' he said.

'Charles, they deliver,' said Lady Jane, an exasperated look on her face. 'We'll send someone around, and they'll send the wine to Lady Nevin's.'

'But I like to go,' was his stubborn reply.

'Then go, and come pick me up on your way back.'

Lenox was not, as many of his friends were, much addicted to the charms of wine, but nobody could enter Berry Brothers and Rudd Wine Merchants for more than a few minutes without wanting immediately to lay down a few cases of Médoc or to rush off and lecture the barman at his club about the importance of grape variety.

The shop, its front painted a dark, rich green, and its vaulted Gothic windows bearing its name in yellow stencil, was dusty, old, and wonderful, located a few paces off of Pall Mall on St. James's Street. The darkened floorboards creaked over a cellar as valuable as any in private hands; at one end of the room was a scale as tall as a man, and beside it an old table crowded with a dozen quarter-full glasses of red wine, which customers had been tasting. Berry's had existed since 1698 and looked as if it would go on forever.

The place was largely deserted. One stooped old man – an oenophile, judging from the excited quiver of his nose over every bottle he smelled – was rooting through a case in the back, but the proprietor didn't pay him any mind, standing instead at the desk in front of his ledger.

Now, this ledger was famous. It was magnificently large, bound in the same hunter green that the shop was painted, and recorded the preferences and history of every client who visited the shop more than once. As soon as Lenox's face had appeared in the doorway, the man behind the ledger was riffling through it to find the *L* section.

'Hullo, Mr. Berry,' said Lenox.

'Mr. Lenox, sir,' said Mr. Berry, with a slight nod of his head. 'How may I be of service to you?'

Lenox put his hands in his pockets and frowned, looking around the glass cases that held the sample bottles. 'What do I like?' he said.

In general conversation this would be a peculiar

question, but Mr. Berry heard it a dozen times a day. 'What are you eating?'

'Probably beef.'

'You have two cases of the Cheval Blanc '62 laid down, sir,' he said.

Lenox frowned again. 'Does Graham know?'

Graham knew everything about wine.

'Yes, sir. I believe you purchased it under his advisement.'

'And I like it?'

'Yes, sir,' said Mr. Berry. 'You took two bottles of it to a dinner party in March. You said it was' – he consulted the ledger – 'tasty, sir.' This word repeated with faint disapproval.

'Well, better give me three bottles.'

'Straightaway, sir.'

This business soon transacted, Lenox and Mr. Berry spent a quarter of an hour discussing Scotch whisky, and before he left Lenox had tasted several samples and was feeling distinctly warm in his belly. He left with a bottle of the darkest sample he had tried, Talisker.

Lenox returned to Lady Jane's to find her ready and was enjoying a quick sip of the Talisker when there was a knock on the door.

It was Graham. Because Lenox and Lady Jane lived in houses that adjoined, their servants often popped back and forth to deliver messages.

'You have a visitor, sir,' said Graham.

'Damn. Who is it?'

'Inspector Exeter.'

'Oh, yes? Well, Jane, do I have time to see him?'

She looked over at the silver clock that stood on her desk. 'Yes, if you like,' she said. 'I'll order my carriage. That should take a quarter of an hour.'

'I'll be faster than that, I hope.'

Exeter was waiting in Lenox's study. He was a large, physically imposing man, who – to give him his credit – had evinced time and again tremendous physical bravery. Cowardice was never his flaw. Rather, it was that he was so hidebound and resistant to new ideas. He had a stubborn face, adorned somewhat absurdly with a fat black mustache. He was twisting the ends of this with two fingers when Lenox came in.

Well, thought Lenox, what will it be: a plea for help or a warning to stay out of the case? The two men stood facing each other. 'Mr. Lenox,' said Exeter with a supercilious smile.

Here to crow, then, thought Lenox. 'How do you do, Inspector? Good evening.'

'I expect you've been following the murders? The Fleet Street murders?'

'I have, certainly, with keen interest. I hope their solution progresses well?'

'In fact it does, Mr. Lenox. In fact it does. We have apprehended the criminal responsible.'

Lenox was shocked. 'What? Poole?'

Exeter frowned. 'Poole? How did you – never mind – no, it's a young cockney chap, Hiram Smalls. He's a short, strong fellow.'

'Oh?' he said. 'I'm delighted to hear it. How, pray tell, did he move between the two houses so rapidly? He flew, I take it?'

The smile returned to Exeter's face. 'We expect Smalls to give us his compatriot, after a few solitary days with the prospect of the gallows in mind.'

'Indeed,' said Lenox and nodded. 'How did you

35

find him?'

'Eyewitness. Always begin, Mr. Lenox – and I say this with the benefit of many professional years of hindsight – always begin with a canvass of the area. Now, that's something an amateur might find difficult, comparatively, given the resources in manpower and time of the Yard.'

Damn the man's insolence, thought Lenox. 'Indeed,' was all he said.

'Well, I thought I ought to let you know.'

'I thank you.'

'I know you've taken an interest ... an amateur interest in several of our cases and even helped us once or twice, but I wanted to tell you that this one is solved. No need for your heroics, sir!'

'I'm very happy for you.'

'Thank you, Mr. Lenox, most gracious. Well – and good day.'

'Good day, Mr. Exeter.'

'Enjoy your party.'

These words he said with as much sarcasm as he could muster, and then he nodded to Lenox and left.

'It's for the best anyway,' Lenox muttered to himself as he poured a glass of sherry at his side table. It was time to focus on politics, after all.

The dinner party that evening was at the house of Lady Emily Nevin, a rather mysterious Hungarian woman (said to be the daughter of some nobleman in her home country) who had married a romantic young baronet just before his death. She had inherited everything but his title, which had gone to an impoverished country cousin who could make no bread by it and still had to till his own earth. Still, people 'went to see her,' as the phrase went – because the Prince of Wales, on whom Lady Nevin exerted all of her many charms, did.

It was Lady Nevin's great conceit that wherever she went she kept a pet on a leash – a hedgehog. It was called Jezebel and waddled around with a surly look on its face, its well-groomed coat glistening with perfume and pomade. She had found it in the basement of her house; indeed, many people in London kept hedgehogs in their basements – the animals slept a great deal in whatever warm corner they could find and voraciously discovered and ate all of a house's insects. Few, though, brought them upstairs as Lady Nevin had. She even took the creature to other people's houses. It was considered either wickedly funny or profoundly tasteless, depending whom you spoke to. Lenox found it primarily silly, although he never entirely discounted the bond between a human and an animal because of a Labrador (Labbie, by name) that he had been given as a child and loved with all his heart.

Despite the hedgehog, Lenox was having no fun at the party. Held in a broad, overheated room with windows overlooking the Thames, it contained few people he knew and fewer of his friends. Lady Jane, with her inexhaustible acquaintance, moved easily among the small groups, but Lenox stood by the window, glumly eating a sherbet. They made a funny sort of couple on occasions like this.

Just then Lenox heard a voice behind him, and every nerve in his body went taut.

'An orchid, for the lady of the house,' it said, in a tone that had once sounded arrogant to his ears but now sounded sinister as well.

'Why, thank you, Mr. Barnard,' said Lady Nevin graciously. 'How kind you are to a poor widow.'

Lenox half-turned, if only to confirm that it was indeed George Barnard.

He was a powerful man, aged fifty or so, who had served time in Parliament and just finished a successful stint as Master of Great Britain's Royal Mint. He had retired into private life with an eye toward the House of Lords; judicious donations to the correct charities (and he was opulently rich, if nothing else) were, society assured him, enough to earn a title to match his wealth. He was a self-made man who had grown up somewhere in the north of England, which London associated, to the region's detriment, with factories and soot, but he had shaken off that dubious birth to rise to his current heights. He was well liked now and known for the beautiful orchids he grew himself and always brought to parties – or, if there wasn't one at its peak, a bowl of the oranges and lemons he grew in his greenhouse.

He was also, Lenox felt with complete certainty, the most dangerous man in London.

For many years his feelings toward Barnard had been neutral. Lenox had gone to the man's parties and suppers and met him in society. Two years before, that had changed.

It was a famous case, which Lenox had been proud to solve. One of Barnard's maids had been killed, and while Barnard was innocent of that crime – his two nephews had committed the murder – in the course of his investigation Lenox had discovered something shocking: Barnard had stolen nearly twenty thousand pounds of the Mint's money for himself. Once he knew this, Lenox began to trace a whole host of crimes back to Barnard, carefully taking notes on the un-solved mysteries in Scotland Yard's files and developing a dossier on them.

It was personal, too, Lenox's pursuit of Barnard, for two reasons. First, he had sent his thugs (he worked with an East End group called the Hammer Gang, who provided him with muscle) to beat half the life out of Lenox; second, and more irrationally, Barnard had proposed marriage to Lady Jane. Ever since she had rejected him and taken Lenox, Barnard had been scornful of Lady Jane, which was more than Lenox could take.

In all this time, though, he had been careful to keep his hatred of the man to himself, to greet Barnard with cordiality, never to let on what he knew.

'George, how do you do?' he said, shaking hands.

'Not badly, Lenox, not badly. There, thanks,' he said, handing a footman his overcoat. 'A lovely party with a lovely hostess, isn't it? How is Jane?'

Lenox didn't like the sneer on Barnard's face. 'Very well, thank you.'

'Good, excellent. I admire her greatly, you know, for looking past your ... profession. Or would you call it a hobby?'

'How are your days occupied now, Barnard?' asked Lenox, in a tone that even he recognized was barely civil.

Barnard wouldn't let go of the subject. 'Fine, fine,' he said, 'but you – are you looking into these murders at the newspapers? It's a great shame about, what are they called, Win Carruthers and Simon Pierce.'

'Did you know them?'

'Oh, no, of course not. Vulgar chaps, no doubt, but we mustn't allow anarchy. Are you looking into it?'

'I'm running for Parliament soon, actually. Everything has fallen behind that priority in my life, I'm afraid.'

Barnard looked bilious at this and only said in response, 'Ah – I see Terence Flood, I must speak to him.'

'Good evening,' said Lenox with a nod.

Lady Jane came back to Lenox. 'Are you almost ready to leave?' she asked.

'Lord, yes,' he said.

They returned to Lenox's house after circulating to say goodbye. Though he was troubled both by Exeter's visit and by seeing Barnard, Lenox threw off his cares long enough to have a late snack – milk and cake – with his betrothed, and an hour's conversation with her put him in a better mood. Walking back up her stoop, she permitted him a short kiss before going inside with a cheerful laugh. Well, he thought; all will be well in the end. This time next year perhaps I'll be in Parliament.

CHAPTER FOUR

The next morning, Lenox was scheduled to visit his friend Thomas McConnell, a doctor who often helped on Lenox's cases, and McConnell's wife, Toto, a young, vivacious woman, with an endearingly cheerful way about her; the most scurrilous gossip, on her lips, seemed little more than innocent chatter. She was a beauty, too, and had married the handsome, athletic Scot though she was some twelve years his junior.

Yet their marriage had been troubled – had even at times seemed doomed – and while Toto's personality had remained essentially the same throughout the couple's troubles, his had not. Once bluff and hale, an outdoorsman with gentle manners, he had begun to drink, and his face now, though still handsome, had a sallow, sunken look to it.

However, things had for a year or so been better, more loving, and it appeared that now the couple had passed the rocky shoals of their first years and settled into a contented marriage on both sides, with more maturity and tenderness, more selflessness, after all of their early turmoil. The apotheosis of this newfound happiness was a pregnancy: In six months Toto would give birth. It had been to check on her that Lenox was going to visit the McConnells' vast house.

When he woke, however, Lenox received a note

from McConnell begging his pardon and asking him to delay his visit until he was bidden come. Lenox didn't like the tone of the note, and visiting Lady Jane for his lunch, asked her about it.

'I haven't the faintest idea,' she said, worried. 'Shall I visit Toto?'

'Perhaps, yes,' said Lenox.

She had stopped eating her soup. 'Despite his request?'

'You and Toto are awfully close, Jane.'

'Yes, that's true.'

'Will you tell me what happens?'

'Of course.'

After she finished eating, she called for her carriage and in time went to her relation's house. Lenox was in the midst of a biography of Hadrian and sat back with his pipe to read it. He was an amateur historian and, without a case, devoted at least a few hours of each day to study of the Romans. His monographs on daily life in Augustan Rome had been well received at the great universities, and he had a wide, international correspondence with other scholars. That day, however, all his thoughts had been on Pierce and Carruthers.

Jane returned sometime later, looking ashen. 'It's bad news,' she said.

'What?' he asked.

'Toto fell ill in the middle of the night.'

'Good God,' he said, sitting by her on his red leather couch.

'They called the doctor in just past midnight. Thomas is worried to the point of utter exhaustion and blames himself for poor – what did he

42

say? – poor medical supervision of his wife.'

'She has a dozen doctors.'

'So I told him.'

'Is it–' He could scarcely ask. 'Have they lost the baby?'

A tear rolled down Lady Jane's cheek. 'It seems they may have. The doctors can't say yet. There's – there's blood.'

With that she collapsed onto his shoulder and wept. He held her tight.

'Is she in danger?'

'They won't say, but Thomas doesn't think so.'

It was an anxiety-filled early evening. After Lady Jane had returned with her news, Lenox had written to McConnell offering any help he could give, down to the smallest errand. Now Lenox and Lady Jane waited, talking very little. At some point a light supper appeared before them, but neither ate. Twice Lenox sent a maid to McConnell's house to inquire, and both times she came back without any new information.

At last, close to ten o'clock, McConnell himself appeared. He looked drawn and weary, his strong and healthy body somehow obscene.

'A glass of wine,' Lenox told Graham.

'Or whisky, better still, with a splash of water,' McConnell said miserably. He buried his head in his hands after Lenox led him to the sofa.

'Right away, sir,' said Graham and returned with it.

McConnell drank off half the glass before he spoke again. 'We lost the child,' he said at last. 'Toto will be well, however.'

'Damn it,' said Lenox. 'I'm so sorry, Thomas.'

Lady Jane was pale. 'I must go see her,' she said.

Lenox thought of all Toto's long, prattling mono-logues about baby names and baby toys, about painting rooms blue or pink, about what schools a boy child would attend or what year a girl would come out in society. Lenox and Jane were to have stood godparents. He thought of that, too.

'She didn't want to see anything of me. May you do better,' said McConnell.

Lady Jane left.

After some minutes Lenox said, 'You have a long and happy future ahead, Thomas.'

'Perhaps,' said the doctor.

'Will you sleep here tonight?'

'Thanks, Lenox, but no. I have to return. In case Toto needs me.'

'Of course – of course.'

McConnell stifled a sob. 'To think I once called myself a doctor.'

'She had every attention a woman could,' Lenox gently reminded his friend.

'Except the one she needed, perhaps.'

'You mustn't blame yourself. Truly.'

After several more drinks and a meandering, regretful conversation, McConnell left. Lenox promised to be in touch the next day and went to bed troubled in his mind.

At four in the morning, as Lenox slept, there was an urgent knock on his bedroom door. It was Graham, carrying a candle, bleary eyed.

'Yes?' said Lenox, sitting up instantly flooded with anxiety about Jane, about his brother, about the future. A nervous day had made for nervous rest.

'A visitor, sir. Urgent, I believe.'

'Who is it? McConnell?'

'Mr. Hilary, sir.'

'James Hilary?'

'Yes, sir.'

Hilary was the MP and political strategist Edmund had recommended Charles speak with. What on earth could he want?

Lenox made his way downstairs as quickly as he could. Hilary was sitting on the sofa in Lenox's study. He was a handsome man, with nobility written on his brow; he had a pleasant and open face usually but at the moment appeared profoundly agitated.

'Goodness, man, look at the hour,' said Lenox. 'What can it be?'

'Lenox, there you are. Come, you must tell your butler to pack a bag. Some sandwiches would be welcome for the trip, too. Even a cup of coffee.'

'What trip, Hilary?'

'Of course – where is my head? We've received a telegram; we need to go to Stirrington now.'

'Why?'

'Stoke is dead.'

'No!' cried Lenox.

Stoke was the Member of Parliament for Stirrington, whose retirement was going to prompt the election Lenox would compete in. He was a rural-minded, rough-mannered old man from an ancient family, who loved nothing but to run after the hounds and confer with his gamekeeper and for whom retirement held only happy prospects. He had never been meant for Parliament, but he had served his time honorably.

'Yes,' said Hilary impatiently. 'He's dead. His heart went out.'

'That's awful.'

'Yes, and in two weeks Stirrington votes.'

'Two weeks?' said Lenox blankly. 'You mean nine weeks. I have pressing matters to attend to here–'

'Two weeks will decide the by-election, Lenox. Come, we must fly.'

CHAPTER FIVE

Stirrington, which lay at the heart of the constituency Lenox hoped to represent, was a modest town of fifteen thousand souls, large enough to have several doctors, two schools, and a dozen pubs but small enough that cattle and sheep were still driven down the long High Street and everyone knew everyone else. To residents there the phrase 'the City' referred not to London but to Durham, with its beautiful riverside cathedral, and as Hilary explained on their ride north, one thing Lenox must be sure not to do was speak down to them, or come off as oversophisticated, or glib, or slick.

'I'll be myself, of course.'

'Of course,' said Hilary. Then he laughed. 'Yet politics often requires certain attitudes. To adopt them one needn't abandon one's character.'

'Yes,' said Lenox uncertainly.

The trip there took hours upon hours. Durham

County was nearly as far north as one could travel without reaching Scotland. The train arrived outside of town well after noon had struck, and both Lenox and Hilary – who had otherwise passed pleasant hours in doing what they loved, talking about the nature and strategy of politics – were famished. A small voice asked Lenox, too, whether he was now definitely beyond the distance at which he might have kept track of the two murders, and of course the great bulk of his thoughts were taken up with Thomas and Toto.

'To be honest, I wouldn't accompany every candidate this far,' said Hilary. 'But we're friends, and perhaps more importantly, the balance is very fine in the House right now.'

'It is,' agreed Lenox. 'I've followed the numbers on each side closely.'

'Every vote will see us closer to accomplishing our goals.' As two lads loaded luggage onto a carriage, Hilary stopped. 'In other words,' he went on, 'we need you to do your level best here,'

'To be sure,' Lenox responded and nodded with what he hoped was appropriate comprehension and solemnity.

Of course, what all this meant was that they wanted Lenox to spend money. The vast majority of parliamentary campaigns were self-funded or else funded by powerful local interests. Lenox was happy to lay out his own money, as his father and brother had. Still, Hilary's message was, even if friendly in delivery, clear in intent. As Lenox already knew, their Conservative opponent, a brewer named Robert Roodle, was quite willing to lay out money on votes. Still, Lenox felt confident that the bank drafts in his pocket would be sufficient to argue his case (for broader civil rights and a firm but reasonable international policy) to the people of Stirrington.

That morning had been a busy one. First Lenox had dressed, as the harried servants packed; then the budding politician had written a brief but loving note to Lady Jane next door, begging her tolerance for his hasty departure, and a similar, more somber note to McConnell, promising his swift return and sending his dearest wish that Toto would recover quickly. Graham, it was decided, would follow on the evening train. Then a dash through dawn to the train station, followed by long hours of travel and conversation. Lenox was ready for lunch and a moment to breathe, in whatever order he could get them. Alas, the first was makeshift, and the second they skipped.

Their first destination was a pub, the Queen's Arms, which dated to Queen Anne's reign. They were going there to meet Lenox's political agent, his chief local strategist and the man whom Lenox and Hilary hoped would deliver a large block of business voters, Mr. Edward Crook. It wasn't a promising name.

'He's the proprietor of the place,' said Hilary as they drove through the town. 'Apparently from a long-standing Stirrington family, much respected here.'

Lenox was observing what he could: maids stringing up laundry, a small but fair church, a slightly more bitter cold than London. 'Any family?'

Hilary consulted his notes. 'Wife, deceased. No

48

children. Crook's niece lives with him and keeps his house, a girl named Nettie.'

'What's Crook's political history?'

'He helped Stoke win – but as you know that was no great achievement. The Stoke name means a good deal in this area, and Stoke has run largely unopposed since he first came into office. Before either of our times, of course. Undistinguished but loyal.'

'So Crook hasn't much experience?'

Hilary frowned. 'I suppose not much, but we've firm knowledge of his stature within the community. Apparently there's a consortium of shop and tavern owners who listen to his every word. Shop owners, Lenox, win elections of this rural sort.'

'Yes?'

Hilary laughed. 'By God, you're lucky to run in such a place. My seat' – he represented part of Liverpool – 'took a good deal more money and a great deal more maneuvering than this one will.'

Soon they pulled up to the Queen's Arms. It was a distinguished-looking public house, with whitewashed walls that had black beams running across them, giving it a rather Tudor feel. An ornately painted, and really rather beautiful, sign depicted Anne with a crown and a detailed image of the world beneath her foot. There were stables to the rear of the house, rooms upstairs, and, from what they saw through the windows, a spacious one-room bar below.

They went in and found a hot, roaring fire at one end and a decent trade for the time of day; in chalk on a board were lunch specials (lamb with potatoes, hearty beef stew, hot wine), and

Lenox's hunger returned to him with a growl. A pretty, busy girl was coming to and fro from the kitchen, while a massive, red-nosed gentleman stood behind the bar, pouring drinks with surprisingly deft hands. He had on a bottle green spencer jacket, and a dirty towel was slung over each shoulder. This, Lenox saw, was Mr. Crook.

'Shall we have a bite?' Lenox asked with barely concealed yearning.

'Best ask Mr. Crook,' said Hilary sympathetically. 'We've much work to do.'

'Yes, yes.'

They approached the bar, a wide, immaculately clean slab of slate, with glasses hanging above it and gleaming brass fixtures at either end. Like the outside of the house, the pub's inside seemed the province of a fastidious, clean, and honest man.

'Gentlemen,' he said in a heavy northern voice. 'Here for dinner?'

'I'm Hilary, actually. I sent word of our arrival. This is Charles Lenox, your candidate.'

Crook gave them both an evaluating look. 'Very pleased to meet you, Mr. Lenox,' he said. 'I promise nothing, let me say from the start.'

'I understand.'

'Still, we shall do our best, and I daresay by the end we'll see you through, and before long you can return to London and forget all about us. Johnson, another pint of mild?'

Before Lenox had a chance to deny Crook's prediction, the tender was already sliding a pint glass of foamy, rich brown ale down the bar. It looked lifesaving to Lenox's eye.

'Thank you for your help,' said Lenox.

'Well – and you look solid enough.' This Crook said rather glumly. 'It will be difficult.'

'Do we have time to sit for a moment and eat?'

'No,' said Crook. 'Lucy!' he shouted. 'Bring a couple of roasted beef sandwiches.'

The pretty girl raised her hand in brief acknowledgment.

'You two must go – with money, mind – straight to the printers. We need handbills, flyers, posters, all that sort of thing – we need 'em before the end of the day. I've designed it all, but run your eyes over what he has. Lucy!'

The girl returned with two sandwiches. Without either of the two Londoners noticing, Crook had poured two half-pints of mild and pushed them across the bar. 'You look peaky,' he said. 'Drink these off and eat on your way. Six doors down, to your left. Make sure you bring cash. The stables have your bags? Good, I've got two rooms for you. Nice to meet you, Mr. Lenox. Mr. Hilary. All will turn out well if you trust me. Clark, one more pint of bitter before you go back to work?'

With that their introduction to Edward Crook was over, and the two men looked at each other, shrugged, and turned away, both taking ravenous bites of their sandwiches before they left.

'What do you think?' asked Hilary as they walked down the street.

'He seems competent.'

'Fearfully so, I should have said.'

'The sort of chap we want on our side, rather than the other,' Lenox added.

'Yes, absolutely. By God, these sandwiches aren't half bad, are they? Look, this must be the printer.'

CHAPTER SIX

Crook, it emerged, was a gloomy, blunt, and practical man; Lenox took to him straightaway. He was honest and fair and had a straightforward way of speaking that engendered in his listeners an instant trust. When that evening he introduced Lenox to the small circle of businessmen and shopkeepers who formed the local party committee, he didn't heap praise on the detective's head. He merely said that he thought they had a candidate who could ably replace Stoke, a candidate with sufficient funds to have his voice heard, a candidate willing to work hard, and a candidate who would be – beyond any doubt – a better representative of Stirrington's interests in Parliament than Robert Roodle, the brewer and Conservative.

After they had returned from the printers that afternoon, Crook had described the situation. 'Roodle's not well liked here, and that's what will matter most. There're no strong feelings about you either way, but Roodle has alienated people in a number of ways. As soon as his brewery grew, he moved it out of Stirrington; he has a farm outside town and has been in a long legal battle with both of his neighbors; and whether it's fair or not his father was known as the most tightfisted, intemperate sod in the county. He used to beat his horses and drove his wife like a donkey. Be that as it may, there's no mistaking Roodle's success. Half of Durham's pubs are Roodle pubs. He also has one other great point, in local terms.'

'What's that?' asked Hilary with some alarm,

'He's from here. In the north we value our own, you see.'

Indeed, as they had walked that day about town Hilary and Lenox had seen numerous flyers on that subject. 'Two weeks in Stirrington, or a lifetime? Who knows you better? Vote Roodle,' read one. 'Vote your own – vote Roodle,' said another.

Lenox saw the fairness of the point. It was a strange political system that led to Hilary representing Liverpool, while the Liberal Party's current leader in the House, William Gladstone, had grown up in Liverpool but for a long time represented Oxford, of all places. Still, he also believed that his platform would genuinely help the people of Stirrington more than Roodle's, and he resented the negative, attacking nature of Roodle's campaign. He was ready to fight.

Lenox's own campaign handbills were, he thought, singularly effective; they advertised what they called his 'Five Promises.' Crook had written it up, and Hilary (who was invaluable for this sort of task) had revised it. The only promise that both the printer and Crook had absolutely insisted upon keeping was for a lower tax on beer. This wasn't self-interest, Crook rather defensively assured them, but the most important issue to many Stirringtonians.

Better still, Roodle was in a bind over the beer tax. He had vocally supported a lower beer tax for many years (as a brewer interested in selling as many pints as possible), but now he found himself on the wrong side of his party, and rather than alienate the aid he received from London he had switched positions. Crook felt this hypocrisy was important, if only to show how weak willed Roodle would be if elected.

At the committee meeting there was a great deal of detailed talk about Lenox's schedule for the next several days; by this time he was faint with fatigue, however – Hilary was still impressively spry, but he was younger – and only half heard the plan for a series of speeches, a debate, a meeting with county officials, and visits to several dances, balls, and livestock auctions. The idea was to make Lenox as visible as possible to compensate for the short time he had in which to present his platform. Through all of this conversation Crook was a gentle but forceful guide. His authority was obvious.

At last Lenox was allowed to go to sleep. In his plain, quite clean room, which had a small warm grate near the bed, he drifted off into a grateful rest, so tired that he only for a passing moment worried about McConnell and Toto.

In the morning, to Lenox's surprise, his coffee appeared via a familiar bearer; it was Graham.

'Thank goodness you're here, Graham.'

'I arrived late last night, sir.'

'You're not exhausted, I hope?'

'I slept very well, sir. May I ask how things have progressed here?'

'Very well, I think, though I'm pulled in five different directions at once.'

'Such is the nature of campaign life, sir, or so I have heard.'

'Indeed it is, Graham,' Lenox took a sip of coffee and instantly felt livelier. 'Well, I'm prepared for the battle.'

'Excellent, sir.'

'I say, though, was there any news about those two gentlemen – about Pierce and Carruthers?'

'I brought yesterday evening's papers with me, sir,' said Graham.

Lenox noticed a bundle under the butler's arm. 'Cheers.'

'I am afraid there is no new information, however. Mr. Hiram Smalls is still in custody. Inspector Exeter is widely quoted in the paper as saying the case is over.'

'Is he now? Insufferable, isn't it,' he murmured as he glanced at the headlines.

'Will you eat breakfast here, sir?' Graham asked.

'Is the pub open?'

'Yes, sir. I ate there earlier and can heartily recommend the poached eggs.'

'Put in an order for me, would you? I'll be down in twenty minutes. Plenty more of this, too,' said Lenox and raised his coffee cup.

'Yes, sir. May I draw your attention to the two letters on your nightstand, sir?'

There were a pair of white envelopes next to Lenox's book. 'Thanks,' he said.

'Thank you, sir,' said Graham and left.

Good to have him here, thought Lenox. It will make life much easier.

He took the first envelope, which he recognized as being on the heavy, cream-colored stationery of Lord John Dallington. The second, however, caught his eye, and he discarded Dallington's note for it; inside was white paper ringed with pale blue. It was from Lady Jane.

Dear Charles,

I pray this finds you well. Thank you for your kind note, and Godspeed in Stirrington. I sit here at Toto's side; under sedation she has lost all her good cheer and effervescence, and their absence does what their presence could not and makes me realize how much I had come to rely on them. Thomas handles himself badly, I'm afraid; and as I would only say to you. His concern for Toto is patent, and he harries the doctors with questions when they come in, but he has also been drinking. Toto instructs me during her coherent moments to bar him from the room, and he's half mad at the exclusion, persuaded that these sorry circumstances are his fault. I try to mediate between them when I tactfully can, to soften words, but there is much I cannot do.

Charles, my mind is so full of doubt! Would that you were here beside me; then I might be at ease for twenty minutes together. I know we are hoping to marry in the summer, six months from now, but witnessing our two friends' difficulties I wonder whether we might delay our union? Do we know that we won't fall into the same traps? If there were days when I couldn't stand the sight of you I don't know that I could go on living.

I can hear your wise words from across England: that Toto and Thomas rushed into marriage; that we have long been friends; that our tempers are quieter than theirs; that our history and upbringing suit us to each other, as well as the content of our minds. Still, I cannot believe that it is right to marry so quickly upon the heels of your wonderful proposal (which I still count the happiest moment of my life, Charles).

May we give it a year? Or longer? Please believe that this is written in love. From your own,

Jane

At the bottom in a hurried and untidy scrawl she had added: *I send this by Graham. Please don't mistake my doubt for doubt in you, dear one.*

Lenox sat in his bed, dumbfounded. What surprised him more than the sentiment of the letter was its wavering fretfulness; for years Lady Jane had been so dependable, the person in his life he knew he could count on should all others desert him. It was out of character. He wondered if there was something more than she confessed to in the letter, to make her feel as she did.

As he was about to read it for a second time, there was a sharp rap at the door, and Hilary came in.

'Good morning, Lenox. Sorry to catch you waking up.'

'Oh – it's quite all right, James, of course.'

'Your first speech is in forty minutes?'

'That's right, yes.'

'Do you know what you're going to say?'

'I'll follow what Crook planned out for the handbills. There are a few words I wrote down after you came and asked me to run.'

'Good, good,' said Hilary.

'Is anything the matter? You seem nervous.'

'Well, Lenox, I'm afraid I have to return to London this afternoon.'

'What? Why?'

'There are committee meetings to be attended, and ... that sort of thing.'

'But you knew your schedule when you came up.'

Hilary sat down and sighed. 'I'm sorry to say it, old chap, but Roodle looks awfully strong here. I got a telegram requesting that I return, in response to my telegram sending them the numbers Crook had worked up of past votes. It's the time, you see – because Stoke died we don't have enough time.'

Lenox felt at a conversational disadvantage, lying in bed, and his heart plummeted. 'How does Roodle look strong?'

'He's spending as much money as you'll be able to, which frankly we didn't expect. He has a much higher name recognition – and, though it's not your fault, and though people here feel respectful of old Stoke, they're ready for a change.'

'How poor do you think my chances are?'

'If you fight hard, you might get within a few hundred votes of him. Then – who knows?'

'But the chances aren't good enough for you to stay?'

'I'm afraid not,' said Hilary with a guilty look. 'You know we're friends, and in the SPQR club together, Lenox, but damn it – politics is a ruthless game, and we have to follow the momentum.'

'I see.'

Hilary looked pained. 'If it were simply up to me, I would have stayed till the bitter end. You know the respect I entertain for you, Lenox.'

'Well,' said Lenox, unsure of what to say.

Hilary stood up. 'I'll be downstairs. Come,' he said encouragingly, 'let's give a fight. This morning will be a good start.'

Lenox sat in his bed and listened to the footfalls

as Hilary walked downstairs. Uncertainty, suddenly, where all had seemed promising. Lady Jane's letter was still in his hand.

CHAPTER SEVEN

It was a long slog of a day, his first full one in Stirrington. Hilary took the latest train back that he could, with another string of apologies for Lenox before he went. More hopefully, Crook said, 'Never mind him. These London types are weak willed, when it comes to politics. There's fighting left to be done.' Strangely, because Crook was so gloomy these words meant much more than they would have coming from a more sanguine character.

Walking around the town that evening, Lenox felt heartened. He had given four speeches that day; the first, before a handful of shopkeepers on the edge of town, had been a timorous, uncertain homily about the importance of lending one another a hand. The line he had concluded with, 'Friends before treasure!' had earned him only a few disapproving stares, not the applause he had hoped for, and he only realized belatedly that the men in the crowd were primarily concerned with their treasure – of friends they had enough. He had gained confidence as he went, though, and having walked around Stirrington all day, he now recognized some of the faces and many of the shops he passed.

He stopped into a chophouse and had a supper of lamb and wine, talking the whole while with several men at the bar. At first they were taciturn, but Lenox did have one gift as a politician, even though he hadn't had time to develop more than a raw way about him – he could listen. He liked to listen, in fact. When these men found that one of the quality was interested in what they said, they found their voices. Primarily they talked about Roodle.

'Bleeding Robert Roodle,' said a thin and thin-voiced one, 'I was workin' in his brewery and lost my job.'

'Did you get another one?'

'Well – yes,' said the man, in that particular grudging way of the English, 'but no thanks to 'im.'

Here a jollier fellow, who had introduced himself to Lenox as the local blacksmith, chimed in. 'What's worse was 'is father, 'e was. A reg'lar tyrant.' Then he braced himself for a long soliloquy. 'The facts about Stirrington, sir, is that we here like hard work, we like our ale, we like our Sunday service, and we like promises kept. That's the secret, Mr. Lenox. Don't make promises you can't keep; we'll find you out, sir, we will.'

'We will,' agreed Roodle's aggrieved former employee.

'Beer tax – you've made a good start, sir.'

'Aye, it's true,' said several of the mute chorus who had been listening to the conversation as they ate.

'One other thing, Mr. Lenox – there's nothing to be gained by attacking Roodle. Everyone here knows his faults, we know his virtues – for he *does* 'ave 'em, Sam, and pipe down – and before anyone votes for you the people of this town will need to know yours.'

'Thank you, gentlemen,' said Lenox. 'I hope I may count on your votes, at least?'

Not so fast, their looks said, though they all nodded agreeably enough.

Finally, after supper, Lenox had time to return to his room and write back to Lady Jane. He sat for some time at the small table at the window of his room; it overlooked a large vegetable garden, but all was dark now, and he felt wracked with doubt. Doubt about Jane herself – never. Doubt in himself. He finally wrote:

My Dearest Jane,

Even your doubtful letter was the sweetest part of my day because it came from you, but I cannot lie: These have been difficult hours in my life. Hilary returned almost instantly to London, expressing grave concerns about my chances here before he left. I have constant visions of Thomas and Toto in their sorrow and feel I have shirked my duty in leaving, whatever the purpose. I can't help but think that the two deaths that I take it still dominate the papers there might have been cleared away under my eye. Yet of all this I feel most sorrowful that you should doubt our marriage in June.

Which is not to say that I do not understand, dearest Jane; for I have analyzed at greater length than you will have had leisure to my own faults, the defects in my character that'd preclude me from making a happy marriage. In fact, I stated them to you before that (indeed happy!) moment when you accepted my offer.

Nonetheless, I have more confidence in my love for you than in all the rest of this doubtful world put together. My dearest hope, to which all my dreams and aspirations have been bent, is our joint happiness, which will begin in earnest when we marry. I hope that is in June, but I will wait as patiently as you like, unto the end of my days.

I cannot help but wish I were in London to speak with you in person and to gaze at your wise and serene face; all would be well then, I somehow believe. Until that blessed moment, believe me to be your most faithful and loving,

Charles

It was a sentimental letter, perhaps, but an honest one. After he had finally started writing it the words had come easily. He blotted the letter and didn't read it over but simply sealed it in an envelope and left it on the small table in the hallway where residents of the inn could leave their letters to be sent.

Going back to his room, feeling somewhat restless, he happened to notice a slip of paper he must have missed coming in. Stooping to fetch it, he saw it was a note from Crook's niece, Nettie, inviting him to have breakfast with them the next morning. Whether this missive came from Crook or the girl herself, he was grateful for it, alone as he was in this strange town.

The next morning he presented himself at the door of the small house adjoining the Queen's Arms, a charming and tidily kept place. A very young maid, not past fourteen, answered the door and took Lenox into a sitting room that was per-

62

haps over-furnished with examples of needlework, with small and amateurish watercolors – in other words, the sitting room of a young woman who spent much time alone and whose diversions were all, or nearly all, of her own making.

Nettie Crook came in at the same moment Lenox sat down. She was a plain girl but with a healthy look about her, and he was surprised she remained unmarried. She could not be below twenty-five years of age. It was entirely proper for them to be alone together – she was evidently the woman of the house – but Lenox rather wished her uncle had been there to introduce them.

'How do you do, Mr. Lenox? I'm so pleased you could come.'

'Thank you, thank you, Miss Crook. I was pleased to receive your invitation.'

'How do you find Stirrington, if I may ask?'

'Altogether charming, Miss Crook. I would have preferred to view it at a more leisurely pace, but it has been pleasant nonetheless.'

'My uncle will arrive downstairs in only a moment or two.'

Lenox nodded graciously. Here was an odd situation, he thought; although he gazed on the strictures of class with a more critical eye than many he knew, it was plain that two people of very different rank were about to dine together. He liked Crook, liked Nettie, too, for that matter, but he hoped it wouldn't be awkward.

In fact, it was not. To Lenox's shock, the glum, agile proprietor of the pub, the shrewd political leader, was at home as soft as warm butter. The reason was Nettie.

'Have you observed my niece's watercolors?' was the first thing he asked Lenox after they exchanged civilities.

It was extraordinary. The man's face, which in the bar was screwed into an impassive and calculating glare, was now softened by emotion. He looked his age.

'I have,' said Lenox, 'and cannot recall a more interesting view of that famous clock tower that I've seen in all my brief time here.'

'Tell him about the clock tower, dear heart,' said Crook with great complacency.

'Uncle,' Nettie chidingly answered.

'Pray, do tell me,' said Lenox.

They had moved by now to a small breakfast nook, which just managed to fit three (though it would have been perfect for two), and she put eggs on his plate.

'I was once very late in running my errands,' she said, 'so late I feared I would miss supper.'

'Miss supper,' Crook echoed softly, gazing with pure love up at his niece.

'I'm generally inside at that hour, of course, but I happened to be in such a rush that I stumbled – and as I stood up saw the clock hanging just between two houses. It was so beautiful, Mr. Lenox, you could scarcely credit! Well, the next evening I went out and drew a few sketches of it – art is a hobby of mine – and then completed the work you see.'

Now, as stories go, Lenox acknowledged to himself, this wasn't *much* of one. Yet through it all Crook looked as enthralled as Thucydides listening to Herodotus in the town square.

'My brother, Nettie's father, was a fine chap,' said Crook, 'but died fighting the Russians.'

'In the Crimea?'

'Yes, I'm afraid so. That would have been 1855, eleven years since. I took her in as a teenager, and she has been my sunshine ever since.'

'Uncle,' said Nettie again in an undertone, 'My mother died in childbirth, Mr. Lenox.'

'I'm terribly sorry to hear it.'

'It was a shame,' Crook said. The bell chimed behind him. 'Blimey – already? All right, dear, give us a kiss.'

This received, he took a great ring of keys from his wallet and left with a scant word of good-bye, already, perhaps, the grim and reliable publican that Stirrington knew.

Lenox was finishing his food when the young girl came in. 'Pardon,' she said, 'but there's a visitor at the inn, sir.'

'Who is it, Lucy?' asked Nettie,

'I've never seen him, ma'am. A gentleman. I'm afraid he's–' Here she stopped.

'Yes?'

'Well – been drinking, mum.'

Lenox had a sinking feeling in his heart. 'What's his name?'

'He said to tell you, "It's McConnell, the poor sod," sir. He said you'd know what that means.'

CHAPTER EIGHT

Lenox spent the next hour tucking his friend safely away in a spare room above the Queen's Arms. McConnell, half in stupor from drink and incoherent about his reasons for coming to Stirrington, was nonetheless as clear as crystal about his reasons for being unhappy. Toto had asked him to leave. He had not only obeyed that request but had decided to absent himself from London forever. He talked wildly of returning to his native Scotland and becoming a groundskeeper at his family's small estate or practicing medicine in the rural parts of the country. Mumbling, he fell into a troubled sleep.

Lenox spent the morning giving speeches. In his spare moments he read the previous day's London papers. They were still full of the two 'Fleet Street murders,' and amid long encomiums to Simon Pierce and Winston Carruthers (journalists, after all, love to eulogize their own; a way of pushing off their own obscurity a little further) were all the details and speculations that papers, high and low alike, could muster about Hiram Smalls, the mysterious man who had been arrested in connection with the murders.

The details were certain, if few. He lived in Bethnal Green with his mother. This picturesque detail the papers dwelt on at great length, and they inquired endlessly about Mrs. Smalls's feel-

66

ings. In person Hiram was a short, solid, muscular figure, with (purportedly) cunning eyes and without discernible scars, birthmarks, etc. He had never been in legal trouble, and while he liked the life of rough pubs and gin mills, he had never (at least that anybody would willingly say) associated with any of London's numerous gangs or thief-taking operations.

For supper one day he had ordered out from prison to a local pub, asking for a pork chop, two large glasses of ale, and a bag of oranges. Ordering food into prison was a common enough activity – *for those with money*, said the papers with dark suggestion – but these oranges! Such an extravagant fruit! Local markets condescended to quote their price for a single orange to the various papers, and all agreed one could not be had for less than a shilling, the price of several meals. As was customary for prisoners, the pub extended no credit. Where, then, did Hiram Smalls get his coin – not to mention his nerve?

There were a few quotes from Inspector Exeter about the case. When the press urged him to explain how Hiram Smalls might have killed two men on opposite sides of town at once, Exeter said that the Yard wasn't ruling out the possibility of a conspiracy between Smalls and several of his local associates. A gang, then, the press very naturally inquired? Possibly a gang, Exeter allowed, though we cannot say more. Did gangs not sometimes have rich or even aristocratic chieftains? Yes, said Exeter. However, it was evident that Smalls was either the sole mover or the leader of a conspiracy – such was clear from interrogation of the prisoner, canvassing of the eyewitnesses, and one particular piece of shocking evidence.

This piece of evidence was that Smalls and Carruthers's maid, Martha, had unquestionably met and conversed within the last month. There were a dozen eyewitnesses who could place them at the Gun pub off of Liverpool Street, including one who happened to know both of them – Hiram from nearby Bethnal Green and Martha because the gentleman made deliveries to Winston Carruthers.

All this Lenox learned from yesterday's papers.

Morning speeches given, he returned at two o'clock in the afternoon to find McConnell at a front table in the pub, gazing with a melancholy air through the small window he sat by. A glass of Scotch whisky sat before him, untouched. He stood up when he saw the detective.

'Lenox,' he said, 'How can I apologize?'

'You've had a difficult week,' said Lenox.

'I had some wild idea of helping you with the campaign, being of some – of some goddamn use in this world,'

Lenox noticed McConnell's hand trembling slightly, whether from nerves or drink. 'Thomas, you must allow yourself to grieve,' he said, 'You're not at fault.'

Dismissively, the doctor responded, 'Lenox, you–'

'Thomas – you're not at fault.'

Lenox held McConnell's gaze until the latter looked away. 'At any rate,' he said.

'How is Toto's health?' inquired Lenox in a neutral tone.

'She's recuperating. Jane is with her.'

'How long will she require rest?'

'She can move already, but her doctor told me that she must first calm her nerves.'

'Of course.'

'It was a fluke, he also said.'

'Of course it was, Thomas. Nobody could have predicted it.'

'Well – be that as it may.'

'Nobody could have predicted it!' said Lenox, driven to a high tone. 'Has it occurred to you that Toto asked you to leave because she feels responsible, *she* feels as if *she* disappointed you, Thomas? Good Christ, for an intelligent man…'

McConnell looked chastened. 'Do you think so?'

'I know it's not because she blames you.'

'Well – thank you, Charles. Excuse me for arriving in that – in that state.'

The tension in Lenox's face relaxed slightly. 'I'm pleased to have you here. Lord knows I need help.'

'I hope I can work on your behalf.'

'I'm running against a brewer. Roodle, his name is. Apparently not well liked, but the local attitude seems to run along devil-you-know lines.'

'Have you any chance?'

'Not a week ago the men who proposed I run were optimistic. Giddily optimistic, even; but Stoke's death has lengthened my odds considerably.'

'Did you see the *Times*, by the way?'

'No, what?'

'They ran a small piece about you and Hilary leaving in the dead of night.'

'How funny!'

'It referred to you as – let me remember – as "Charles Lenox, notable for his successful intervention in the infamous murder of Bill Dabney and the disappearance of George Payson, as well as the final capture of the so-called September Society." In the clubs there was quite a buzz about your campaign.'

'What did people think?'

'That it was celebrity chasing by the Liberals, I'm afraid. Those who knew you emphasized your long interest in politics, but the general opinion was derisive, unfortunately.'

'I've dealt with worse, of course.'

Lenox saw McConnell eye the Scotch whisky. At that moment Lucy, the energetic waitress, sailed by. 'Eating, Mr. Lenox?'

'I'd love something. Whatever looks good,' he said.

'Straightaway.'

'Is there much talk of Pierce and Carruthers?' asked Lenox.

'Well – you'll understand I haven't been lazing about Pall Mall. I only went by my club yesterday afternoon to escape the house. I do know Shreve' – this was the McConnells' funereal and corpulent butler – 'has been censoring a great deal of below-stairs gossip. I can't imagine there's any more tact evident in the high houses.'

Lenox laughed. 'Of course not. Oh – I say, McConnell, would you mind if I was rude for a moment? I've been carrying this letter about with me all day looking for a moment to read it.'

McConnell acceded with a wan nod. It was the

letter from Lord John Dallington, who for the space of four months or so had been filling an awkward and new role; he was Lenox's apprentice.

It was a strange fit. Dallington was well known in London as a dissolute and disheveled, if charming, scion of the aristocracy and the eternal worry and disappointment of the Duke and Duchess of Marchmain, whose youngest son he was. The duchess was one of Lady Jane's very closest friends, and so for years Lenox had known Dallington without ever paying him undue attention. He was a short, trim, and handsome man, whose face was unblemished by his dissipation, dark eyed and dark haired, something of a dandy; a perfect carnation always sat in his buttonhole.

Most third sons of the aristocracy chose the military or the clergy, but Dallington, in part encouraged by his parents' leniency, had repudiated these traditional paths and instead devoted the first years of his twenties to the Beargarden Club and pretty young girls. Then, shockingly, one day in September he had approached Lenox and requested an education in detective work. Lenox had warned the lad that it was a profession whose only rewards were internal, that it took dedication to work at a vocation held in such low esteem. Dallington pointed out that his own reputation was not high, and Lenox had taken him on. Since then, the lad had been surprisingly adept at his new work, and diligent besides, even if there had been several rocky moments. Those, though, were forgotten: Dallington had either saved Lenox's life or come close to it, and their bond – indeed, their friendship – was now secure.

His letter was brief.

Lenox,
I once met Simon Pierce at a party – crashing bore.
Nevertheless, one does feel a certain sorrow. Are you
doing anything about this? I would like to help, if so.
Hope you had a jolly Christmas and everything like
that.

Dallington

This note raised in Lenox a sense of guilt, which combined with the poor chances of his campaign made him feel suddenly that his real place was on the trail of whoever had murdered the two London journalists, not here courting votes among people who had no affection for his presence.

'From Dallington,' he said. 'Asks about the journalists. I do feel I should be there, rather.'

McConnell did something strange then – he literally smacked his forehead. 'How could I have forgotten, Lenox! I come bearing news.'

'What is it?'

'We had just spoken about the matter,' said McConnell with a bemused shake of his head. 'It's the drink – it puts me awkward – I'm not...' He trailed off nervously. 'My memory.'

'For the love of Christ, what is it?' Lenox asked.

'Hiram Smalls? The chap in jail?'

'Yes?'

'He's dead, apparently. Just before midnight yesterday evening. I was in the train station when I heard about it.'

CHAPTER NINE

Lenox was stunned. 'Are you sure?'

'Yes,' said McConnell.

'You're absolutely certain of that?'

'They were selling an extra edition of the paper with a story to that effect – I'm sure of that anyway.'

'Did you buy it?'

McConnell looked embarrassed. 'I'm afraid I was – not myself,' he said.

With any luck the late papers from the night before *might* make it up to Stirrington tonight. Otherwise he would have to wait until the morning. It was maddening, just maddening. For a tenth of a second every fiber in Lenox's body strained against the town and his task there.

'What did it say? Do you remember? Murder? Suicide? Was it unclear?'

Rather lamely, McConnell answered, 'Only that he had just died, actually.'

Then Lucy arrived with a bubbling pie of some kind or other for Lenox, which despite his focus on Smalls was a welcome sight after a morning of what had been cold campaigning.

'Lucy, a moment – do you take telegrams here?'

'No, sir, but the boots will take a telegram to the post office for a small tip.'

'Could you send him over?'

The boots, when he appeared, turned out to be

a lad of not more than thirteen or so, with a pronounced overbite and black hands from his work
shining shoes. Lenox had quickly scribbled out a
message and an address, and he handed these to
the boots along with a large tip, in addition to the
money it would cost to send the telegram. Admon-
ishingly, he instructed the boy not to lose it or to
tarry on his way to the post office. Thinking it
over, he took back the tip and promised to hold it
until the lad returned with a receipt. Perhaps this
wasn't the most trusting thing to do, but Lenox
remembered what he had been like at thirteen.

'To whom did you write?' asked McConnell,
who was looking slightly ill again.

'Dallington.'

'Telling him?'

'Asking him for information, primarily. Also
telling him to keep an eye on matters there.' Lenox
looked at his pocket watch. 'I wish I had time to
wait for a reply, but I'm afraid I'm scheduled to
speak soon. Excuse me, will you?'

'Where?' asked McConnell.

He received no reply, though, for Lenox had
already walked up to Crook at the bar for a brief
consultation. Either Crook or Hilary had introduced him before all of his speeches so far, but
Hilary was gone, and Crook was working; another
member of the Liberal committee, Sandy Smith,
was going to meet Lenox at his first speech and
accompany him for the rest of the day.

'I must go,' Lenox said to McConnell. 'I'll see
you for supper?'

'Can't I tag along and help you campaign?'

'Tomorrow, certainly – but have another afternoon of rest, won't you?'

McConnell still looked disheveled, and Lenox, though he had never been embarrassed by a friend before, felt he couldn't march around Stirrington with the doctor now. How politics had already changed him! It wasn't clear whether McConnell understood Lenox's motives, but without any further protest he agreed to spend the afternoon on his own.

Lenox's mind fairly swarmed with ideas. It would have been useful, in fact, to ask McConnell to look at Hiram Smalls's body, but now the doctor was here; still, work might be the best thing for him. If there was any possibility of foul play, Lenox might ask him to return.

Sandy Smith turned out to be a small, dark-haired, and precise-looking man, a contrast to the vast Crook. He wore glasses, a short-brimmed hat, and a snug gray waistcoat, and constantly checked a gold pocket watch that sat in a small pocket therein. He shook Lenox's hand enthusiastically and repeated several times that he thought their chances were better than anyone realized, which was cheering to hear.

Soon enough they arrived at a small, square park, full of bright green grass and low, well-maintained trees.

'This is Sawyer Park,' said Smith. He gestured to the arcades that ringed it. 'Many of our finest shops are here – there you see my law office – and the apartments above the arcades are very eligible indeed. Mr. Roodle's agent has that shop, the milliner's.'

'I don't see much of a crowd.'

Smith looked at his watch. 'We have twenty minutes yet. Nobody wants to close shop or leave work much before they have to, but there'll be a hundred people here, give or take. How many have you been speaking to generally?'

'Yesterday? Only twenty or thirty at a time. More like meetings than speeches.'

'Well, I hope you're in good voice.'

'I think I am. The issues shall carry us, I expect.'

'Well,' said Smith doubtfully, 'people around here are fond of a good speech.'

'Shall I take questions?'

He laughed. 'Yes, whether you like to or not.'

'I see.'

Smith and Lenox spent the next few minutes shaking hands with people who happened to pass by. Some of these stayed in the park, others left and then returned with a friend, and soon there was a sizable crowd amassed on the small green, even larger than a hundred people. Lenox felt nervous, but he had practiced on the smaller crowds and knew he could deliver his speech. His anxiety now went toward the questions, which might well be rude or mocking. I must remember to maintain my own manner, he thought; there's nothing I can do about anybody else's.

At last he went to the small raised platform that served as a kind of Speakers' Corner and delivered his speech. It went off fairly well, drawing appreciative laughter and confirming hisses at the right moments.

Then came the questions.

The first was already dangerous. 'Why would

you care about Stirrington?' a man a few feet off to the side asked.

'Because there's an election here!' somebody farther back shouted, and everyone laughed.

'It's true that I'm here because of this by-election,' Lenox said when the noise had died down, 'but I'm here because I care about every corner of England and all her people, and Stirrington is just as much a part of this country as Sussex, where I'm from, or London, where I live. People here, like people anywhere, want a decent wage, a strong government, and' – here Lenox gulped back his pride – 'a fair price for beer.'

This answer earned Lenox a round of applause.

'What's a fair price?'

'Less than you're paying,' the candidate answered.

'Do you drink?'

'Not right now, thanks.'

Another laugh, and Lenox felt he was getting the hang of the questions. A little humor mixed with broad answers.

Then a short, fat, sharp-faced man standing not five feet away said, loudly enough for everyone to hear, 'You should go back to London, Mr. Lenox.'

Smith's voice behind Lenox whispered, 'That's Roodle.'

'I will when I'm elected, Mr. Roodle, so I can represent this wonderful town.'

In the crowd there was total silence, almost an anticipatory inhale of breath, as the two candidates faced each other for the first time.

'So you can prance around in Parliament and

forget all about us back here.'

'No man who knows me could deny that all of my convictions, all of my beliefs, are directed toward the protection of people like these. A better life for people here in Stirrington, and everywhere across England. I'll never forget that.'

'You don't know "these people",' he said with a scoffing laugh. 'I've been here my whole life, sir.'

Lenox felt a riposte forming somewhere in his brain. 'Your whole life?' he said.

'My whole life,' confirmed Roodle.

'Yet your brewery hasn't.'

There was a moment of silence, followed by an absolute roar of laughter. When it subsided just a little, Smith said, 'Thank you!' and pulled the candidate offstage.

The small man was thrilled. 'Leave 'em on a high note,' he said. 'That was wonderful! You showed Roodle! Round one to Lenox! Come, come, we must wade into the crowd and shake every hand we can find! Come! "Yet your brewery hasn't," he says! Wonderful!'

CHAPTER TEN

Flushed with success, Lenox spent an hour in Sawyer Park, until he had indeed shaken every hand he could find. Smith was invaluable – had grown up in Stirrington and seemed to know every soul who lived within the town limits and a good many that lived beyond. On Roodle's behalf

78

several beefy-looking gentlemen were circulating in the park, saying that glib talk would get them nowhere, that the beer tax would probably be lowered regardless of this election's outcome, and most importantly that Lenox was an interloper and a fraud – but all to little avail. Lenox was the man of the hour, and people of every stripe crowded around him, congratulating him and asking him questions (often very personal ones – one young man asked what Parliament could do about getting him onto the county cricket team, which Lenox still wasn't sure had been a joke).

Finally Smith and Lenox had met everyone there was to meet, and Lenox, who after the headiness of the speech remembered again that Hiram Smalls was dead and began speculating in his mind about the Pierce and Carruthers murders, inquired what they were to do next.

'It's a fearful proposition, but I thought perhaps we might call on Mrs. Reeve.'

'Who is that?'

'Has Crook not told you about her, then? Perhaps we should wait.'

'Who is she?'

'Mrs. Reeve is a widow, about fifty. She was married to Joe Reeve, famous in these parts as Durham's best horse trainer. He left her with a comfortable living, and her house is a kind of stopping point for every woman in town. There's always food and tea, and people agree to meet there as if it were a shop or a train station. Mrs. Reeve herself is very influential with all of the women I know.'

'She sounds a fascinating character.'

'Aye, and a powerful one. Men with little time to waste on politics will often listen to their wives, I believe.'

'What is she like in person?'

'Oh – fat – exceedingly fat.'

'What else?'

'Well – I don't think she's ever properly left Stirrington. It's *possible* – and mind, I don't say probable – that she's never left town. She may have been to Durham once, but I can't remember hearing of it.'

'On the provincial side of things?' Lenox asked, with what he hoped was delicacy.

Smith laughed. 'I didn't want to say it.' Then he paused. 'I've been to France, actually.'

'Mr. Smith, I hope you don't think I class you in such a way? I really don't look down on Stirrington, you have my absolute word. Whatever Mr. Roodle says.'

'No, no, of course,' said the lawyer, red faced. 'At any rate – to Mrs. Reeve's?'

However, Mrs. Reeve was – and Mr. Smith called it an aberration – away from home. According to her housekeeper, who looked flustered, Mrs. Reeve was at her doctor's.

'And if people would stop visiting until she returned I wouldn't complain,' she added. Then rushed to say, 'Not meaning you, Mr. Smith.'

It was just past four o'clock by then. 'I hate to waste any daylight,' said Smith, 'but perhaps we should visit Mrs. Reeve after supper?'

'Will she be up that late?'

'She keeps very late hours – requires next to no sleep, apparently.'

'She does sound a peculiar woman,' Lenox said.
'Well – quite.'

Back at the Queen's Arms, Lenox found Crook serving pints of ale to the first men who were getting off work. He had already heard all about the speech and congratulated Lenox on the success of his conversation with Roodle.

'Dirty trick,' the bartender added, 'but we'll see him done for.'

'I hope so, anyway.'

'If he wants a fight, he'll have a fight.'

'I've never asked you, Mr. Crook: Why do you involve yourself in politics? Is it of special interest to you?'

'I've always thought a man ought to believe in something, Mr. Lenox, and if he believes in something he ought to support it. Good evening, Mr. Pyle. A pint of mild, I expect?'

With that Crook was at the other end of the bar.

'Perhaps we could see Mrs. Reeve tomorrow, Mr. Smith? I don't feel my most vigorous.'

'Of course,' said Sandy, although he looked chagrined.

Lenox didn't care a fig at the moment, however, and bade farewell to his companion even as he began to walk tiredly up the stairs to his room.

'Wait, sir!' said the voice of Lucy, the waitress, behind him. 'Here's your telegram!'

With some excitement Lenox took it from her, enfolding a few pennies' tip in her hand.

It was from Dallington, sent in at Claridge's Hotel. Lenox knew this was one of Dallington's watering holes and hoped the young man wasn't reverting, as he occasionally had even under Lenox's tutelage, to his old, dissipated ways. Still, the telegram was coherent.

GLAD YOU ARE INTERESTED IN THE CASE STOP LONDON TEDIOUS AT THE MOMENT STOP SMALLS FOUND HANGING BY BOOT-LACES FROM WALL HOOK IN HIS CELL STOP APPARENT SUICIDE STOP EXETER CON-VINCED MURDER STOP VERY FEW DETAILS RELEASED BUT SPOKE TO WARDEN TODAY STOP SMALLS LEFT BEHIND SEVERAL TORN BITS OF PAPER AND ON TOP OF THEM THE FAMOUS ORANGES STOP GOOD LUCK THERE STOP DALLINGTON

As Lenox was reading, McConnell knocked at the door and came in, looking fresher after his day's rest but troubled nevertheless.

'Read this,' said the detective.

'Interesting,' said McConnell when he was fin-ished. He handed it back. 'What do you make of it?'

'Well – I wonder whether it was murder. If Exeter believes something, I always examine the opposite possibility.'

'Suicide?'

'Doesn't it seem more likely than murder? Why murder Smalls if you were his partner? Wouldn't it draw attention to you?'

'Of course,' said McConnell. 'Hence the appearance of suicide.'

Lenox sighed. 'You're right, of course, and it's easy enough to enter a prison if you wish to –

those guards will look away for a price, no matter what you do. Only it seems so transparent. Still, there was always the risk of Smalls ratting out whomever he worked with.'

'Yes.'

'I wish I knew what "several torn bits of paper" meant, exactly.' Lenox paused. 'McConnell, how are you feeling?'

The doctor shrugged. 'Well enough physically, I suppose. Full of regret as well.'

'I know you came all this way, but how about some work?'

To Lenox's surprise, McConnell fairly leapt at the idea, 'I would like that beyond anything.'

'It would be back in London.'

'About Smalls?'

'Yes – and to see if you could find any information others missed about Pierce and Carruthers, too.'

McConnell laughed. 'I haven't been here twenty-four hours,' he said.

In part Lenox was hoping a trip to London would force McConnell to see Toto, but he didn't say that, 'Still, I'm glad you came,' he said. 'I felt terrible having to leave at the moment of your loss.'

'Does this mean you're looking into the Fleet Street murders?'

'I suppose I shouldn't. I shall have to stay here.'

'Yes,' said McConnell. 'This is important.'

'Please let me know of your progress, however.'

'By telegram, yes.'

The two men, each unhappy in his own way – Lenox to be out of London and because of Lady

Jane's worries, McConnell for more profound and sorrowful reasons – sat for another moment and spoke. Then McConnell stood up and said he'd better pack.

Lenox rang for Graham then. He hadn't seen his valet since that morning.

'Graham,' he said when the man appeared in the doorway, 'take a look at this.' He passed over Dallington's telegram.

'Yes, sir?' said Graham when he had finished reading it.

'Well? What do you make of it?'

'Are you inclined to believe it was murder, sir, as Inspector Exeter does?'

Lenox again expressed his ambivalence on the question.

'With so few facts, I suppose there's little to speculate about, sir.'

'Yes,' said Lenox. 'Wait, take this telegram to the post office, would you?'

Graham waited while Lenox wrote out a note to Dallington asking for more information.

'I guess we're stuck here,' Lenox said as he handed the note over.

'Most certainly, sir,' said Graham somewhat severely.

'Oh, I know, I know, I'm curious, that's all.'

CHAPTER ELEVEN

The next morning Sandy Smith picked Lenox up at the Queen's Arms after breakfast, and they went again to see Mrs. Reeve. This time she was in.

McConnell had left by the early train, assuring Lenox that it would be a marvelous distraction to work and promising to give Lenox's best to Toto and Lady Jane. (Especially Jane, wished Lenox in his silent heart.) Meanwhile Graham had asked Lenox what help he might be in the campaign, and Lenox asked him to take over the various forms of propaganda that candidates had usually found necessary in parliamentary campaigns: the printing of further handbills and flyers, the circulation of Lenox's name by a new patron who stood everyone in the pub a pint, the quick word to servants and livery about the by-election. Lenox could think of nobody better suited to the job. He and Graham had for many years now been more friends than master and man, and he knew now that Graham had a particular talent for sliding into unfamiliar situations and earning quick friends and allies. He could speak deferentially to a (perceived) superior and confidentially to a (perceived) equal, and his good looks meant young women were often willing to listen to him.

'Plenty of beer,' said Lenox. 'Hilary tells me that's crucial in these matters.'

'Shall I state baldly that I represent you, sir?'

'I think probably. Your discretion shall dictate what you do, of course. Here are a few notes.'

As Smith, in his usual snug gray waistcoat and with his favorite gold watch bulging on one side, led Lenox to Mrs. Reeve's, he advised the candidate what to say.

'Flattery is poison to her,' he said. 'Equally, however, she's always watching out for what might be an insult or condescension. Her back will be up because you're from London. It works to your benefit, though, that you've gained some fame even here for that case.'

'The September Society business?'

'Yes, exactly. Mrs. Reeve rather collects celebrities, if you see what I mean.'

'I do, unfortunately. Who has she collected so far?'

Sandy Smith frowned, thinking. 'Well, there was a lad who fell into a well and lived. An actor named Crummies who comes through sometimes and does a decent show. There are more, though I can't think of them.'

'I'm honored to be in such company,' Lenox said with mock formality.

Smith laughed. 'You'll find her a strange woman, no doubt. Still, she's sharp enough in her way, I can promise you.'

They arrived at her well-maintained house, which was white with two tidy gables, and the maid let them in, then guided them down a front hall and into a sitting room that seemed purposely designed as a kind of permanent salon for guests. There were small clusters of chairs and couches spread throughout the room, each centered around a sizable tea table; all of these bore tea rings and hot water stains, bespeaking long hours of intimate conversation. On the walls were a few portraits in black and white of what might be deemed 'Olde Stirrington,' sentimentalized pictures of rural lanes and young couples in bygone churchyards. The largest of these pictures was of a blacksmith shop from some impossibly halcyon time, with a brawny man at the hammer and tongs and awed small children watching him, as a row of ducks passed in the foreground. All of it made Mrs. Reeve's vision of the world very clear.

As for the woman herself: She sat on the largest of the sofas, perhaps because it was the only one that fit her, wearing a regal maroon gown the size of a ship's sail and reading Dickens's latest novel, *Our Mutual Friend*.

'How do you like it?' asked Lenox before they had been introduced.

'Have you read it, Mr. Lenox?' she asked in a low-pitched voice, one with more charm and power in it than he had expected.

'I have indeed.'

'It's very black, I think – but funny, too.'

'They say he's sick.'

'Mr. Dickens? I hope he lives forever, as long he can always write.'

Lenox laughed. 'I'm Charles Lenox,' he said. 'Although you already know that.'

'Alice Reeve. Sally, fetch some tea, will you?'

'I'm awfully pleased to meet you, Mrs. Reeve.'

'And I'm glad you came to see me. I suppose you must view me rather as a local monument –

yes, I see you, Sandy Smith, please sit down – a monument, along the lines of a church or a museum, to be respectfully and duly visited?'

'On the contrary, I've heard the best conversation in town is to be found in this room.'

'In town, yes.' She arched her eyebrows appraisingly. 'Not quite London, though.'

'I grew up in the country, in fact.'

'Oh, yes – but in some vast house.'

'Well – big enough.'

'We're sharper in these small towns than you might expect.'

'After meeting your fellow townsmen, I've little doubt of your sharpness here in Stirrington.'

'We don't appreciate interlopers or arrivistes, either. Still, I bear no love for Robert Roodle.'

'No?'

'My nephew worked at the brewery before it left. A young lad with a family. He looked for six months before he found work again – and at a mill, terrible work at a lower wage.'

'I'm sorry to hear it.'

'Well, we need jobs, no doubt of that. The men here may care about this beer tax, but the women know better.'

'I'm relieved to hear you say that – I thought beer might be the local god from the way some people talk,' said Lenox.

At this Sandy Smith looked terrified, but after a moment of silence Mrs. Reeve gave her first real laugh, warm and long. Lenox liked her, in fact. A strange woman. She had gained some of the outward symbols of the gentry by virtue of her small fortune and intellect but retained the sense of a workingman's wife, he saw. She corrected her maid when she brought out the largest teapot.

'Wasteful, Sally,' she said as she poured. 'Well, and what can I do for you, Mr. Lenox?'

'Ma'am?'

'Sandy?'

'We would appreciate your support.'

Lenox hastened to say, 'Although before we can ask for that, I thought I'd meet you.'

'Well – let us see,' she said, but in a benevolent enough way. 'Would you call again tomorrow evening? There's a group of women who meet then, who I'm sure would like to meet you.'

'Of course I should be honored.'

Just then there was a knock at the door, and Sally ushered in a woman who said she 'absolutely *must* talk privately with you, my dear Alice,' and after brief introductions Lenox and Sandy Smith left their teacups mostly full and made their way outside.

'That was painless,' said Lenox.

'I thought it went very well indeed. Lucky you'd read that book. I forgot to mention that she's a great reader.'

'What do you think will be the effect of our visit?'

'Cigar? No? I think probably you have her support. She's one of ours, by tradition. Only I think she wanted to be courted a bit, and old Stoke never had to set foot in Stirrington to win his seat. The Stoke name means a lot here.'

That was the second time Lenox had heard words to that effect. 'Are there any Stokes remaining?'

Smith looked pained. 'Stoke's daughter married

a local landowner – very respectable chap, no title, but a family that stretches straight back to the Domesday Book. Quite religious, she is, and rarely comes to town except on Christmas.'

'So I've just missed her.'

'Indeed – both for that and for Stoke's funeral, As for Stoke's son – that's a sadder tale, I'm afraid. There were bright hopes for him at Cambridge, but after he went down from university he fell in with a gambling crowd in London and lost great sums of money. Eventually his father paid the debts – and was severely the worse for it, if local rumor means anything – and banished his son to India to make his fortune. There he contracted yellow fever, and nobody's quite sure if he's dead or alive. This town always loved Anthony Stoke, however. Such a merry lad, he was.'

By now they were coming to Main Street. 'Where are we going?' Lenox asked.

'I'm going to drop you off now. You've your speech at the library this afternoon – nothing until then. This evening will be important, however. You're meeting with a group of businessmen, those who would favor Roodle in the normal course of things but want to see what sort of man you are.'

'What time shall I see you?'

'I'll be at the library.'

'You're not coming with me?'

'Oh, no – Crook will. His niece, Nettie, volunteers there. Very loyal to the library.'

CHAPTER TWELVE

'Telegrams, sir!' sang Lucy as Lenox came in the door. She made her usual rounds, picking up empty glasses and bringing full ones, until she met Lenox again and reached into her pocket, gone again before he could thank her. The first people for lunch were at the pub. Interesting, staying here, to watch the ebb and flow of it. Crook was too busy to acknowledge him.

The telegrams were from Dallington and Scotland Yard. With great curiosity Lenox put the latter aside and tore open his apprentice's note. Which hand had killed Hiram Smalls, he wondered? Perhaps Dallington would know the answer.

DO YOU REMEMBER JONATHAN POOLE THE TRAITOR STOP THEY HAVE ARRESTED HIS SON STOP MET THE CHAP ON MY TOUR SOMEWHERE IN PORTUGAL AND HE SIMPLY COULD NOT HAVE KILLED ANYBODY STOP AIRIEST FELLOW I KNOW STOP EXETER IS CROWING TO THE PRESS STOP TORN BITS OF PAPER ARE SMALL SHREDS OF PAPER STOP WOULD HAVE THOUGHT THAT WOULD BE CLEAR TO THE MEAGEREST INTELLIGENCE STOP NOBODY KNOWS WHAT THEY SAY STOP RETURN STOP LONDON NEEDS YOU STOP POOLE NEEDS YOU STOP DALLINGTON

Scotland Yard couldn't afford such extravagance when telegrams cost by the word, but the other note was just as arresting.

FEAR EXETER ARRESTED WRONG MAN STOP PRESS EXCITABLE STOP CAN YOU SPARE TIME STOP JENKINS

With these two telegrams Lenox's mind flew into motion. Exeter had arrested Poole's son, a lad no more than twenty who had never seen England since he was a child and been brought up in the softest ways by his maternal family, and here were a character witness and an evidentiary one (perhaps?) from two people whom Lenox trusted? There was a chance, of course, that young Poole really had conspired with Hiram Smalls – or indeed independently of the man – to kill Simon Pierce and Winston Carruthers. However, Lenox held Exeter's certainties in very low esteem and at the moment felt disinclined to believe him about Poole.

The two implorations to return to London tempted him powerfully. Both because of the case and, less consciously, because of Lady Jane's letter, he had been uncomfortably longing to go back since he arrived at Stirrington. Moreover, while he liked Crook and Smith and still held his dream of entering Parliament, he wasn't sure but what the campaign didn't suit him. It made him uneasy. He would stick it out because the prize was so great, but it was another feeling that pushed him homeward. Often in his adult life he had told people that he was a Londoner and hated to be away from the metropolis, but it had always seemed a pro forma rather than a meaningful statement. Now it rang true to him again, and he remembered why he had begun saying it when he was a youth.

Counterweighing all this was Lenox's inborn, or at any rate early taught, feeling of responsibility. He couldn't possibly turn his back on Stirrington when he had vowed to Hilary, Edmund, and now Crook to fight his hardest and do his best.

Still, couldn't they spare him for forty-eight hours?

'You look thoughtful, Mr. Lenox,' said a female voice.

Lenox's distracted thoughts vanished, and he looked up. 'Why, hello, Nettie.' He stood up. 'Would you care to sit down?'

She shook her head. 'No, thanks. I've come to give Uncle his lunch.'

Lenox laughed. 'He doesn't have what all these gentlemen are having?'

'Oh, he likes the little meals I make him. If you work in a public house long enough, Mr. Lenox, you grow weary of steak and kidney pie with ale.'

'I can imagine.'

'I trust you're coming to the library this afternoon?'

'Yes, I shall certainly be there.'

'I'll see you then.'

Lenox watched as she took her uncle his midday meal, noting the momentary softening in Crook's eyes as they spoke. He promised to return the plate unbroken. Then he signaled to Lucy that he was stopping to eat, filled the pint glasses that

93

were empty, and went to a quiet back table with his food and a glass of fizzy lemonade. Lenox was loath to interrupt Crook's only respite of the day, but as soon as the publican had taken his last bite the detective went over.

'How do you do?' he asked Crook.

'Quite well enough, thank you.'

'I fear I may need to return to London. Only for two days or so – three days perhaps.'

Crook was astounded. 'With scarcely a fortnight until the vote!'

'Call it two days. Less than forty-eight hours.'

'Mr. Lenox, I've never been so shocked in all my life!'

'It's because of a murder.'

'Let there be twenty murders, see if I care! You cannot leave!'

'I'm aware of my duties here, but I feel I can still discharge them. What if I were to add another hundred pounds to our budget for advertising?'

'The town is pretty well covered.'

'My man, Graham, has been buying beer.'

'Not here,' said Crook, temporarily distracted.

'I thought it would look ill.'

'Because it's my public house?'

'Well – precisely.'

'Be that as it may, you simply cannot leave. Think of all that they say about you being a creature of London, and caring nothing for our Stirrington – and as soon as you arrive you leave!'

Gradually, though, as Lenox convinced Crook of his seriousness and promised further funds for all the sundry expenses of a campaign, the bartender's position altered. Promising that he would leave Graham in place, Lenox reached a compromise – he would leave that evening on the last train, stay in London for one day and one morning, and return in time to speak at Sawyer Park again on the second evening. He would be in London for something less than thirty-six hours.

'We'll have to tell them you're going to Durham to meet with county officials about the issues of Stirrington. That's all.'

'We cannot lie,' said Lenox, frowning.

'Ha! Ha!' said Crook, coughing as he laughed. 'You've been in politics a very short time! Make that face all you like, but lie we must, and lie we shall. Luckily Durham is a very impressive place to many of these voters, and they'll like that you have the power already to meet with those who control the city. Roodle could never get in.'

'Well – if we must.'

'We must.'

For another ten minutes (by which time there were several disgruntled drinkers clattering their pint pots on the bar with meaningful strength) Crook and Lenox discussed the matter.

As a sort of final condition Crook said, 'You must promise me that this afternoon and when you return, you will shake the hand of every person you meet on the way to and from your appointments.'

'Well – all right.'

'Promise me! It's no easy thing.'

'I promise I shall speak to as many people as I possibly can. Surely I'll miss some while I talk with others.'

'Well – yes,' said Crook begrudgingly. 'Very well.

95

Now you must knock at the door of my house. Nettie will walk you to the library. I'm afraid I won't be able to come, Mr. Lenox.'

'No?'

'I've wasted enough time away from my business.'

Lenox went through the afternoon shaking every hand that would reach out to meet his and speaking to people with a sunny optimism he didn't quite feel until he was hoarse. He impressed the town burghers at the library and earned the respect, if not the vote, of perhaps three-quarters of the severe-looking businessmen he met with that night. True to his word, he shook the hand of even the waiter who brought postprandial coffee into that meeting.

Even so, it must be owned: All the time his thoughts were bent toward London, toward Pierce and Carruthers, toward Dallington, Jenkins, and McConnell, and above all toward Lady Jane Grey, whom he hoped was still his engaged love.

Graham took him to the station.

'Don't stint on the pints of beer!' Lenox said to his man. 'Spend money where it must be spent!'

'I shall, sir.'

'Would you like me to take any messages back to London?'

'No, sir, thank you.'

'Did you pack my gray checked suit?'

'You're wearing it, sir.'

'Ah – so I am.'

'Return quickly and safely, sir.'

The train began to move, 'Good-bye, Graham! Conciliate Crook, if you can! Remember, money is no object!'

The detective turned into the train with a wave and found his empty compartment. It was something past midnight after a long, wearying day, yet as he felt the train gather pace beneath him and knew it was headed toward his home, he felt his heart lighten and his senses refresh themselves.

CHAPTER THIRTEEN

London.

In all its variety it seemed to put Stirrington out of existence, or at any rate out of thought. Lenox looked through the window of his phaeton and saw dustmen and shoeblacks darting among the traffic. The streetlamps were still lit at that early hour, but he had slept on the train and felt more excited than tired now. At eight o'clock Dallington and McConnell were coming to meet him, but before then he wanted to see Newgate Prison, the place where Hiram Smalls had died. According to the papers the warden there was a great advocate of abstinence and clean living (as almost by necessity a good warden must be) and preferred to begin the day early rather than end it late. Lenox hoped to find him at the prison, though it wasn't past six yet.

It was modern times, now, 1867, and for some years the prison system had been subject to close scrutiny from Parliament. This was primarily because of a remarkable woman named Elizabeth

Fry, who had died some twenty years before. In her life she had toured prisons such as Newgate and found herself profoundly shocked by the treatment of prisoners there, especially women prisoners – in particular because if a female prisoner had a child, that child often accompanied its mother to the prison and stayed there as long as the prisoner had to.

Only in the last decade or so had a comprehensive overhaul begun. Prisons now were by law better ventilated, served heartier food, endured less theft by the guards, and allowed prisoners time outdoors and with visiting family. It was a change Lenox was all in favor of, though his more conservative friends decried the money it meant spending on common criminals.

Those were prisons in general, though, not the most famous prison in the world. For so Newgate was.

It stood at the corner of Newgate Street and Old Bailey, near the primary criminal court of London. Though it had some architectural distinction, its dark walls and low roof gave it an ominous aspect, as if the building had learned its purpose and rushed to take on an apt appearance. It had housed any number of famous people: Jack Sheppard, the most infamous thief of the previous century, who had managed to escape three times before he was finally hanged; Daniel Defoe, who wrote Robinson Crusoe; the playwright Ben Jonson, Shakespeare's rival; and the pirate Captain Kidd. Gruesomely, most public hangings in London had for more than three-quarters of a century been done outside of Newgate's walls, where the prisoners could hear the crowd's bloodthirsty cries. Although there was now a widely embraced movement to stop such barbarity, one Lenox suspected would lead to the end of the practice.

The detective had several times in his career occasion to visit the prison and always left feeling slightly desolate. It was improved now, to be sure, but still had the eerie feeling of a place where mayhem and death are almost as prevalent as their constriction. A place of high walls, little light, and constant sorrow.

Also a crowded one. As Lenox entered by the main gate and asked the bailiff if he might have an audience with the warden, signs of overcrowding were everywhere. It was another marker of the times. In previous eras punishment had been largely corporal, but now that men and women were staying in prison for long stretches instead, space came at a premium. The cells Lenox passed on his way up to the warden's office were all full by one or two too many, and he marveled that Hiram Smalls had received his own space.

The warden was in. The man who had led Lenox up to the warden's office went in and had a quick word and then poked his head out of the door to nod Lenox inside.

The man in charge of Newgate was fifty or so but looked strong and healthy. He was standing at a window that overlooked the courtyard, watching a group of thirty ill-looking men straggle around below him. A cup of tea was in one hand.

'How do you do, Mr. Lenox?' he asked. 'I was surprised to hear you had come. I thought you were in the north.'

'How do you do, sir. Yes, I was, but have returned for a day.'

'Plus I may help you, I take it?'

'If you would be so good.'

'Inspector Exeter was here.' A small smile formed on the warden's face. 'Do you agree with his suppositions about this case, Mr. Lenox?'

'I haven't had the honor of hearing your name, sir,' said Lenox stiffly. He disliked the warden's savoring of the situation.

He stuck out his hand. 'I'm Timothy Natt, and very pleased.'

'Pleased. I'm not sure whether I agree with Inspector Exeter, to answer your question. A friend has asked me to look over this matter, and I thought I would begin here.'

'With 122?'

'Excuse me?'

'With prisoner 122. Mr. Hiram Smalls.'

'Ah – indeed.'

'We give all of our prisoners a number when they enter Newgate.'

'I see.'

'I often hear from prisoners – I speak to them regularly, you see, in keeping with our modern trend of better inmate care – that they tire of being called only by their number. It's 74 this, 74 that, 74 everywhere, as one man – prisoner 74 – remarked to me.'

Lenox concealed a smile. Some pomposity here then. 'I had hoped to see Mr. Smalls's cell?'

'If you wish, yes.'

'Has anybody inhabited it since he left?'

'No, Mr. Lenox. Because the case attracted such

attention, we have been scrupulous in our handling of 122.'

'Well – in most ways,' said Lenox wryly.

'Sir?' asked Natt rigidly.

'Only – well, he died.'

Natt drew himself up. 'I can assure you that had we known he was in any danger from another prisoner, as Inspector Exeter thinks, or had we known he was a threat to himself – we would have – we would have – this is a well-run prison, sir.' With this piece of bluster complete, the warden took a violent sip of tea.

Lenox was quick to conciliate him. 'Oh, of course,' he said. 'I never meant to imply otherwise. A model, from what I've seen.'

'Well,' said Natt, with a definite 'humph.'

'What about his personal effects, sir?'

'Excuse me?'

'His personal effects? The things you confiscated from him on his entrance to Newgate – pipe, purse, that sort of thing?'

Natt stared at Lenox for a moment before saying, 'I'm ashamed to admit this, sir, but neither Exeter nor I thought to look at them.'

'What?'

'It's quite possible – indeed, probable – that they have been remitted to the care of his family.'

Lenox cursed. Natt couldn't have been expected to think of it, but Exeter! 'Well, do you keep a list of what the prisoners arrive with?'

Natt brightened. 'Ah! We do! Rime,' he shouted out to his assistant, '122's list of effects! On my desk! I see that you're a sharp one, Mr. Lenox. The papers were right. The Oxford case, I mean to say.'

Not wanting to be drawn, after a moment's pause Lenox said, 'Shall we see the cell, then?'

'Certainly, if you wish.'

To reach the cell they walked through a series of dank corridors, some lined with cells and some not. The prisoners they met along the way were alternatively listless or loud, though when they saw the warden they all went quiet. At last, when Lenox could smell fresh air for the first time since he had entered Newgate's walls, they stopped at a cell.

'The prison yard is just down here, the place where prisoners may exercise and socialize.' The guard following them opened the door. 'You see we left the cell intact.'

It was a poor little place to spend one's final days in. A narrow cot with rumpled sheets took up most of the space, with a small, ill-made, but solid nightstand just by it. The hook Smalls had hanged himself from was just to the right of the cell's front bars.

'The bits of paper – the oranges – they were on the night-stand?'

'Precisely. Inspector Exeter took those as evidence.'

'Did he say of what?'

'No, Mr. Lenox. Not that I can recollect. Exeter and I suspected that whoever did this, if 122 was murdered, tore up the papers to conceal their meaning.'

'No,' Lenox murmured.

'Excuse me?'

'Ah – you'll pardon me, I didn't know I was

speaking out loud. I doubt it, though, that's true. A murderer would either have taken the papers or left them. Smalls himself tore them up. Whether meaningfully or not remains to be seen.'

'Inspector Exeter was certainly of the opinion,' said Natt shaking his head with certainty, 'that the murderer did it.'

'Would it be easy for a guard or a prisoner to murder someone here, Mr. Natt?'

'Not a guard, certainly.'

'A prisoner, then?'

'Yes, sadly. Before 122's death we left vacant cells open while their inhabitants were in the yard. It would have been easy to sneak into a cell and lie in wait, I suppose. There's a great deal of chaos, unfortunately, and since some cells are overcrowded a person *might* not be missed for – say, half an hour.'

'Then bribe a guard to return to his own cell?'

'Well–'

'I take your point, Mr. Natt, There are also deliveries and so forth to the prison?'

'Yes, sir. All prisoners with sufficient funds may order in food, books, pen and paper, etc.'

'Is the delivery person admitted to the cell?'

'Yes.'

'So again – it wouldn't be impossible to pretend you were a delivery person and somehow gain access to a cell?'

'Not impossible.'

'Is there a list of incoming deliveries?'

'We have – er – discussed it.'

'I see. Well – may I look over this room?'

'Yes, of course you may.'

CHAPTER FOURTEEN

Lenox began, as was his wont, by searching from the ground up. With a lack of ceremony that plainly surprised Natt, he lay flat on his stomach and took a preliminary look under the bed. Lighting a match from a matchbox in his pocket, he then made a more comprehensive survey of the space. He took enough time for Natt to offer an impatient throat clearing, but in the end the time he took was worth it. Behind one of the bed's feet he found a pile of coins, stacked in order of size so that they made a small pyramid. He picked it up carefully and spread the coins in his palm.

'A farthing, a halfpenny, a penny, threepence, sixpence, and a shilling. All the coins of the realm up to the shilling,' said Lenox.

'You would be surprised what people hoard in here.'

'Of course. Wouldn't he have kept money on his person, though?'

'In fact, no. There are frequent incidents of theft and mugging, I'm afraid.'

'It's to be expected. What could this buy?'

'A pair of trousers?'

'I know what it could buy in *our* world,' said Lenox, 'but in here?'

'Oh – oh. Perhaps five breakfasts? Four suppers?'

'Tobacco?'

'To be sure.'

With this Lenox resumed his search, looking under the nightstand, removing its one drawer and searching for false joints, and trying to pry off its top, until he was convinced it was innocent of further contents. Then he searched the visible floor, then the walls, and after that the ledge of the tiny window.

There was very little else in the cell, and finally he turned his attention to the hook Smalls had died on. It was slightly loose, no doubt from bearing all the weight it had. Lenox couldn't make much of it but noticed a brown square about a foot below it, the size of another hook.

'What's this?' he asked.

'There used to be two hooks. Still are, in a few cells.'

'Why did you take them away?'

'They had fallen out of use. From the color of the stain I'd say this one has been gone for three or four years.'

'I see.'

Lenox felt discouraged. He made it a policy to visit the freshest crime scene first but now wished he had gone to Carruthers's or Pierce's house instead.

They walked back to the warden's office by the same grim route, and Lenox felt glad he had been born into a position that made crime an unlikely choice for him. Which was not to say there weren't men of his station within these walls. Some of them were there because of him.

'Ah,' said Natt when they were in his office, 'here is the list of 122's effects.'

'Thank you.'

It was a short list that Lenox took in his hands. 'One suit, gray serge; one piece of paper; one pouch, shag tobacco; one pipe, mahogany and match scarred; one penny blood, *Black Bess.*'

Lenox knew his compassion ought to be reserved for Pierce and Carruthers, but something about this list struck his easily reached heart. It was the magazine perhaps, the penny dreadful. He knew *Black Bess.* It was about a legendary highwayman, Dick Turpin, who had in truth been a stupid man, a robber of old ladies, a murderer, but who in these glamorized stories was the owner of a beautiful horse, Bess, on whom he rode the country, bad but never evil, a rogue with a conscience. What appeal would *Black Bess* have to a man like Hiram Smalls? It seemed to tell its own tale, the man's choice of what to read.

'Did the paper have any markings or writing on it?'

'There will be a note on the reverse of the sheet if it does.'

'Ah – thank you.'

In fact, there was an addendum. In careful handwriting, a clerk's probably, it read, 'Note dated Dec. 20, no signature or address, beginning "The dogcarts pull away" and ending "No green." Thirty-two words, nonsense or code.'

Well, this was maddening.

'Is there no way to get hold of the note?'

'You might inquire about it with 122's mother.'

'Indeed I shall. You have her address, I hope?' Lenox said, trying to contain his ire.

'Here it is, somewhere on my desk.' Natt shuffled through his things. 'Ah, yes, here.' He copied the address down for Lenox. 'Will that be all?'

'Yes, thank you. I appreciate your help.'

'We strive for transparency, and in particular as you're now in – in the public eye, as it were...'

So this was why it had been so easy to see the prison.

'Yes?'

'If you do make it into Parliament, Mr. Lenox, I can guess you won't forget us?'

'Of course not.'

Natt fairly beamed. 'Topping! Yes, well, I wish you all of the best luck in your campaign and your – your case alike.'

'Thank you, Warden.'

CHAPTER FIFTEEN

It was nearing eight o'clock in the morning now, and as Lenox rode homeward his thoughts turned to Lady Jane, whom he pictured in the small pale blue study, across from the rose-colored sitting room, where she spent her mornings. She would be reading her letters and answering them with a cup of tea beside her, and Lenox wondered whether perhaps his own note lay on her mahogany desk. It was foolish, but he felt afraid of visiting her. Still, he believed in facing things that frightened him and decided that after speaking with McConnell and Dallington he would go to her house.

He arrived at his own familiar door and found that the moment he touched the knob it flew open, with McConnell behind it. Mary, who was in charge of the house in Graham's absence, stood a few feet behind him with a worried look on her face.

'How do you do, Lenox? I'm a bit early.'

'How do you do, Thomas? Shall we go to the library?'

'Yes, yes. I have news.'

About Toto or the case? It wouldn't do to ask in front of Mary, however, who had taken Lenox's coat and now trotted down the long front hallway behind the two men, whispering in Lenox's ear that his suitcase had arrived, sir, and would he like breakfast, and that she had offered Dr. McConnell a seat, but he had insisted on waiting by the door. Lenox dismissed her with as much tolerance as he could muster, instructing her to admit Dallington whenever the young man arrived. Mary, who was always overawed by her responsibility when Graham was gone and Lenox spoke to her directly, blushed and stammered and left.

In Lenox's library a fire had just been lit, and to his agitation the papers on his desk were now neatly stacked.

'Will you come sit by the fire?' Lenox asked. 'I've a bit of a chill. Winter weather.'

'With pleasure,' said McConnell.

The doctor's face was flushed, and his eyes were slightly wild, darting a little too often to his left and right, never quite focusing. His hands trembled just slightly. His hair was combed back, but his clothes certainly hadn't been changed in twenty-four hours, maybe more.

Gently, Lenox said, 'May I ask after Toto's health?'

'I haven't seen her,' said McConnell. 'I'm staying at Claridge's. Even so, her doctor says she's well.'

'I'm so glad to hear it.'

McConnell nodded. 'Yes,' he said. Then, a little less certainly, he said it again. 'Yes.'

'How are you?'

'I've found something out, I believe.'

'What is that?' said Lenox, pouring two cups of coffee. McConnell looked as if he could use it.

'I think Smalls was murdered.'

'Not a suicide?' asked Lenox sharply.

'No.'

Now, McConnell was truly a world-class doctor. In his time he had been one of the most gifted surgeons on Harley Street, the epicenter of the empire's medical community, and had treated the royal and the destitute side by side. Toto's family had considered it beneath their dignity that their scion should marry a medical man, however, and though he had resisted for three years after his marriage, in the end they had persuaded him to sell the practice to an impoverished relation for a mere song.

It had been the catastrophic mistake of his life. Work had given him purpose and identity; left to his own devices, to the endless hours of an unoccupied day, he had begun to collapse inward. Now he only practiced when he helped Lenox. Because of the doctor's state, however, Lenox felt less confident in the man than usual.

'How do you know?'

McConnell breathed a deep, steadying sigh. 'It comes down to his bootlaces.'

'Yes?'

'I saw them. I visited your friend Jenkins, at Scotland Yard.'

'I'm seeing him this morning.'

'He managed to show me the bootlaces. He had to risk getting caught when he pulled them out of evidence, but I impressed the urgency of it on him.'

'What was so telling about the bootlaces?'

'That they weren't broken.'

'Well, of course they weren't – they–' Then Lenox saw it. 'They couldn't have borne Smalls's weight.'

'Precisely. I nosed around at the coroner's a bit. I couldn't manage to see the body, for which I'm sorry–'

'Not at all.'

'I did find out that Smalls weighed roughly eleven stone. I measured the bootlaces, looked at the report Exeter drew up to see how they had been arranged around his neck, went out and bought a dozen pair of identical laces, and then did some experiments at the butcher's.'

'And?'

'I tried hanging every hog and cow in the place – even a few that were much lighter than eleven stone – and every time the laces snapped. They were thin ones.'

'The butcher let you?'

'I gave him a bottle of whisky.'

'Brilliantly managed,' said Lenox.

McConnell's eyes steadied for a moment and shone with the happiness of a job well done. 'Thank you, Lenox,' he said.

'Yet how did Smalls stay up on the wall?'

'I believe I figured that out, too. According to the Yard's report, his belt was unusually worn – with the buckle in back.'

'His back was to the wall, correct?' Suddenly Lenox thought of the colored square on the wall where a second hook had once been, 'They turned his belt around, so it would hitch to the metal bit?'

'Yes.'

'I wonder if Exeter saw that.'

'Perhaps,' said McConnell. 'Perhaps.'

'Then what killed the man?'

'I've no doubt it was strangulation. I know the coroner who wrote the report. He's very good.'

'Strangulation that was then made to look as if it were suicide? There's one problem remaining, of course.'

'Do you mean – what his belt was hooked to?'

'Exactly. Can Natt have been lying?'

'Who?'

'The warden.'

'I don't know,' said McConnell.

'Well – it was awfully well done, anyway,' said Lenox, 'We know what we're facing now.'

Just then there was a ring at the door. It would be Dallington. Glancing up at his clock, Lenox saw it was just past eight.

But no.

'Lady Jane Grey,' announced Mary and held the door for Lenox's betrothed.

CHAPTER SIXTEEN

It was very awkward, because Lenox had strode toward the door of the library when he heard the ring, and as Jane came in she saw only him at first.

'Charles!' she said with high emotion after Mary had closed the door behind her. 'I saw you come home.'

'I was just on my way to see you,' he said, 'after keeping two short appointments.'

'Hello, Jane,' said McConnell just then, apparently without perceiving her fragile state.

She started. 'Why – hello, Thomas.'

'How do you do?'

'Fairly well, thank you. I come from your house.'

Of course she wouldn't have been in her pale blue study, Lenox thought. She would have been at Toto's side.

'Yes?' said McConnell stiffly.

With uncharacteristic directness – she was a tactful soul – she said, 'You ought to return there this instant.'

'Oh, yes?' he said, looking even more unhappy. 'I believe that the household might be more comfortable if – if–'

'Don't be proud, for the love of heaven. Toto pines for you, and these are the hardest days of her life. Go back to her.'

'Well – I–'

'Oh!' She stamped her foot in frustration. 'Men waste half their lives being proud.'

Even in this fraught situation, Lenox felt a burst of pride that she was his – if she was, anyway.

'Well–' said McConnell in a halting voice. 'Good day, Lenox. Good day, Jane.'

With that he left the room.

Lady Jane went to the sofa in the middle of the room and sat, a heavy sigh escaping her lips as she did. 'What lives we all lead,' she said. 'Poor Toto.'

Lenox went to sit beside her but did not embrace her. They were a foot or so apart. 'How are you, Jane? Well, I dearly hope? Did you receive my letter?'

'Yes, Charles, it reassured me. Still, these two days I've sat at Toto's bedside–'

Just then there was another ring at the door, and, as Lenox had instructed her to, Mary brought Dallington into the library.

He was a cheerful-looking young man, a carnation in his buttonhole, and genially said hello to Lenox and Lady Jane. There were dark circles under his eyes, the legacy no doubt of a long and debauched night in some music hall or gambling room. He bore fatigue better than McConnell, however, being younger and, because of his long years of carousing, perhaps better used to it.

'I hope I don't interrupt your conversation?' he said.

'No,' answered Lenox.

Dallington went on, 'I'm late, as I daresay you'll have observed.'

'John, will you say hello to your mother for me?' asked Lady Jane. 'I've missed her twice in the

113

past two days.'

'Of course,' he answered.

'Charles, I'll see you in a little while?'

Lenox half-bowed.

'Then I must be off.'

She hurried out of the room, and as she did Lenox thought of her usual movements, how graceful and languid they were compared to the agitation of her carriage now. It was the stress of seeing Toto, he thought, in combination with her doubts about their marriage. Jane Grey had striven for her entire life to act well and honestly, and she felt miserable when she didn't see the right course ahead. Suddenly a solemn sense of fear overtook Lenox. He had to master himself before addressing the young lord.

'Thank you for your telegrams, Dallington,' he said. 'They were most welcome when the newspapers' information lagged.'

'Don't mention it.'

'What can you tell me about this young suspect?'

'About Gerald Poole? Well, Exeter arrested him yesterday. You've seen the papers?'

'Not yet. I've had a steady stream of appointments since getting back this morning.'

'How is the campaign, incidentally?'

The relationship between the two men was a funny one. Not quite friends, they had nonetheless been through more than most friends already – for Dallington had saved Lenox's life, while Lenox had witnessed many of Dallington's flaws firsthand; and though student and pupil, they knew too much of each other and moved too closely in the same circles to retain the formality of that connection. It was never clear whether their conversations should stay professional, but Dallington settled the matter by seeing that they didn't. Still, Lenox never felt entirely comfortable confiding in the young man, whose tastes and habits were so different than his own.

'Well, thank you. It will be difficult to win, but I have high hopes.'

'I once gambled with old Stoke's boy.'

'Did you?'

'Dissipated sort.'

'What about Poole?'

Dallington offered Lenox a grim smile. 'To business already?'

'I'm only here briefly.'

'Well – can that blushing creature of yours fetch a paper?'

Lenox rang for Mary and asked for the morning's and the prior evening's newspapers.

Dallington said, 'Asking for one is the same as asking for a hundred – they all have the same information. Inspector Exeter placed Gerry Poole under arrest for the murders of Simon Pierce and Winston Carruthers.'

'Have they cottoned on to his father's history yet?'

'Oh, yes. They all mention the treason.'

'Has Exeter given up on Smalls, then?'

'On the contrary – he's convinced that they did it together.' Gravely, Dallington said, 'In fact, that's the strongest piece of evidence linking Gerry to the murders. The rest of it is circumstantial.'

'What's the strongest piece of evidence?'

'About fifty witnesses have Gerald Poole and

Hiram Smalls meeting in the Saracen's Head pub the night before the murders. Even if none of them had seen it, however, he's admitted it's true.'

'Hiram Smalls must have been a busy pubgoer, from the sound of things. He met Martha Claes and Gerald Poole both at pubs.'

The papers came in just then, and Lenox perused them without much close attention. They were in concord with Dallington's account of the matter.

'What's his explanation for being in the pub?'

'I haven't been in to see him, and he hasn't told the papers, but he admitted it readily enough.'

'As an intelligent person would if denial were useless. He went into prison after Smalls had already died there, I take it? No overlap?'

'No, no.' Distressed, Dallington said, 'Listen, won't you, he simply *can*not have killed anyone.'

'No?'

'I met him years ago on the continent and have kept in touch with him since. He's the friendliest, least sinister chap I ever saw. Not to mention that he couldn't tell you the time without losing his watch. The idea of him planning a murder is laughable.'

'Yet his father was guilty of high crimes, almost certainly.'

'Gerry always lived in a sort of permanent, jovial daze. Never said a cross word to anybody, happily won and lost money alike at the track, drank himself into a friendly stupor – I can't describe accurately how incapable of malice I believe him to be.'

'A more cynical man than myself might say you

saw him through a friend's eyes.'

'Am I such a poor judge of character as all that?'

'No,' said Lenox quietly. 'I don't think you are.'

'Well, then.'

Trying to sound detached, Lenox said, 'You know, you look a bit tired, Dallington.'

The younger man laughed. 'You always smoke me out, don't you, Lenox?'

'Well?'

'A friend of mine was in London. I've been sleeping for the last fifteen hours, but we did chase the devil for a day and a night.'

Lenox sighed. It wasn't his place to say anything, but the lad had talent, definite talent, in the art of detection. 'I hope it was worth it.'

'Excuse me?' said Dallington, who was used to his own way.

'By God, man, do you realize I have a day here, not more than a day and a half? Much of this case must come down to you – to you! Or the Yard,' Lenox said as an afterthought.

A look of determination came onto Dallington's face, 'I had hoped as much.'

'Well,' said Lenox, standing. 'Let us go and see Mr. Poole. Newgate twice in one morning! What a depressing thought.'

CHAPTER SEVENTEEN

Because of the hook on the wall of the prison cell that must have been propping up Hiram Smalls from the waist – and Natt's comment that it had been gone for 'two or three years' – Lenox felt distinctly suspicious of the warden as he entered Newgate again. In the end, however, he wasn't forced to confront the man and merely signed in with Dallington to see Gerald Poole in a small room where prisoners could receive visitors.

They went in and found the prisoner sitting at a small table with three rickety stools around it. The room was otherwise empty, though a guard remained outside the door.

'That can't be John Dallington, can it?' Poole said with transparent shock on his face,

'How do you do, old friend?' said Dallington.

'Only middling,' said Poole, then laughed and turned to Lenox, 'Gerald Poole. Won't you sit down?'

'Charles Lenox,' said the detective, seeing right away the way Dallington had been trying to describe Poole. He seemed as unconcerned at finding himself in prison as he would have been at finding himself in Buckingham Palace. An unflappable lad. Of course, criminals often *were* unflappable.

'I'm pleased to meet you.'

'I wish it were under happier circumstances,'

said Dallington.

'Whatever can bring you here?'

'It's funny, actually – I'm an amateur detective now. Or training to be one. Lenox here made the daft decision to take me on as his student. Perhaps you've seen his name in the paper?'

'The Oxford case, wasn't it?'

'Yes!' said the young lord and beamed.

'But – a detective, Dallington?'

Now here was a conversation Lenox had had a hundred times in his life. Peers and elders who had once considered him promising greeted the news with barely concealed consternation, while those less familiar with him idly wondered if he had lost his money on horses or women. How much easier to be like Edmund, a stolid MP, part of the great mass of respectable aristocrats who clustered around Grosvenor Square! Lenox loved his work dearly and felt it was noble indeed; nevertheless, ignoble though it was, part of him yearned for the comfortable respect of being a Member of Parliament. It wasn't the main reason he was running, but if he admitted it to himself it was one of the reasons. No more uncomfortable moments like this one.

Dallington, predictably, was more open than Lenox. He laughed. 'Just a fancy,' he said. 'I haven't been disowned or anything like that. I felt I could do some good. Neither of us was cut out for the old military and clergy line of things, were we, Gerry?'

Poole laughed merrily, accepting Dallington's explanation at face value. 'No, indeed not,' he said. His accent was very definitely English, though he had passed so much of his life abroad. Lenox thought of the traitor Jonathan Poole and suddenly found himself curious.

'I told Lenox you couldn't possibly have killed either of those journalists, and he agreed to come over and see you. He's the best, I promise.'

'I'm awfully grateful. I seem to have few friends in this city – if visitors are friends. My cousin visited but could never rid himself for a moment of his feeling of superiority, and a childhood friend came but found me changed beyond his liking. I've ordered in a few books, but these have been worrisome hours, I confess.'

'I have faults,' said Dallington, 'but at any rate I'm a good friend.'

Here Poole broke into a magnificent smile, a truly radiant smile, and in that moment Lenox felt with great power that he must be innocent. All the incarcerated lad said was, 'Yes, you are, John. A good friend.'

'Will you tell us about your meeting with Smalls?' asked Lenox.

'Business – yes. Well, it was the damnedest thing I ever knew.'

'Oh?'

'I only returned to London three and a half months ago, when I finally turned eighteen, Mr. Lenox, and came into my inheritance. Before then my education had been on the Continent, and my tastes had run toward that part of the world anyway.' Very openly, he added, 'You've heard of my father?'

'Yes,' said Lenox in a measured voice.

'London was a bitter place to my mind because

of him, you see, but my lawyers contacted me and said that I had to return to see to business – and anyway I was finally growing restless in Porto, where Dallington and I first met.

'I've found it pleasant enough here, although I had no friends and little enough acquaintance. I spent my time corresponding with friends abroad, seeing shows, walking in Hyde Park, dining at my club – in short, adjusting to London – when the man named Hiram Smalls contacted me.

'He called himself Frank Johnson, however, not by his real name. He said in a letter that he had worked for my father at our house in Russell Square when I was very young and that he had always been fond of me and longed for a reunion, having heard that I was back in London. I'm not sure *how* he heard that, and it strikes me as strange, frankly.'

Poole lit a cigar and seemed to ponder this for a moment.

'What happened at your meeting?'

'It was the strangest thing. At first he began reminiscing in such broad terms that I was instantly sure we had never met in this life. After ten minutes I felt I had listened enough and asked him his true business. He denied lying, and I did all I could do – stood up and left. As I went I heard a barmaid who quite clearly knew him address him as Hiram. It left a strange impression upon me, but I didn't think a thing of it after a day or two had passed. Then yesterday Inspector Exeter knocked on my door and arrested me for the murder of two men I've never heard of in my life. It's the strangest damned thing under the sun.'

'Singular,' Lenox agreed.

'Clearly Smalls wanted to meet him in public for some nefarious reason!' said Dallington with passion.

'Yes,' said Lenox, 'and he took you to a pub where they knew him and could testify to the meeting. It's strange indeed. I remember something slightly like it, that I heard of once – though that was in France. I doubt the solution there meets the facts here, however. In that instance they needed the man out of his house in order to steal from it. Nobody has stolen anything from you, I hope?'

'Not that I know of, no.'

'Well – I certainly trust Dallington when he avers your innocence, Mr. Poole. He and I shall do our level best to figure out what happened to Pierce and Carruthers, not to mention Smalls. I take it the man you met at the pub was like the description you subsequently heard of Smalls?'

'Oh, yes – short and stocky. The very man, I would say.'

'Very well, Mr. Poole. Is there anything you wish to add?'

'I scarcely need to say that I'm innocent, I think.'

'Of course not,' said Dallington indignantly.

'In that case we shall bid you good day.'

Outside of the prison again, Dallington said, 'What did you think, then?'

'There's a chance he's guilty.'

'There certainly isn't!'

'A small chance, of course. Still, one must say it, a chance.'

'What on earth would his motive be?'

Lenox stopped. Around the two men London's business milled. 'You can keep a secret?'

'Yes,' said Dallington expectantly.

'Carruthers and Pierce testified against Poole's father. Whether Gerald knew that or not I couldn't say.'

Dallington whistled softly. 'I didn't know that,'

'Yes.'

'Gracious.'

'Can you blame Exeter for his certainty?'

This question snapped Dallington out of his reverie, 'By God, I can! Gerald Poole is simply – is simply not a killer. I know it with every fiber of my being!'

'We shall have to work to prove it, then,' said Lenox, a doubtful grimace on his face. 'Consider, though, the clear motive he had and his open admission that he met with Hiram Smalls, and Exeter's case seems a difficult one to disprove.'

'Yet equally impossible to prove – because Gerry didn't kill anyone.'

'I hope so.'

'Where are you going next, Lenox?'

To Jane's, the detective wished he could say, but he had other appointments to keep. 'I expect I shall go see Inspector Jenkins. Then I think I'll go and see Smalls's mother. That will require tact.'

'What can I do?'

They stood on the corner, and Lenox examined his protégé. 'If you want a job–'

'With all my heart.'

'Then you might go to Fleet Street and speak to Pierce's and Carruthers's friends and colleagues. You might find out whatever you can about Jonathan Poole. You might speak to Pierce's family and find out about the landlady of Carruthers, the Belgian woman who vanished.'

'Then I shall,' said Dallington stoutly. 'Will you be at home this evening?'

'God willing,' said Lenox.

CHAPTER EIGHTEEN

Lenox was closeted with Inspector Jenkins of Scotland Yard for some twenty minutes and came away from the meeting with a copy of the frankly unrevealing police report. Jenkins was pessimistic about the case. He felt far from sure of Poole's guilt, as his telegram to Lenox had indicated, but admitted now that no other leads had emerged to contradict Exeter's theory. He promised to meet Dallington and keep Lenox apprised of any news by telegram, but when the two men parted it was in a melancholy mood.

It was ten o'clock in the morning by then and had already been a long, long day for Lenox. He left the headquarters of the Metropolitan Police by hansom cab to see Hiram Smalls's aged mother but had the driver let him out a few doors early so he could stop into a public house. A warm brandy braced him to no end and took some of the cold ache out of his bones, and he walked up Liverpool Street with a renewed sense of purpose.

'What is she like?' he had asked Jenkins.

'You understand I haven't been involved in the

case at all – or rather, simply as a spectator with better access than the public.'

'Still, I know you speak to the constables on their routes, the other officers.'

Jenkins shook his head. He was an intelligent, sensitive young man, who found fault with Scotland Yard but served it faithfully. 'Nobody saw her other than Exeter,' he said. 'Who reported back that she was entirely intractable.'

'What a wasted opportunity.'

Jenkins, who had heard with horror that Exeter had neglected to ask for Smalls's personal effects at Newgate, nodded. 'Then again, many people in the East End fear the police. With reason, sometimes.'

'She's in her right mind, however?'

'I believe so. Exeter said nothing on that score.'

Lenox rang at the door, and a small, plump, red-cheeked girl of two or three and twenty answered the door. She had sharp little eyes.

'Yes?' she said.

'I'm here to see Mrs. Smalls, miss.'

'Are you, then? Well, I'm sure I don't know whether she's receiving visitors.' The girl put her hands on her hips. She had a pronounced cockney accent. 'May I ask 'oom I 'ave the pleasure of meetin'?'

'Charles Lenox, ma'am,'

'Fair enough, Mr. Lenox, and your business?'

'I'm investigating Hiram Smalls's death.'

Instantly the tone of the conversation shifted from the suspicious to the outright combative, 'We don't want none of your kind here, Mr. Lenox.' His name as if it were a curse word.

'Good day.'

'Are you Mrs. Smalls's landlady?'

'Am I her – well, I'm sure it's no concern of yours, but I am, yes.'

'I believe Hiram was murdered.'

She inhaled sharply, and her eyes widened. 'No!'

'I'm not with the Yard, ma'am. I'm a private detective.'

'Well.'

'I only want justice.'

'For Hiram?'

'If he was wronged.'

'Of course 'e was wronged! Hiram wouldn't 'urt a fly!' Her outrage was in its way as persuasive as Dallington's on behalf of Gerald Poole. 'Come into the 'allway, come in. I'll speak to Mrs. Smalls.'

After a series of complex negotiations, in which the landlady went back and forth and inquired who Mr. Lenox was, first, and then who Mr. Lenox *thought* he was, second, and finally whether he was quite sure he didn't belong to Scotland Yard – only after all of these questions had been posed by the doubting go-between and satisfactorily answered by Lenox did she lead the detective up one flight of stairs to see Mrs. Smalls.

Now, Mrs. Smalls was, anybody with a rudimentary faculty of perception could see straightaway, a particular type – a faded beauty. She retained all the ornaments and outward accoutrements of beauty, including a beautiful velvet dress, profuse jewelry, and massive, heavily curled hair. There were gaudy cameos of a pretty young girl on half the surfaces in the cramped

126

sitting room, and on the other half sat framed and dusty notices of a variety of plays.

Although the woman herself was pale, painfully thin, and red eyed, and Lenox speculated to himself that perhaps this tragedy had punctured her vanity for good. She lookcd as if the cares of the world had all crowded around her at once.

'How do you do, Mr. Lenox?' she asked in a somber voice and gave her curled forelock a vicious twist and tug as she curtsied.

'Fairly,' he said, 'I'm so sorry about your son, Mrs. Smalls.'

'You believe my Hiram was murdered?'

'It may be the case.'

She sighed heavily. 'Mr. Smalls was a fishmonger, Mr. Lenox. I was on the stage, you know, and Lord Barnett once asked at the stage door for me–'

Here she paused for a moment to give Lenox the opportunity to appreciate her accomplishment, which he did with a lift of his eyebrows.

'Still, we always figured Hiram would follow his father into fish.'

There was something ludicrous about this that under other circumstances might have provoked laughter in Lenox. Despite that, there was the weight of grief in the apartment, and he merely nodded.

'He didn't, I take it?'

'Put it this way, Mr. Lenox – he never worked a proper job, but he always had money.'

'Something illegal, you think?'

'Ah, but he was so sweet, Mr. Lenox! You ought to have seen him, in his blue suit. He worked hard, whatever he did – and like the fool I am, I was proud of him whatever he did.'

'It's a becoming pride in a mother,' said Lenox gently.

'Well,' she said, with a theatrical but genuine sob – in fact, the theatrical *was* the genuine in Mrs. Smalls, perhaps. 'Oh, but he was sweet! Did you know I owed a man a hundred pounds – think of it! – and was only a few months away from debtors' prison when Hiram paid it off? Months away!'

'Where did he find the money?'

'Oh, he always found the money. You should've seen him as a lad, you know! Always wanted a ha'penny for candy, he did. Little nipper.'

Lenox sighed inwardly and to forestall any further reminiscences said, 'May I ask you one or two questions, Mrs. Smalls?'

Instantly her look sharpened. 'Now, where do you come from, Mr. Lenox?'

'Not Scotland Yard, ma'am. I'm an amateur detective.'

'How do you come to involve yourself in the case, sir?'

'A friend of mine knows Gerald Poole and has asked me to intervene on that young man's behalf.'

'Who is intervening on Hiram's behalf?' said Mrs. Smalls angrily.

'Nobody, as yet. I shall see what I find. As I understand it, the prison remitted your son's effects to you?'

'Yes, as why shouldn't they?'

'Of course, ma'am, of course. I had hoped to

see a letter he was in possession of.'

'I know the one.'

'I didn't quite understand what it was.' Now, here was a fib: He recalled that it was thirty-two words, beginning *The Dogcarts Pull Away* and ending *No green*. 'Do you have the letter?'

'You have a trustworthy face,' she said and half-sobbed again.

'Thank you.'

'Well – here it is, then.'

It was on a coarse piece of paper such as might be had for a penny in any shop, unfortunately, and looked new – relatively clean, written recently. It was in an unsophisticated hand; there was a greeting but no farewell, nor was there a date. There were two paragraphs: a short one of thirty words and another that was even shorter, only two.

Mr. Smalls–
The dogcarts pull away. I'll see that Messrs. Jones get all the attention and care they need. For the others, George will rely on you and on your worthy peers.
No green.

Now this was, at best, puzzling. It seemed as if Messrs. Jones (but wasn't that a strange locution, in fact?) were in for something sinister, as were the 'others' to whom George and Smalls – if indeed the letter was addressed to him – were to give attention and care. Although clearly the keys to it were the first sentence and the last: *The dogcarts pull away* and *No green*. Both of them seemed like utter nonsense to Lenox, anyway. A dogcart was a rough-and-ready farmers' equipage used on country roads. No green perhaps meant 'no money.'

Lenox read it two or three times, skipping words ('The-pull-I'll' – 'The-away-Messrs.' – no), reading backward, and adding one letter to every word, then to every other word – first t, then r, then s – but no. It had to be written in some prearranged language that the reader would understand without resort to any trick. So faithfully he copied the note down and thanked Mrs. Smalls, promising her he would give it his further consideration.

The puzzling thing about the note was *why* Hiram Smalls would have taken the letter to prison. Either he had acted very stupidly, had been sure of the code's impenetrability, or else he had wanted to be caught for something – or perhaps it wasn't his! That was the possibility that shook Lenox slightly. What if after all Hiram Smalls was innocent of any involvement in the murders of Simon Pierce and Winston Carruthers?

'Mrs. Smalls, do you see any meaning particularly in the oranges that Hiram ordered while he was at Newgate?'

She shook her head vehemently. 'There's been too much discussed about that, Mr. Lenox. It doesn't mean a single thing! I don't remember Hiram enjoying oranges, but he has very refined – erm – parentage, sir, and there's no reason why he wouldn't enjoy the finer things in life.'

'Of course,' said Lenox sympathetically. 'What else was there among his possessions that the prison gave you?'

Her trust in the detective was more or less complete now, and she brought out a bag of things –

and slightly sad things they were, a little rough, of coarse fabrics and cheap paper. The serge suit, the copy of *Black Bess*, the pouch of tobacco. Methodically Lenox searched through these but found nothing.

'May I ask you one other question?' he said as he returned Hiram's things to her.

'Yes?'

'Do you think your son was capable of murder?'

She shook her head violently. 'Never! Never in a million years!'

Lenox thought again that this was as persuasive as Dallington's fervent advocacy of Gerald Poole, in its way. Apparently everyone was innocent. With a sigh, Lenox wished Mrs. Smalls good-bye and went back out to the street.

CHAPTER NINETEEN

Back at home there was a telegram from Sandy Smith, Crook's associate, with a list of commitments that Lenox had to return in time to fulfill the next day. He would have to be on the train by six the next morning, he saw with frustration. Still, it had been a productive half day. He had some grasp of the case, however uncertain.

As he passed the threshold of his home, he traded the uncertainty of the three murders for the domestic uncertainty that mattered far more to him.

'Has Lady Jane returned here, Mary?' he asked

after he had changed into a new suit.

'No, sir. Shall I see if she's in next door?'

'Yes, please do.'

She curtsied and left. With dismay he saw the stack of unanswered letters that had built up in his absence, sitting on his desk. He shuffled through them listlessly and waited for Mary to return. She was downstairs now, ringing a bell strung through to the servants' quarters next door. If they rang back once Jane was in, twice and she was out. Lenox smiled as he thought of this – the ties between them both literal and figurative.

He hoped so.

Mary returned. 'Lady Grey is in, sir,' she said.

'Thank you. I'll go over there, then. I'll want lunch when I get back.'

'Sir?'

'Oh–' Lenox waved his hand. 'Graham would know. Something warm. Ask Ellie.'

This was the house's cook, 'Yes, sir,' said Mary. 'I did, sir, and she says she – well she didn't know.'

Ellie had a salty vocabulary, and Mary blushed.

'I suppose we must have some sort of potato lying around, gathering dust? No doubt a single homely carrot might be procured from the fruit and vegetable man? If I dream I can imagine a very small cut of meat with sauce?' He snapped. 'Tell Ellie if she values her job she'll put two or three things on a plate by the time I return. The same goes for you.'

'Very good, sir.'

Even as the door closed behind her he sighed. It was rare for him to lose his temper, and he always regretted it instantly. Mary would know his threats

132

were hollow, in all probability – Ellie certainly would – but they still might distress her. It was all because of his fear of this tête-à-tête with Jane.

He strode outside and over there in a burst of determination, however, and once Kirk, Jane's very fat, very dignified butler had admitted Lenox, he felt silly. It was a house that made him comfortable in all its details, for it reminded him of her, and suddenly things seemed as if they might be all right.

She came out at the knock of the door and saw him. 'Hello, Charles,' she said.

'Hello, Jane. I'm so pleased to see you, now that I have a moment to breathe.'

'Will you eat something?'

'No, thanks. Ellie's cooking.'

'Come into the sitting room, then.'

She wore a plain blue dress with a gray ribbon at her slim waist and a matching one in her hair, which was slightly different now, lying in curls down her neck. Her thin, graceful hands, which had more than once shown surprising strength, were folded over each other, and it was slightly awkward that the two didn't touch as they went to the sofa and sat down.

'I've missed you very much, Jane,' Lenox burst out. 'Your letter made me miserable.'

'Oh!' she said. Tears came into the corners of her eyes.

'Did you mean what you wrote?'

'I don't know, Charles.'

There was a moment's unhappy and uncomfortable quiet, while each of them pondered the letter she had written – which as Lenox had thought at

133

every stray moment since then was so out of character, so flighty in contrast to Lady Jane's stable, undramatic personality.

He forced himself to speak of something different. 'How is Toto?' he asked.

'Physically, entirely well, but as I wrote you – well, you read what I wrote.'

Now he took her hand and, looking straight at her, said with conviction, 'Can't you see how different and how well suited to each other our temperaments are? Haven't all our years of friendship revealed our true compatibility?'

This eruption led to some silence while Jane cried. Lenox looked at his hand and realized with some detachment that it was shaking.

'I fear I must tell you a secret now, Charles.'

His stomach plummeted. 'What can you mean?'

She sighed and looked pale. 'You remember my first marriage, I know.'

Indeed he did. At the age of twenty she had made a spectacular marriage, one entirely apposite considering her beauty and nobility, to Lord James Grey, the Earl of Deere and a captain in the Coldstream Guards. It had been the wedding of the season, breathlessly gossiped about, with an invitation seen by those who were on the borderline of receiving one as more precious than rubies and emeralds.

Lenox had sat next to his brother and his father in the third row, a flower in his buttonhole, and the queer feeling he had in his stomach as he watched her walk down the aisle, straight backed and lovely, was the first intimation he had that he might feel something more than friendship for her.

Her father, the Earl of Houghton, was Lenox's godfather, and Lenox and Jane had always been playmates – never more.

Then, not six months later, tragedy – James Grey had died in a skirmish with locals in India, where he was stationed with his regiment.

'I do, of course,' said Lenox softly. 'Was it unhappy?'

'We hadn't time to be either happy or unhappy, I think, only joyful, as newlyweds are. Yet I never told you Charles – it's a difficult thing to talk about–'

'Yes?'

'I found I was pregnant just a few weeks after the wedding.'

'But that makes no sense–'

He stopped.

'Yes,' she said. 'Just the same as Toto.'

All he could say, after a minute of silence was, 'I'm so very sorry, Jane.'

'It has made these few weeks difficult for me, you must understand, and I need – I simply need more time, Charles.'

Tears stood in her eyes. His heart went out to her, undercut by a thin stream of jealousy of her first husband – a decent chap, Lenox had always thought, except that now he stood on through time noble, handsome, and flawless, an idol rather than a man of flesh and blood. How could Lenox compete against her memories?

It took all of his courage to say, then, 'If you wish me to release you from your word, I shall consent, of course.'

At that Lady Jane did something unexpected:

She laughed. It broke the tension between them, and Lenox found himself smiling, too.

'What?' he said.

'It's not funny, I know,' she said, still laughing, 'but of course I want to marry you! As dearly as I did the moment you asked. Oh, Charles! Can't you understand? I need time, that's all.'

He put his arm around her waist, and she put her head onto his shoulder. 'Then you shall have it. I know I'm selfish.'

'Can we wait until the fall? Next fall? Wouldn't it be lovely to marry next September? None of our plans yet are definite?'

'September,' he said. 'Of course.'

'We have our long lives ahead of us, you know. I want some time – so we can know each other better.'

'Is that possible?'

'Say – say know each other differently, then. It's frightening, isn't it?'

He laughed. 'A little.'

'I know we'll be happy, Charles. I shall never doubt that.'

After this their conversation devolved into all the endearments and stolen kisses and long laughs that belong to any new love – and that scarcely need to be repeated here.

Half an hour later Lenox left Jane, promising he would dine with her that evening after he spent the afternoon out. He ate lunch in front of his fireplace, reading over a new journal on Roman history and having a wholesome sort of meal for a cold day, with a glass of red wine to go along. Finally he finished eating, and Mary came to clear the things.

'Thank you,' he said. 'Oh, and Mary? Please excuse me for losing my temper with you. You did nothing wrong.'

'Sir,' she said and curtsied. 'There's bread and butter pudding if you care for it.'

Lenox smiled. 'Only to be given should I behave?'

'No, sir! Of course—'

'Only joking, Mary.'

'It's quite tasty, sir.'

Normally Lenox, a thin man, skipped dessert, but he decided to have some today. Mary brought the flaky pastry, doused in a sauce of sweet vanilla cream, and it was so good that when he was done he asked for a second helping and ate that too.

By now he was thoroughly warm and thoroughly sated, and as he sat reading, whether he realized it or not the cares of his life at that moment – the election, the murders, Toto and Thomas, and Jane – began to fall away from him. An observer might have seen his face relax, just slightly at first, and then into a smooth kind of repose. The warmth of the room was wonderful, really, he thought.

He would just rest the journal on the table and look into the fire for a moment – ah, and then perhaps rest his weary eyes – he felt his cheeks relax – his eyelids closed ever so comfortably – and soon the detective was deep in sleep, and not even Mary, who tripped into the library with the coffee a little while later, could wake him up.

CHAPTER TWENTY

Shadows fell along the floor of the library, and that particular golden glare at the edge of the windows showed that it was late afternoon. With pleasantly heavy eyes Lenox stirred and awoke, his gaze on the fire, which sparked and flared when its logs shifted. When at last he was entirely back in the world, he noted the time – it was nearly four – and thought with lazy happiness of his reconciliation with Lady Jane. Soon they would be married, whether in six months or a year, and all would be right with the world. He trusted her judgment – more than his own, perhaps.

He rang the bell, and after some delay Mary came into the room. 'Sir?'

'You were busy?'

'I apologize, sir, I was polishing silver,'

'Will you bring me some tea, please?'

'Yes, sir.'

'Then take the rest of the day off, would you?'

She didn't know quite what to make of that. 'Sir?'

'I'm eating next door, and I can find my own clothes. Go to the theater. Here–' He handed her a couple of coins.

'Thank you, sir, I shall,' she said, with a glad curtsy.

'Tea first, though, please.'

'Of course, sir. Straightaway.'

Though she blushed easily, could be awkward around guests, and fumbled with some of her tasks, in the matter of making tea Mary was supremely assured. Lenox liked Indian leaf brewed strong, and between the first cup she had made him and this one there had been no variation in the perfection of her technique, whatever it was. She brought it in with a plate of cookies. Lenox ignored these but took a deep draught of the tea and found his senses tingling and his skin a little warmer.

He wandered over to his desk, which sat by the high windows overlooking Hampden Lane. What was he to make of this case? Who was Hiram Smalls? From a pocket Lenox pulled his copy of the cryptic note Hiram had taken into prison.

He wondered again, as he had before, *why* take it into prison? Either he had assumed the code was impenetrable, he was stupid, or he wanted some small artifact of his crime with which he might blackmail his partner. Lenox strongly favored the latter theory but couldn't dismiss any of them at this moment.

The dogcarts pull away.

It was a strange, forced style of prose, which made Lenox again wonder about the nature of its encryption. Of course, it was just as likely that 'dogcarts' was a prearranged synonym for any number of words – drugs, money, even people. The same held true for the names in the letter, Jones and George. It was a hopeless jumble. Soon after picking it up he threw the letter aside in disgust and stood over his desk, tea in one hand, trying to puzzle through some itch in his mind he couldn't quite scratch.

There was a knock at the door then, and Mary, in direct contradiction to Lenox's order that she take the rest of the day off, flew up the servants' stairs to answer it as the detective came out of his library. She opened the door and gasped involuntarily.

It was Inspector Jenkins, Lenox's sole friend within Scotland Yard, and he looked awful. A painful red and black welt had risen on his cheekbone, and there was a cut just under his left eye. In the normal course of things he was an efficient and serious-looking fellow, but between his face and his disheveled clothes he now looked like a reject from one of the gin mills by the docks.

'There you are, Lenox,' he said, peering around Mary. 'I didn't know where I ought to go.'

'Come in, I beg of you. Mary, take his coat and clean it.'

'Yes, sir,' said Mary, though there was a doubtful note in her voice. She wasn't used – as Graham was – to the frequent admission of outwardly insalubrious characters to the house.

'You don't have anything like a hot whisky, do you?' he asked,

'Of course,' said Lenox. 'Before you see to his coat, bring one, won't you? Bring two, in fact. I'll drink with you, Jenkins. Now, what the devil has happened?'

Lenox motioned him down the hallway, and Jenkins came forward. The two men shook hands, and Jenkins smoothed down his ruffled hair.

'It's been a long day,' was all he said.

There was a jittery kind of energy left over in

him from whatever altercation had painted him black and blue. When the whisky arrived, he gulped at it gratefully, then took a deep breath.

'Well,' he said, 'I think it very likely that before the day is out I shall have been officially dismissed from the Yard.'

'No!' said Lenox, genuinely shocked, 'Why on earth would they do that?'

'They've just suspended me for showing Dr. McConnell our internal reports. Exeter did it, in fact. Called me a traitor. I asked him if he would say it again, and he did, and I jolly well showed him he shouldn't have.' Jenkins laughed bitterly. 'Although I didn't come out of it unscathed, mind. He walloped me twice.'

'I'm shocked! Exeter has tolerated my involvement in cases of his before, even asked me for help.'

'It was a pretense, I believe,' said Jenkins, taking another sip of his whisky. 'Exeter has resented me for some time. One of his lackeys saw me closeted with Dr. McConnell and reported me to the great man.' Another bitter laugh.

'There's been tension between the two of you?'

'Yes, and I made it pretty plain that I didn't think he was right about the Pierce and Carruthers murders. The great joke is that he may have been.'

'Why do you say that?' Lenox asked.

Jenkins shrugged. 'Poole met with Smalls, and the two dead journalists had his father hanged. The motive is ironclad, and the meeting is a strong piece of circumstantial evidence.'

'Did Gerald Poole even know the details of his father's case?'

'I don't know, but the meeting with Smalls... I confess it seems damning.'

'Are they bringing him to trial?'

'Within a fortnight. All of Exeter's men are out looking for evidence.'

'Do they have any idea who killed Smalls?'

'None, but Exeter certainly believes it was murder.'

'It was.'

'How can you say so?'

Lenox explained McConnell's hypothesis about the bootlaces and the second hook.

Jenkins shook his head, as if the enormity of his loss were sinking in. 'For once Exeter has it all right,' he said.

'It's maddening,' Lenox agreed, thinking of his meeting with Exeter some days before, when the inspector had assured Lenox the case was well in hand. Had lorded it over him, in fact.

Still, even if he was right about Smalls's death he might be wrong about the man's involvement. Or Poole's, for that matter. Dallington seemed so sure of his friend's character.

'I say, have you any ice?' Jenkins asked.

'Of course.' Lenox called for Mary. 'Will you bring ice?' he said when she came. 'And two more glasses of hot whisky.'

'Yes, sir.'

'How long is your suspension meant to be for?' Lenox asked when he and Jenkins were alone again.

'Two weeks, but Exeter has far more power than I do. Fighting him was damnably stupid.'

'Still, you'll get a fair shake, won't you?'

'I hope so. In point of fact, I *was* wrong to show Dr. McConnell those documents, but police inspectors generally have a fair amount of latitude. Exeter has chosen to follow the letter of the law in this one instance, despite breaking it a hundred times himself.'

'What do you think you'll do?'

'I don't know. Search for another job, I suppose. This is the only one I want.'

It pained Lenox. 'I'm so sorry,' he said.

'I'm an adult,' said Jenkins. The ice and whisky came then, and he applied the first to his face and the second to his gullet, both liberally. 'Anyway, there are always small-town jobs for the taking, even if you've left the Yard under a cloud. I rather fancy the South Coast. It's beautiful, I've heard.'

'It is indeed,' said Lenox, 'but we must keep you in London. May I speak to people on your behalf?'

'If you wish. I know you have friends in high places, of course, but you must remember that the Yard keeps to itself. We don't generally abide the interference of others, be they ever so powerful in other spheres of life.'

'Of course,' said Lenox, although his mind had returned to the letter Hiram Smalls had carried with him into prison.

'It's just the way of our profession, I'm afraid.'

'Wait here a moment – I've got use of your faculties even if Scotland Yard has disposed of them.'

'By all means,' said Jenkins stiffly.

The joke had fallen flat, and after an apologetic grimace, Lenox fetched his copy of Smalls's letter.

'The dogcarts pull away,' Jenkins muttered. He

read the rest to himself.

'What do you make of it?' Lenox asked when the other man had done.

'I don't know. I've never had a knack for these codes. Unimaginative on the part of the criminal underclass, I've always felt. Been reading the penny bloods.'

Lenox laughed. 'You're right. Still, something about it bothers me. I can't quite put my finger on it.'

'I wish I could help.'

'Well – thanks anyway.'

'Keep me apprised of any breaks in the case?' said Jenkins, standing up.

'I shall. Be of good cheer.'

'It's difficult.'

'Exeter has moved hastily before, and it rarely ends up well for him. You'll be back at work soon.'

'Perhaps,' said Jenkins and shook hands.

Lenox stood still for a moment, contemplating his friend's unhappy fate, and then took a last sip of tea. He had another errand to run before his day was through.

CHAPTER TWENTY-ONE

Thomas and Toto McConnell lived in one of London's grandest houses, her parents' wealth visible in every aspect of it – everything new or just replaced, everything shiny and fresh. It had a ballroom, where McConnell played solitary games of horseless polo, and more bedrooms than they could ever use. These must have seemed a bitter reproach to Toto, who hadn't yet filled them with the festive decorations of childhood though her entire family expected her to.

Lenox sighed as his carriage stopped. It was near dark, and the flickering candlelight in the windows felt gloomy. All the banal ornaments of sorrow sat upon the house. The stoop and sidewalk were dingy, unswept, the servants having more serious charges than cleanliness for once. Or congregating in corners to whisper, just as likely. There was a black crepe sash over the knocker, though that sign of gentility was at Toto's house usually pink or white. The black, color of mourning, warned visitors away perhaps. Curtains were pulled shut over the window of the McConnells' bedroom.

Lenox knocked at the door, and duly Shreve came to answer.

Now, Shreve was by general consent the most depressing butler in all of London, a present to the newlyweds from Toto's father. He was surpassingly tactful and skillful in the discharge of his duties but in personality couldn't have been more different than the effervescent and eternally happy Toto. Saying hello, Lenox thought that perhaps Shreve *ought* to have seemed an oppressive figure in this now sorrowful house but that in fact he was some comfort. Strange. He only hoped Toto felt so, too.

'I'm here to see Mrs. McConnell,' said Lenox, handing over his hat and coat.

'Please follow me, sir.'

He led Lenox down the front hall and to a

145

large, well-appointed sitting room. Nobody was in it.

'May I bring you anything to eat or drink while you wait, Mr. Lenox?' asked Shreve in his gloomy baritone.

'Thanks, no. Is she up and about?'

'At certain hours of the day, sir. Excuse me, please.'

Shreve left, and without much interest Lenox picked up a copy of *Punch* that sat on a nearby table. He leafed through it, preoccupied – both by his concern for the McConnells and by that note Smalls had taken to jail. He had truly believed Mrs. Smalls's protestation of innocence, but was it possible that both Poole and Smalls were innocent of all wrongdoing? On the other hand, Smalls had a criminal background of some kind, though it was obscure what his specific crimes might be.

'My lady will be down shortly,' said Shreve, jerking Lenox out of his daydream.

'Thank you, thank you,' he said, 'Shreve, has Mr. McConnell been home today?'

'No, sir,' said the butler with a slight tone of rebuke. It was an intrusive question.

'Thank you.'

At length Toto came into the room. Lenox rose to meet her and with a chaste kiss led her to the sofa he had been sitting upon.

'My dearest Toto,' he said, 'I'm so sorry I left London when I did.'

'I understand,' she said in a quiet voice. 'Thank you for coming to see me now.'

'Of course. Has Jane been here since this morning?'

'She just left.'

'I hope she has comforted you.'

'She is so – so good,' said Toto, and a sob caught in her throat before she could compose herself.

She did not wear the traditional black but a dark blue dress that was unlike her usual clothes, colorful as they were. Her face was somber and not in the least frantic, as if the hours of manic anxiety had passed and left one encompassing, mountainous feeling behind: grief.

'I saw Thomas this morning,' Lenox said. 'He's helping me. Those two journalists who died.'

'Oh, yes?' she asked coldly.

'He is – may I speak plainly, Toto?'

'I would ask that we discuss another subject.'

'Ah,' said Lenox, nonplussed.

A silence.

'How do you feel?' he asked.

'I think my health has returned,' she said. Her voice was still so terribly cold. It was jarring, when he was so used to her good spirits lifting his. 'Thank you.'

It was as if she had decided Lenox belonged to McConnell's camp, Jane to her own. Some barrier had gone up between them, after years of the closest intimacy. He didn't know quite how to break through to her.

He sighed. 'I came here for two reasons.'

'Oh, yes?' she said, without any apparent interest in this piece of information.

'I was worried about you, of course.'

Here she softened slightly. 'Thank you, Charles.'

'I also need advice.'

147

'Do you? Thomas can't help you?'

He waved a hand impatiently. 'Not like that,' he said. 'It's about Jane.'

'Oh?'

'About our wedding. You know I'm fond of travel, perhaps?'

'I do know that, Charles.' The roll of her eyes as she said this was the first glimpse of the Toto Lenox knew.

Indeed, it might have been a rhetorical question. Travel was one of Lenox's great passions, and he spent much of his leisure time planning elaborate trips to far-off lands – the Middle East, Asia, the Americas. Sadly, these trips (which always included Graham) remained largely theoretical. True, he had spent a blissful two weeks in Russia some years earlier, and after Oxford had toured Italy and France, but every time he was on the verge of leaving London nowadays something interrupted his plans. Usually a case, which he could never resist. Nonetheless, he was an enthusiastic member of the Travellers' Club, whose charter decreed that all its members should have traveled at least five hundred miles in a straight line from Piccadilly Circus, and a frequent patron of several mapmakers, purveyors of durable luggage, and travel agents.

'I've promised Jane that I would decide on the itinerary of our honeymoon and surprise her with our destination on the day we left.'

'Charles,' said Toto with a scornful laugh, 'she won't want to go to India or somewhere dreadful like that!'

Lenox laughed, too. 'Precisely. That's why I

need your help.'

'How can I help? You know the capitals of all the countries, and which rivers are where, and how many windmills are in Holland, and all the tiresome things I could never remember at school.'

Again he laughed. 'I'm afraid none of that will do me any good in this situation. Therefore I propose that the two of us form a committee and choose the best spot for Jane's honeymoon. I want it to be perfect, you see, and you know Jane as well as anyone.'

'That's awfully sweet,' she murmured and seemed to favor him with a smile. 'Perhaps Switzerland?'

Sternly, he said, 'No, no, idle suggestions won't do. I've brought several travel guides for you to look over, with watercolor drawings and picturesque descriptions and – I'm afraid – a very few facts. The sort of thing that drives me mad.'

He pointed to the parcel he had left on a nearby table.

'I love that kind of book!' she said.

'I know. That's why we'll make such good collaborators – I can look for train schedules while you look for beauty. Shall we meet the day after I next return from Stirrington?'

Perhaps it was the idea of a project, or because Lenox spoke so earnestly, but Toto laughed, a real, genuine laugh, and with far more animation than before said, 'We shall call it an appointment, then.'

She stuck out her tiny hand, and with a show of solemnity Lenox shook it. 'Thank you,' he said. 'What a weight off my mind!'

'I warn you that I'm a slow study.'

'Where did you and Thomas go, remind me?'

The smile vanished from her face. 'We went to Scotland and then to Paris,' she said.

'Ah. I recall now.' In an attempt to rectify the mistake of mentioning McConnell, he said, 'Did you like it?'

'I loved it,' she said with emotion in her face. 'It was the happiest I've ever been.'

It was easy to forget, Lenox thought, how in love they had been – how profoundly in love. McConnell's manly, kind bearing, Toto's enthusiasm and loveliness – how happy they had seemed! The thought disturbed him for some reason.

'At any rate, I know Jane has been to Paris half a dozen times, and even I managed to spend a few months there.'

She laughed, her goodwill reinstated. 'I'm glad I can help you,' she said, 'I'm so looking forward to the wedding.'

'As am I,' said Lenox. 'In that case, I shall take my leave.' She stood and accepted another kiss on her cheek. 'Will you tell Jane – do you mean to see Jane?'

'Yes.'

'Will you tell her, just one more night, perhaps?'

She had been staying there, then. Poor Toto. 'I certainly shall.'

'I said she needn't bother, before – but–'

'I'll tell her first thing,' Lenox said. 'Of course.'

Some moments later he was out on the steps, and in the cold evening air he stopped and gazed at the horizon. It was pink and blue, and overlaying those colors a deepening violet, and seemed to reflect back to him all the sorrow that filled his heart, cheerful though he'd tried to be. Poor, innocent Toto, he thought. For so long, even through her troubles with Thomas, she had been everything fresh, everything unblemished, everything pure. Now, no matter how well she recovered, that was gone. How various, he thought, are the punishments this world may inflict on us. He stepped with a burdened heart toward his carriage.

CHAPTER TWENTY-TWO

Eating supper with Lady Jane restored Lenox's good cheer. His own dining room was low-slung and comfortable, with a casual air about it even when he had a dinner party; by contrast hers was a marvel both of grace and intimacy, with candles glowing along rosewood walls. To eat they had a hearty beef and vegetable stew, which Lady Jane knew was Lenox's favorite autumn supper, and for dessert what had gradually come to be called Victoria sponge, after the queen – an airy cake with cream poured over it. Jane offered Lenox the wine she kept in for him, but he declined it. They spoke of every subject that occurred to them, ranging between old memories and new gossip, and by the end both felt that despite their separation all was again well in the world.

He had told her straightaway about Toto's request that Jane return that evening, and she had ordered an overnight bag prepared. As a consequence there was less time to sit in the parlor after supper than either would have liked, but they were happy moments, Lady Jane quizzing Charles about Stirrington, Crook, and Roodle and expressing over and again her wish that she might visit him there.

Finally, as a gentle rain began to slope down over the city, she left.

'Good-bye, my love,' he said.

'Good-bye,' she answered and kissed him swiftly on the lips before he handed her into her carriage. 'Be well there. Don't worry, Charles. I know you worry.'

With that, he knew he wouldn't see her for another fortnight.

He made the short walk back to his own house as slowly as he could, savoring the raindrops on his tired face. Indeed, on his steps he stood and smoked a pipe, looking up and down the small, tidy lane they lived upon. It saddened him. The trees, the shops, they were his own, and he hated to leave again. Especially without having solved the murders of Pierce and Carruthers. He had wasted his energy, perhaps, in returning – but it had been necessary.

Inside he found he had a visitor; it was Dallington, his feet up by the fire, chuckling over the same issue of Punch Lenox had inspected before seeing Toto.

'Hullo, old chap,' the young lord said and sprang to his feet with unnatural energy to shake hands.

Lenox shook hands and sat down heavily in his armchair. 'How are you? Excitable, I see.'

'Well enough. You? You must be tired?'

'No, not tired. Uneasy.'

'Because of the case?'

'In part, anyway. Do you bring news?'

Dallington shrugged. 'Nothing consequential, I'm afraid.'

'More's the pity.'

'I spent much of the day wandering around Fleet Street, speaking to whomever I could find.'

'Yes?'

'I understand both of the men better now. The link between them – that's difficult to say.'

'Other than Jonathan Poole.'

'Yes, other than that,' said Dallington. 'Anyway, I know Gerald Poole didn't do anything.'

'So you say,' Lenox answered slowly.

'So I know,' Dallington insisted, a flash of temper in his voice. 'There was one interesting thing, however. About Carruthers.'

'Yes?'

'There's a pub you may know on Fleet Street, called Ye Olde Cheshire Cheese?'

'I know it well,' said Lenox. 'Dickens works there.'

'Exactly, has since he worked at the Morning Chronicle. Well, I checked in with the bartender there, a gent named Ransom, stout fellow with a red face and a great belly. Apparently Carruthers ate there every day.'

'Go on.'

'Buck rabbit, Ransom said. Can't stand the stuff myself. All that cheese. In any event, according to Ransom it was well known up and down the street that Carruthers had his price.'

'What do you mean, exactly?'

'He accepted bribes. A few quid in his pocket

and he would write an article or edit one, cut things from the paper, add things. Quite shamelessly, said Ransom.'

'Did you ask at the *Daily Telegraph?*'

'Oh, they were pretty indignant. Both men I spoke to would have thrown me out if I hadn't taken a hasty leave of them.'

'Do you think it's related to the case?'

'It's something to know, anyway.'

'That's true. And Pierce?'

Dallington's eyebrows furrowed. His handsome, open face looked healthier, as if he had recovered from his hangover and was the better for a day of hard work. 'Quite to the contrary,' he said, 'apparently Pierce was scrupulously honest. Many men had tried to bribe him, but he was untouchable. Religious, apparently.'

Lenox sighed. 'This is all according to the knowledgeable Mr. Ransom?' he asked.

'Scoff if you will, but he was very specific about Carruthers's misdeeds. Had all sorts of examples to give me. I had the feeling that he spent a lot of time eavesdropping on men in the newspaper business.'

'That's true, I daresay.' Lenox stood up and walked to his desk. 'Here's the product of my day.' He handed Dallington the copy of the note Smalls had had in prison.

The younger man read it. 'What does it mean?' he asked.

'I don't have the faintest idea.'

'Still, there's something about it.'

'I know,' Lenox murmured, taking the copy back. 'It's been on my mind ever since I read it.'

154

'At any rate – Carruthers bad, Pierce decent, That's the bottom line.'

Lenox froze. 'Wait a moment. Pierce.'

Peers.

'Lenox?'

'Wait, for pity's sake.'

He studied the letter for thirty seconds, his face the picture of intense concentration. When at last he looked up, there was a small, twisted smile on his face. 'That poor woman,' he said.

'Whom do you mean?'

'Mrs. Smalls. Hiram was guilty, I think. I feel sure, in fact. He killed Simon Pierce.'

'How do you know?'

Perhaps it had been the repetition of the name 'Pierce' that had finally allowed Lenox to see what had been on his peripheral vision since he saw the note. He read the note with 'peers' as a keyword, counting out its letters and words, until he realized that every fifth word of the middle paragraph held the message.

'Listen,' he said to Dallington. He read the note aloud:

Mr. Smalls–
The dogcarts pull away. I'll see that Messrs. Jones get all the attention and care they need. For the others, George will rely on you and on your worthy peers.
No green.

'Well?'

Lenox handed him the note. 'Try every fifth word – but only of the middle paragraph.'

Haltingly, Dallington read out, 'I'll – get – care

155

– others – you – peers.' He shook his head. 'It still doesn't make any sense.'

'Think about it – "care others" – Carruthers. "Peers" – Pierce. It says, "I'll get Carruthers, you Pierce." Or am I mad?'

With dawning recognition, Dallington said, 'No, you're brilliant. Of course.'

'The names Jones and George distracted me,' said Lenox. 'It's a tidy little thing. I wonder how Smalls knew to sound it out.'

'And why he took it to prison,' said Dallington.

'That seems clear – to protect himself. He probably warned the author of the note that his effects included the letter.'

'The author believed in his code, though.'

'Exactly.'

'What of that last line– "No green"?' asked Dallington.

'I'm not sure. It doesn't appear to fit with the rest.'

'No,' said Lenox.

'Still, it's a start. We may surmise Smalls killed Pierce.'

'Yes. I should say we might.'

CHAPTER TWENTY-THREE

The next morning Lenox woke early, with the sun not yet out and that pale white of dawn covering the sky, gray and blue mingled in silken layers behind it. The rain had stopped and left behind it a new cold, but the coals in the fireplace across the room were still orange. He lay under his covers, warm, drowsy, comfortable, for a few moments longer than he ought to have, savoring the sense of being inside his own home. It meant something – but Stirrington beckoned.

He dressed in a dark suit with a dark cloak and found that Mary had packed new clothes in a tidy overnight bag for him. Downstairs he had coffee, apple slices, and toast, a scoop of marmalade spread over the last. He thought of Jane and wished she were next door, or better yet next to him. He was melancholy, for some reason. An identical note to each of two men, Jenkins and Exeter, informing them of the previous night's discovery, and he was prepared to leave.

Although there was a small surprise first – an early visitor. It was James Hilary.

'How do you do?' Lenox asked, answering the knock at the door himself. 'I'm pleased to see you.'

The young Member of Parliament had a slightly awkward air about him, standing on Lenox's stoop, but spoke plainly. 'Are you?' he said. 'I rather wondered whether you would be.'

'Because you left Stirrington?'

Hilary nodded.

Lenox shrugged. 'I understood,' he said. 'It wasn't a personal decision.'

'That's true, but nevertheless.'

'We've been friends for a while now, Hilary. It's politics.'

'That's good of you, Charles – but it was a bad decision.'

'Oh?'

157

'Apparently you're pulling even in local support.'

'We worked hard after you left.'

'I heard about your encounter with Roodle,' said Hilary. 'Sounds like you scored one off of him.'

'I had little taste for it, I confess,' said Lenox.

'You oughtn't to have left, however.'

'I know Crook thought so, too.'

'I hope you don't learn how precious time is in a county campaign too late.'

'I'm returning now,' said Lenox.

Hilary gave him a searching look, 'You'll stay? Scotland Yard can take care of themselves, you know.'

Lenox laughed. 'Yes, I'll stay,' he said. 'I had to come down, James, I promise you I did, but I've scarcely been gone a full day, and I won't leave again.'

Hilary nodded, apparently satisfied with this intelligence. For ten minutes he stayed and discussed strategy with Lenox, promised to keep close track of the election, and generally made himself agreeable in the way he knew how to.

The truth was that Lenox *did* feel slightly betrayed by Hilary, his friend; and yet when he thought of the man as a political associate rather than as a friend it seemed better. He saw Hilary away with a cordial smile, and as he put on his overcoat he had a small smile on his lips. *Pulling even in local support*, the phrase had been.

They would see; perhaps he might nose out Roodle in the end.

As the sun slipped over the horizon and burnished London gold, Lenox was stepping into his carriage, on the way to King's Cross Station. As he rolled through the streets he silently contemplated his fellow men, those just setting out for their days and those just getting home from their nights – the aristocratic gamblers who were stumbling home in a daze, the elderly ladies who preferred Hyde Park at this unhurried hour, the deliverymen who gave these rich houses their milk and fruit and meat as the day began. A sense of his own inconsequence stole over Lenox. This rented world. He discovered that he did care about marrying Jane sooner rather than later. All he wanted was to be beside her, Parliament and Hiram Smalls both be damned. The low fire of love for her that always burned in his chest flared and filled him.

At the train station he sat at a café with a cup of coffee, his third of the morning, and read the *Times*. According to a lead column, Exeter had definitive proof that Smalls and Poole had acted in concert. 'Inspector Exeter had already ascertained that Mr. Poole and Mr. Smalls met in the Saracen's Head pub,' said the article, 'but he now has further proof of their complicity. When reporters asked him to reveal the new information, Exeter said, 'You'll see, you'll see.' Speculation centers on some link between both men and the Belgian housekeeper employed by Winston Carruthers, Martha Claes, whose whereabouts are currently unknown, with Scotland Yard eager to learn them.'

Lenox sighed. What proof could it possibly be?

Suddenly, across the vast expanse of King's Cross Station, he heard a shout. It was coming from near the ticket booths.

'Lenox!' the voice shouted. 'Lenox!'

Charles stood and turned, patting his pocket nervously to make sure his ticket was still there.

Then he saw who it was: Dallington. The young lad ran up to Lenox, people staring as he passed before they returned to whatever they had been doing.

'What on earth can it be?' asked Lenox. 'How are you?'

'Quite well, quite well,' said Dallington breathlessly. 'It's Poole.'

'What happened?'

Dallington gulped the air, apparently unused to the exercise. 'I didn't think I'd catch you.'

'What happened to Poole?'

'The knife they found in the back of Carruthers's neck? The long one?'

'Yes?'

'Poole bought it. It was Poole's.'

'How do you know? How did you discover this?'

'Poole sent for me himself.'

'What are the details?'

'It's a hunting knife with a red and black handle. Poole has always hunted and bought it three weeks ago.'

'Go on.'

Dallington nodded with an anguished look on his face. 'Furthermore, what's worse, Poole denied buying it at first. Now he says he can't remember. It's all so dreadfully suspicious – but I know he didn't do it.'

'This looks black, Dallington. Exeter can prove the murder weapon was Gerald Poole's knife?'

'The shopkeeper who sold it entered all of

Poole's particulars into a ledger.'

Lenox sighed. 'I'm afraid he may be guilty,' he said.

'He's not. I can tell you that flatly.'

The older man looked at the younger with pity. 'Yes,' was all he said.

'What can we do?'

'I must go to Stirrington.'

'What! You can't think of leaving, can you?'

'Indeed I can.'

Dallington looked dumbfounded. 'An innocent man goes to trial in a week's time.'

This pierced Lenox. 'I will write to Exeter,' he said. 'Forcefully.'

'You must stay!'

'I cannot. If you keep me apprised of every detail you learn, I will try to help. Yet if Poole is convicted, I can always return and try to exonerate him. Still, if he is truly innocent – then I hope he won't be convicted.'

'Hope?' said Dallington, and a faint look of disgust passed across his face. 'Parliament will go on forever. This is a man's life!'

Lenox knew the justice of what Dallington said, but he thought as well of all the people who were paid to be discovering who had killed Pierce and Carruthers, and the thought of his visit with Hilary that morning – *you're pulling even in local support* – and wondered why *he* had to be the one who fixed everything; and a small selfish voice rose in his mind. He wanted to be in Parliament.

'John,' said Lenox in an utterly reasonable voice, 'you must understand. I have obligations. I came down expressly against the wishes of those with an interest in my campaign and have done my best. We know Smalls must be guilty, don't we?'

'Because of the note? Everybody may write anything they please on a piece of paper.'

Lenox sighed. 'You're right, of course.'

'Stay, Lenox. You must.'

'I can't, but you shall have all of my attention when you write, and as goes without saying I shall follow every detail of the case in the newspapers.'

Dallington threw his hands in the air. 'I can only ask you to stay,' he said.

'I can't. You can handle this.'

'I don't think I can, Lenox. I'm afraid I simply can't.'

'I must go, Dallington. Keep in close contact.'

'If you must, then,' said Dallington, his face suddenly forlorn. 'I'll write to you this evening.'

Lenox turned, ran for his platform, and just in time caught the train headed north.

CHAPTER TWENTY-FOUR

It was a busy afternoon. Guilt gnawed at Lenox, but he knew Dallington's request had in its own way been unreasonable, too. It was important to do the work of the nation, and if he could make it to Parliament, what untold good might he not accomplish? It was an uncertain business, being an adult, trying to be responsible. Nonetheless, he wrote Exeter a letter full of the precise details of

Lenox's day in London, congratulating him on apprehending one murderer – Hiram Smalls – while on the other hand cautioning the inspector that Gerald Poole's role in the business was far from certain. Alas, his cajoling would likely be futile, unless Exeter's theories were somehow thwarted, when he might turn to it. He was a bullheaded man.

Lenox sent that letter and then wrote a telegram to Dallington, half-apologizing for the scene in the train station and asking him to keep in close touch. He also advised the young lord to continue investigating Carruthers's and Pierce's history on Fleet Street. Something besides Jonathan Poole's treason years before had to link them.

Lenox wondered about the knife, though. He felt uneasy about Gerald Poole. The young man was hiding some secret.

After he had written this letter and this telegram, there was nothing left to do but turn his attention to the work at hand. Fortunately, Graham had been on the job.

'How do you do, sir?' Graham had asked when Lenox stepped off the train in Stirrington.

'Tired,' the detective had answered, 'and sorely tried.'

'I'm sorry to hear it, sir.'

'And here?'

'My task went tolerably well, sir.'

'You bought everyone beer?'

'Yes, sir.'

'What about Crook? Is he upset?'

'He reconciled himself to your absence, sir.'

'Wonderful.'

Graham nodded and said, 'Of course, sir.'

They bumped through the small town, and Lenox found that he recognized certain shops, even certain faces, and it increased his affection for the place. He would be honored to represent it should they let him.

The Queen's Arms remained as he had found it on first arriving in Stirrington; the fire burned hot and high toward one end of the bar, and a chalk-board menu offered venison with apple-sauce for the midday meal. Crook, his massive bulk and great red nose intact, nodded in a cursory but friendly manner to Lenox. One thing was different, however: At Lenox and Graham's entrance, a cry went up and people crowded around them.

Am I so beloved so quickly? thought Lenox.

A moment later he was laughing quietly at his vanity – for they were all talking at once to Graham.

He ought to have known; Graham had the most extraordinary way of listening, such that his inter-locutors felt grateful to him when they parted, and he had evidently been true to his word, had stood any number of rounds, and become intimate with all the usual inmates of the pub. No fewer than seven men came up to them. All had looked slightly suspicious, slightly aloof, when Lenox first entered the Queen's Arms, and all now cheerfully clasped his hand and vowed that a friend of Mr. Graham's was a friend of theirs. It was an un-looked-for success and encouraged Lenox greatly.

'Mr. Crook,' he said, approaching the bar.

'Pleased to see you, Mr. Lenox. London?'

This lone word was evidently a question, so

Lenox said, 'Yes, it was good I went back.' He thought of Jane. 'Very good I went back. Do you think my absence dooms us?'

Crook chuckled at that. 'I reckon not,' he said. 'It didn't hurt to leave Mr. Graham behind. You shook every hand you could within Stirrington city limits?'

Lenox laughed and remembered his promise to do so. 'I did, yes,' he said.

'Then we shall be all right. Sandy Smith has spread it around that you were in Durham, speaking with the right people.'

Lenox shook his head doubtfully. 'I can't say I like that.'

'It's politics, you know,' said Crook. 'You *will* speak to them within this next week or two, but folk around here would take it poorly if they knew you had scarcely been here any time at all before you felt the call back to London.'

'I understand.'

The candidate and the political agent (though he was still a bartender when Mr. Smith, at stool seven, asked for another pint of bitter) then spoke about the day's schedule, and about their strategy for Roodle, and about the further handbills and flyers they would print up, and Crook confessed to writing Hilary with the promising news of Lenox's popularity – in sum spent fifteen minutes or so in the pleasant and easy conversation that men who love politics are able to expend an infinite amount of time on. The last thing Crook said was to remember the importance of that evening's dinner. Now, Lenox didn't remember with whom he was dining, or why it was important, but, eager to stay in Crook's good graces, he nodded solemnly and resolved within himself to ask Graham what dinner it was.

'Then I'll see you at the meeting of corn and grain merchants, Mr. Lenox?' Crook said.

'Certainly.'

Lenox nodded to Graham then, and the valet extracted himself from a large group of friends to accompany the detective upstairs.

'You know what I'm to do today?' asked Lenox when they had reached his room.

'The corn and grain–'

'Yes, yes, but for supper?'

'Oh – yes, sir. You have supper with Mrs. Reeve, sir. Many local merchants and officials will be in attendance. Men who determine public opinion, sir – for instance, Ted Rudge, the wine merchant, who dislikes Mr. Roodle intensely. Mr. Crook impressed upon me that these men are the sort who determine elections, sir, and that you might not meet them without Mrs. Reeve's patronage.'

'I'm not a pet, Graham.'

'No, sir,' said the butler, nodding to indicate the verity of Lenox's statement. 'Nonetheless, these men are far more important than the corn and grain merchants, for example, sir. Although the corn and grain merchants *do*–'

'Blast the corn and grain merchants,' said Lenox grumpily.

'Very good, sir.'

'Save your corn and grain stories for the long winter nights, Graham.'

'Yes, sir.'

'If I lose the respect of the corn and grain merchants, life will go on, you know.'

'Yes, sir.'

Lenox sighed. 'I'm sorry. I don't know if I'm suited to politics, you know.'

'Sir?'

'I wish they wouldn't tell everyone I was in Durham.'

'Men often need time to settle into political life, sir. The story about Durham is an exigency of your position.'

'I know it.' Another sigh. 'Anyway, Graham, what about you?'

'Sir?'

'What are you going to do today?'

'I thought I would discharge my usual duties, sir, now that you are returned.'

Lenox waved a hand. 'We can't have that. These chaps would elect you if they could. No, you must stick by me. Unless you mind?'

'Not at all, sir. The servants at the Queen's Arms are most competent, I have found.'

'Capital, then. The blue tie?'

'Here it is, sir.'

'With this tie I could face a legion of corn and grain merchants,' said Lenox, putting it on in the mirror.

'Excellent, sir,' said Graham.

CHAPTER TWENTY-FIVE

With every person he met, Lenox could feel himself gaining ground. In his absence, ironically, the town had adjusted to his presence. The speech in Sawyer Park – and the subsequent talk of it – had doubtless played its part, as had the confident energies of Crook, Smith, and Graham. Whatever it was, Lenox was well met everywhere, men and women stopping to shake his hand as he passed. Each stride through Stirrington encouraged him further.

He expected the worst when he met the corn and grain merchants but found them to be in fact a pleasant lot, and when he stopped in for an afternoon cup of tea at a teashop along Foul Lane he had a long and interesting conversation with the proprietor, a woman named Stevens who promised she would have her husband vote for him. Lenox's ideas on the cost of beer would persuade Mr. Stevens, she said, while his plan to lower taxation persuaded her.

By the time of Mrs. Reeve's dinner, then, Lenox was feeling assured and happy; Roodle seemed an altogether smaller figure in his mind, and the cacophony of good and supportive voices that had followed him through the day rang in his ears.

All of that lasted about ten minutes into the party.

Now, Mrs. Reeve herself was perfectly nice, a

fact from which Lenox took some solace. So was Mr. Rudge, the wine merchant who detested Robert Roodle. Here were two supporters.

Not so nice, on the other hand, were several of the other party guests, whose personalities seemed calculated to grate on Lenox's nerves. Worst among these was a woman whom for years afterward he thought of with a shudder. Her name was Karen Crow. She was a fervent Roodleite.

'Mr. Lenox,' she said when they were all sitting at the table for supper, soup before them, 'is it true that you have never visited a brewery?'

'That is true, yes,' he said.

'Mr. Roodle has been in the brewery all his life,' She said this with great significance – greater than Lenox could perceive it to have – and turned her head from side to side, as if to say to her neighbors, 'Now, did you catch *that?*'

'I understand that beer is important in Stirrington?'

'Mr. Lenox,' she said, 'is it true that you have *always* lived in London?'

'No,' he said shortly.

'Surely Mr. Lenox's provenance is well enough known?' said Mrs. Reeve.

'But you have lived in London *most* of your life,' clarified Mrs. Crow.

'Yes,' he said.

'Mr. Roodle has lived in Stirrington all his life.'

After relating this wonderful anecdote, she set to her soup with a dainty ferocity.

'His factory hasn't, though,' said Rudge, the wine merchant. Lenox shot him a grateful look.

After this Mrs. Crow retracted her claws until

dessert was served, when she again began to de-
lineate the biographical differences between
Roodle and Lenox. Picking up the baton in the
meanwhile was a man named Spronk, who managed a clothiers on the High Street. Spronk's plan
of attack was to associate Lenox with every mis-
deed of any member in the history of the Liberal
Party. All of his sentences either began or ended
with the phrase 'Now, isn't it true...' For instance,
he said, 'Now, isn't it true that Gladstone visits
prostitutes?'

'In an attempt to reform them, I believe,' murmured Lenox, 'though I scarcely think that in
this company it is appropriate to discuss–'

'The party betrayed Russell, didn't they? On
his reform bill? He was a radical, to be sure, but
nonetheless it indicates a certain slipperiness.
Now, isn't it true?'

'Perhaps,' said Lenox. 'Who better to be a radical
than the son of a duke, however, like Russell?'

'Now, isn't it true as well that Palmerston was a
Tory first, and only changed parties to gain power?
You can scarcely claim credit for Mr. Palmerston,
I think, Mr. Lenox,' Spronk said with a chastising
chuckle, as if Lenox had been taking credit for
Palmerston all over Stirrington.

'He shifted parties wisely, in my view,' was all
the candidate managed.

After several other questions of this variety,
Spronk sat back with a satisfied 'humph.' Thus he
and Mrs. Crow between them spoiled Lenox's
appetite before the lamb arrived.

Almost worse than Spronk and Crow, though,
was the way in which Mrs. Reeve, after having

invited him into this lions' den, constantly tried to 'save' him by interjecting a soft word or two when the assaults on him became intemperate. He appreciated her intent but bridled against her proprietary manner. It made him feel a slight snobbery. It occurred to him that, having lived in his own small circle in London for so long, he had without knowing it narrowed his social life to exclude the Mrs. Reeves of the world; and then it occurred to him in the same moment that perhaps the men and women in Stirrington who were suspicious of him for being from London were right. He didn't understand them as well as Roodle did, in all probability. Previously he had assumed it was an unenlightened and fearful sort of instinct in the locals, but maybe they knew their business. It was a depressing idea.

According to the Bible, though, all things pass under heaven, and despite Lenox's doubts that it would, the supper eventually did, too. Mrs. Reeve offered him a few words of consolation as he parted, but he returned to the Queen's Arms in a foul mood.

The place was humming, voices and laughter mingling in the eaves of the ancient building. It was warm inside, and whether from that or from drink, nearly all of the patrons at the bar and at the tables were red faced. Crook was dispensing pints at a rapid rate but paused to greet Lenox.

'How was it?' he asked, shaking hands.

'Rather like hell,' said Lenox.

Crook laughed. 'I'm afraid we let you in for it. Mrs. Reeve keeps a mixed company – politically, I mean to say. Anyway, now they've vetted you,

171

whether they like you or not. You must trust me that it was important.'

'I do,' said Lenox.

'We didn't want to warn you – felt you might do a runner.'

'I'm not some skittish pony,' said Lenox irritably.

'There, there,' said Crook with another expansive laugh. 'How about a pint of ale on the house?'

'It wouldn't go amiss, I suppose. Thanks.'

Crook drew the dark, golden liquid into a pewter pot and slid it across the bar to Lenox. 'There you are,' he said. 'Cures what ails you.'

'Have you seen Graham?' asked the detective after a long pull at the drink.

'He accepted an invitation to supper as well, just after you left. A few men were off to a chophouse and brought him.'

'He's been valuable, has he?' asked Lenox.

Crook nodded. 'To be sure.'

'What do you think our next set of handbills should be?'

'You didn't like the last ones? The five promises, Mr. Lenox?'

'I do like them, but I worry that Roodle's signs are more direct, more effective.'

'*Vote Roodle – Vote Your Own*, you mean?'

'Hm.'

'How about *Vote Lenox – Vote Your Wallet?*' said Crook.

'I like that. *Or Vote Lenox – Vote Your Interest.*'

'Folks care more about their wallets than their interests, I reckon.'

'*Vote Lenox – Lower Roodle's Beer Tax.*'

'That's much better. Roodle will hate it.'

'It's not quite his, is it?' said Lenox.

'It don't do to be too fine in politics.'

'No,' Lenox said with a smile.

'We'll print a few hundred more of the five promises and add in some of the more blunt handbills, then?'

'Glad it's decided.'

'You'll need to go back to the printers in the morning.'

'Graham can do it.'

'I'll think about it overnight, see what I can come up with. I like *Lower Roodle's Beer Tax*, though.'

'So do I,' said Lenox.

'We'll call it settled, then,'

'And tomorrow?'

'A speech at the theater. That will be crucial. In two days' time you have the debate, of course. The debate will be crucial, too, Mr. Lenox.'

'I debated at Harrow.'

'Sir?'

'At school.'

Suddenly the gap between them was tangible; perhaps only to Lenox, after his long supper. Talking politics leveled their perspectives, however, and he was glad to have work in front of him.

'Then you'll do well,' said Crook. 'Johnson, another half of stout?' He flew off down the bar.

Lenox stood and realized that he was bone tired. It had been the longest two days he could remember; all he wanted was sleep.

CHAPTER TWENTY-SIX

In the morning there was a telegram from Dallington.

Lenox had had his breakfast with Crook and Nettie and was again in his room, eating an apple, when Graham brought it in. It was the first Lenox had seen of him since the night before.

'How was dinner with the lads?' he asked.

'Productive, I hope, sir.'

Good. 'Thank you.'

Graham nodded and withdrew. Lenox tore open the telegram and read it with curiosity.

EYEWITNESS PLACES SMALLS AT PIERCE HOUSE AT TIME OF MURDER STOP WIDOW IN HOUSE ACROSS LANE STOP SMALLS WALKED UP TO HOUSE RAN AWAY MOMENTS LATER STOP IMPOSSIBLE TO SEE DOORWAY FROM WINDOW ONLY STREET BUT MAN SHE SAW MATCHES STOP SEE EVENING PAPERS STOP HOPE IT HELPS STOP GOOD LUCK THERE STOP DALLINGTON

Dallington was profligate in his style of telegram, but on this occasion Lenox was glad. It was confirmation of what that coded letter to Smalls had already implied, but, he hoped, more conclusive. Unfortunately it drew the noose a little tighter around Gerald Poole's neck. With a guilty start

174

Lenox crumpled the paper and threw it into the wastepaper basket. He took a final bite of his apple and tossed the core on top of the telegram. With a moody sigh he stood up. Another day of campaigning.

The speech at the theater went moderately well. It was on the opposite side of Stirrington and drew a different crowd than his speech in Sawyer Park had. There were a few lively questions afterward, which Lenox parried as well as he could, and encouragingly several men stopped by the stage to meet the candidate and promise him their vote. Two of these men asked to be remembered to Graham, and Lenox silently marveled at the man's energy. He seemed to have met more people in Stirrington in twenty-four hours than Lenox had in a week. Another gentleman, though, came up and with a rude smirk vowed that only Roodle could possibly win the hearts of his 'local brethren.' A prominent abstinence pin on the man's chest meant he probably didn't care about the beer tax.

'Only a handful of days to go now,' said Crook, 'The debate tomorrow is important.'

'Have we got the new handbills yet?'

The bartender shook his head. 'He's working all night. We should have them in the morning. They'll work a treat, I reckon.'

'I hope so.'

'Roodle's had a bad day, too.'

'How so?'

'He gave a speech and didn't get much of a crowd. Those who did go were all being paid. You're more of a novelty, it would seem.'

'Whether that bodes well for election day is anyone's guess. Novelty wears off.'

Crook shrugged. 'If the novelty gets them in the door, it's up to you to get them to your side of things.'

'True enough.'

As Dallington had directed him to do, Lenox took in all of the evening papers and looked at them, but the news of Smalls's guilt had yet to reach Durham and the north, and he had to content himself with rehashed stories from the papers he had read on the train that morning. It was dreadful to be beyond the reach of information – how he depended on it, how vital it seemed when he couldn't have it!

One of the evening papers had an article that caught Lenox's eye. It was about George Barnard – Lady Jane's former suitor, the Royal Mint's former Master, and Lenox's bête noire. The thief of – Lenox was certain – nearly twenty thousand pounds from the mint. Apparently Barnard was on a tour of French foundries, in preparation for a report to Parliament. Shaking his head with disgust, Lenox thought of all the crimes he had proved Barnard guilty of – though only to his own satisfaction. The evidence was too tenuous for the courts, but Lenox recognized the same hand behind various thefts and shakedowns, many of them in connection with the Hammer Gang. What was he doing up here in Stirrington, he wondered doubtfully. Wasn't his place among the criminals of London? At Gerry Poole's side? Investigating George Barnard, as he had off and on for a year? Was it simply vanity, this candidacy?

No – he wanted to make a difference. He must remember that. It would be crucial to have the confidence of his beliefs the next afternoon at the debate.

It was about ten thirty now, and the Queen's Arms was packed. Every ninety seconds or so the bell over the door signaled another entrance or departure, more often the former than the latter. The line to get drinks at the bar was three or four men deep, and the high chatter of voices was more like silence than noise, so used had everyone inside become to it. Crook was sweating and red, his agile hands flying up and down the taps. The lad who washed dishes was running to and fro with dirty and fresh pint pots.

Then there was another ring of the bell, and when a man entered all of the commotion stopped. Silence.

It was Roodle.

His eyes scanned the room, 'Mr. Lenox,' he said when his eyes lit on the Liberal candidate, 'May I have a private word with you?'

'If you wish,' said Lenox gamely.

'Perhaps you would consent to visit the Royal Oak, down the street, with me?'

'Terrible place, that,' said a voice in the silence.

'Terrible beer, too,' said another.

There were snickers all over the room. The Royal Oak was a Roodle pub, which served Roodle beer.

'After you,' said Lenox, putting down his newspaper.

They left and walked the short way to Roodle's pub without speaking.

Compared to the Queen's Arms, the Royal Oak

177

was an entirely different kind of place. The lights were dim, and under them morose patrons sat singly and doubly, nursing their beers. Its charm lay perhaps in its quiet nature; it lacked the slightly rowdy good cheer of Crook's bar.

'Well? What can I get you?' Roodle asked.

'Nothing, thanks.'

'It's free, you know.'

Lenox smiled. 'That certainly is an inducement,' he said, 'but I don't want a drink.'

Roodle ordered a pint of stout, and the barman skipped over two customers to deliver it. That attempt at ingratiation failed, however; the brewer chastised his employee and told him to give the two customers free half-pints. He then led a bemused Lenox to a table in the back, next to a cobblestone wall.

'You know why I asked you here, Mr. Lenox?'

'On the contrary, I haven't the faintest idea.'

'You ought to leave the race.'

At this Lenox laughed outright, though he knew he ought not to. 'Why, pray tell, should I so gratify you?'

In a sudden passion, Roodle said, 'Is it dignified for a detective to seek a seat in Parliament? For a Londoner to visit a town he has never seen and compete against a candidate with roots there? Is it dignified for you to seek the seat of Stoke, whose family has been here for generations? No, it is not. It is not.'

Lenox was no longer smiling. For a moment there was tense silence.

'My party has seen fit to let me stand here,' he answered at length, 'and I can pay my bills. Your opinion of my profession is your concern, but I will answer for it to any man in the world. As for my being a Londoner – seeking Stoke's seat – that is the politics we have, Mr. Roodle. Whether we think it ideal or not, it is the politics we have, and by which we must abide.'

'A gentleman's code stands above politics.'

This whipped Lenox into a lather. With all the restraint he could muster, he said, 'Let us each define what a gentleman's code is for ourselves, Mr. Roodle. I am at ease with my own definition.'

'You ought to leave,' muttered Roodle.

'Yet I shan't.'

'I come to you civilly with that request, sir.'

'On the contrary, you have insulted my profession, questioned my honor, and attempted to bully me.'

Roodle glared. His heaviness had not obscured his sharp, intelligent face. 'Then we are at an impasse,' he said. 'I take my leave of you.'

He left the pub by the front door, his pint standing untouched on the table, and after a moment Lenox stood and followed him through the door. Suddenly he remembered why he was running for Parliament, and it seemed important again to him – as important as any murder – to keep small-minded men away from the nation's big decisions. He walked back to the Queen's Arms feeling a renewed determination.

CHAPTER TWENTY-SEVEN

The prior evening's London papers arrived the next morning, bringing Lenox in fuller detail the news Dallington had relayed to him by telegram. He was breakfasting in his room on eggs, bacon, and dark tea, and between practicing snatches of dialogue for the debate he ran his eye over the news.

A letter came up the stairs; he recognized Jane's handwriting on the envelope. It read:

Charles—
How wonderful to know that your foot fell somewhere in London again yesterday. You left this morning, and already I miss you. Your house, though you couldn't know it, looks quite desolate when you aren't there.

There is only one piece of news to relate to you—Thomas and Toto have made up, and Thomas is living in their house again. Needless to say I am relieved. It happened in a roundabout way. I was in Toto's bedroom when the card of a gentleman named Dr. Mark Lucas came up. The doctor was waiting downstairs and said he arrived on medical business. Toto was disinclined to admit him (her mood has been a little happier in the past day or two, but she still has black stretches of time; I wish for her above all an occupation) until he said he came at the behest of Thomas. She asked I stay but consented to see him.

He was a strange little man, but quite evidently profi-

cient. He asked poor Toto, who seems to have seen every doctor London could dredge up, an exhaustive series of questions about her diet, her pregnancy, her habits, and every other thing under the sun. At last he said, 'In my medical opinion no doctor could have predicted your misfortune. Not even one in daily contact with you.'

'Does that change anything?'

'Not even Dr. McConnell,' he said with a significant glance.

Toto groaned. 'That fool,' she said. 'Does he think I blame him?'

'I've offered my opinion,' he said.

About half an hour later Thomas came in, as formally as you like, and though I left the room they soon called me back again. Neither looked happy but both quite relieved, and some of the anxiety of Toto's face was gone, thankfully. I agree with her – what a fool. It is for the best, of course. I am glad of it.

James Hilary was at the duchess's last night. He is full of excited plans for your political career. I told him it was all the same to me whether you were Prime Minister or a pauper, which he frowned at and couldn't agree with at all. Still, it is true.

I send this by fastest post, that it may carry my love to you all the more quickly. Please know me to be your very own,

Jane

Lenox folded the two sheets of paper carefully (two sheets – since one paid by the sheet, this was an extravagance) and put them on his dresser with a contented sigh.

Graham, who'd brought the letter in and then gone out, knocked at the door again and entered.

181

'You have an uncanny ability to know when I finish letters,' said Lenox.

'Thank you, sir.'

'Is there something else?'

'I came to ask whether you require any assistance in your preparations for the debate, sir.'

'How do you mean?'

'I could play Roodle, for instance, sir, or simply pose questions to you.'

'Do you think you know Roodle well enough?'

'My new ... acquaintances have thoroughly briefed me on his character and tactics, to be sure.'

'He gave away his hand a bit last night.' Lenox described Roodle's visit to the Queen's Arms and the two men's subsequent meeting. 'Well, let's give it a try. You be Roodle. Shame we don't have a moderator, but we can either of us offer the subject of discussion.'

So the two men sat for above two hours, practicing. Now, Lenox considered Graham a member of his family and would have done anything in the world for him, but by the time they were finished he comprehensively disliked the man. His insinuating manner and obnoxious insistence on Lenox's London background were irritating beyond all reason. Still – Lenox was better prepared than he had been that morning. His soul was a little lighter, too, now that he knew Toto and Thomas were on the mend.

Soon Sandy Smith showed up, dancing a little jig of nervousness, and Lenox slowly and neatly dressed, with Graham's discerning aid.

'The debate is at the Guild Hall,' said Smith as

Lenox put a tie on.

It was a tie from the local grammar school, in what the shop there had referred to as 'Stirrington purple and gray.' He fleetingly hoped it would be recognized, only to think how silly politics could be.

'Oh, yes?' Lenox said,

'It's important to speak calmly and evenly, Mr. Lenox, because a loud noise will do funny things up among the rafters.'

'Yes?'

'At the Christmas play last year – we did *The Cricket on the Hearth* – the director barked orders from the wings all night long, and we could hear every word he said. It was a disaster.'

'All right.'

'A disaster!' said Smith fervently. 'Now, the year before that, it was a wonderful show – everyone spoke evenly and calmly – there was a little girl in the lead, and she was–'

Lenox, though he considered himself broad-minded about regional theater, was impatient. 'Evenly, calmly, yes, yes.'

'Well – exactly,' said Smith. 'If you raise your voice in anger, the building turns it into a kind of squeal.'

'Thank you,' said Lenox.

'More ridiculous than impressive, you see.'

Graham, who had popped out to freshen his own attire, came back now. 'I neglected to mention, sir, that there are several gentlemen in the audience who are prepared to offer gentle questions during the final period of the debate.'

'Excellent,' said Smith.

'Of what nature?' asked Lenox.

He was cut off by a knock on the door. It was one of the lads who cleared dishes about the place.

'Telegram, sir,' he said.

Lenox gave the boy a coin and took the paper, expecting it to be another missive from Dallington. Instead it was from Inspector Jenkins.

Lenox blanched when he read it. Then he scanned his eyes over it twice more. 'Christ,' he muttered.

'Sir?' said Graham.

'Mr. Lenox?'

It was to Graham that the detective looked. 'Christ,' he said again.

'What is it, sir?'

'Exeter has been shot. He's not dead, but he's close.'

CHAPTER TWENTY-EIGHT

Half an hour later all three men were at the Guild Hall. Lenox, shaken but determined, was trying his best to concentrate. Crook arrived. All four of them now looked around the hall.

'Adlington,' said Smith, and Crook nodded knowingly.

Adlington was apparently officiating the debate, and Lenox already knew him to be an important personage: the mayor of Stirrington.

Now here was a grand figure. As the crowd filed into the hall he sat at the center of the stage in a dignified manner, with a look that showed his abstraction from the petty cares of the world. Years of diligent work at the dinner table had earned him a shape more akin to a small building than to any of his fellow men. He had a proud paisley waistcoat stretched taut across his girth, and strung along it was a (by necessity) very long gold watch chain.

Crook leaned over to Lenox as they stood on the wings of the stage. 'Do you know what the most important part of a public house is, Mr. Lenox?'

'What's that?'

'The brass. Even more important than the beer, you know. Gives everything that golden gleam, reflects the fire and the faces – makes it out of the normal, if you see my meaning. Not like home.'

Lenox smiled. 'How interesting.'

Crook nodded. 'Great man taught me that, you know. My Uncle Ned, who had the pub before me. Now, that watch chain on our gracious mayor – it serves a similar purpose. Adds to the dignity of the office, you see, to have ten yards of gold chain stretched across your belly.' Crook laughed loudly, and Lenox joined him. 'I haven't been called slim recently, but I could never hope to pull off that watch chain. It would hang down to my knees.'

Lenox was grateful to Crook for trying to lighten his mood, but butterflies still stirred in his belly and anxiety for Exeter, the fool, in his mind.

Exeter. For years Lenox had alternately aided and squabbled with the man. His bullheadedness had jeopardized more than one case, and his lack of imagination had made Lenox a necessary evil in his life. Half of the time he warned Lenox off, and the other half he came to see him hat in hand, asking for help. It was maddening.

Yet – Lenox couldn't help but recall meeting Exeter's small, quiet son, and the look of paternal love in the inspector's eyes as he gazed at his lad. How painful it was to think of Exeter's family now. His sins, in the end, had been mostly venial ones; a little too rough with a criminal now and then, obstinate about taking advice. He abused his power, too, but he wasn't a malicious man.

Furthermore, who on earth would be either stupid or brazen enough to shoot one of the most important figures in Scotland Yard? None of the gangs; they knew how to skirt attention and didn't bother with the police when they could help it at all. Of course, Exeter had been working on the deaths of the two journalists. Standing beside Crook, watching the auditorium fill, Lenox felt a chill run down his spine. He was grateful to be here in Stirrington.

Lenox couldn't help but think that a boy like Gerald Poole, full of years' rage, would be more likely than anybody to lash out without regard for the consequences. Yet Dallington seemed so sure – and Poole so airy. Besides, Poole was behind bars.

A booming voice startled Lenox from his reverie. It was the portly Mayor Adlington. He had stood. 'Stirringtonians!' he said and then allowed a moment for the hall to quiet. 'Welcome to the parliamentary debate!'

A ragged cheering.

'The participants today are Mr. Robert Roodle and Mr. Charles Lenox. Gentlemen, if you would come to the stage.'

Lenox felt Crook's hand push him in the back, and he walked onto the stage, meeting Adlington and Roodle in the middle. All three men shook hands, and then Roodle and Lenox went to their podiums, about six feet apart. He heard Lenox supporters calling his name and Roodle supporters calling Roodle's, and then Adlington held up a hand.

'We meet under sorrowful circumstances, friends. The Honorable Mr. Stoke, who served our corner of England so admirably and for so long in the great halls of Parliament, is dead. Please observe a moment of silence with me.'

Only reluctantly did the Roodleites and Lenoxites stop their bickering. The silence was not very good, as silences go – there were coughs, for one thing, and outside a woman was yelling at either a husband or a horse, which caused a few titters. The mayor dealt with these by staring severely at a spot in the middle of the crowd. For a moment then there was perfect silence, which was broken when a baby toward the back of the hall began to caterwaul. Sandy Smith had been telling the God's honest truth when he described the strange acoustics of the room; the lone baby sounded like all the demons of hell. Lenox had to stifle a laugh.

The mayor, persevering through the noise, said, 'Now let us begin.'

When he described it to Lady Jane and his friends later on, Lenox said the first twenty minutes of the debate had been a blur, and they truly were. He answered as well as he could, but he couldn't remember from one moment to the next what he had said. All of his focus was on the question at hand. The three men conversed for some time on the question of the British navy and then moved to the more parochial subject of the beer tax. When Lenox called for it to be lowered, his supporters cheered fervently, and among the neutrals there was a murmur of agreement.

The next question was addressed to Lenox. 'Mr. Lenox,' said the mayor, 'as someone who has lived in Stirrington all his life' – Lenox tried not to groan – 'I must say that I agree with Mr. Roodle that it would be difficult for you to comprehend all of the issues that matter to us here. Do you disagree with that?'

'Yes,' said Lenox, 'with all proper respect, I do. The issues of Stirrington are the issues of England, Mayor. Not enough money in your pockets. Lads off to fight throughout the empire. The beer tax. Mr. Roodle could live in Stirrington for a hundred lifetimes, and his positions on these issues would still leave his townsmen and women behind. It simply won't do. Liberals look out for the common man. Conservatives – like brewers – look out for themselves.'

'See how he panders,' said Roodle in response to this. 'Look at Mr. Lenox's tie, gentleman. He thinks that a few quick words and a local tie will convince you of his legitimacy as a candidate for Stirrington's seat in Parliament. That's nonsense! He hides behind a knowledge – a knowledge he may or may not have – of England in general. Well, Mr. Fordyce, there in the fifth row, and Mr. Simpson, there in the third – we live in England, to be sure, but we don't live in the slums of London, or in Buckingham Palace, or in some snobbish house on Grosvenor Square, like Mr. Lenox here. We live in Stirrington. We have Stirrington manners and Stirrington concerns.

'I don't blame Mr. Lenox. He thinks he can put on a tie and understand us, and it may appear to him that he can. But *we* – we know that only a true son of Durham, a true son of this wonderful town, can understand its people. And I am that son. I am that son.'

Lenox felt the force of this. He would never acknowledge his inferiority to Roodle in terms of genuine interest for the people of Stirrington, but as rhetoric he knew it was powerful. He drew in a breath, as Mayor Adlington and the entire hall stared at him, awaiting his response.

'I'm reluctant to bring Mr. Roodle's business into this argument, but I feel I must. I am only now coming to understand Stirrington manners and Stirrington ways, it is true, and it is also true that I feel my qualifications lie in the positions that would benefit all of England.' He saw Sandy Smith wince in the first row. 'Stirrington especially,' he added hastily, 'but at least I'm trying. My opponent took a lucrative business away from this town he claims to love – and perhaps even *does* love. So it is surely hypocritical, is it not, to criticize me of putting Stirrington second? If you care so very much for the town, then bring your brewery back here. You either care for yourself and your own prospects or for the town's and its people's. We know how you chose the first time around. Why should it be any different this time?'

Surprisingly to Lenox, there was a cheer. He realized some of these men, or at any rate men they knew, must have worked at Roodle's brewery.

Roodle, red faced, prepared to respond. In the pubs that night they debated what he had actually intended to say; all that came out, however, was the phrase, 'Damn and blast your impudence!'

In addition, here all of Sandy Smith's predictions were borne out. Roodle's high-pitched words rebounded and buffeted every surface in the hall until they came out as a kind of squeal, a high-pitched and angry yelp.

There was a moment of silence, and then every man and woman in the auditorium, with the exception of a few stern Roodleites, burst into laughter.

After some time the mayor managed to calm the crowd and resume the debate; but for all intents and purposes it was finished already.

CHAPTER TWENTY-NINE

'Well, Graham? What did your new friends think?' It was the evening, and Lenox and Graham sat at a table in the Queen's Arms, eating supper together as they had many a time in their younger days, during Lenox's early years in London. In fact, Lenox remembered the first day he had slept in his new house – now his for some twelve years – when he and Graham had eaten a supper of wine and cold chicken amid the boxes and debris of moving house.

They were seeing each other for the first time in

several hours. After the debate Lenox had gone to three separate receptions (including, to his own amusement, one with the famous corn and grain merchants) while Graham had done what were now his usual rounds, among the pubs and shops.

'There is no doubt that Mr. Roodle has made himself a figure of fun, sir. Nearly every man I met either did an impression of the gentleman or asked for an account of his behavior.'

'That's good, I expect,' said Lenox glumly. 'I'd infinitely prefer a fair fight.'

'I would concur, sir, if Mr. Roodle had chosen to fight fairly as well.'

'Yes, that's true – and politics is a dirty thing, of course.'

'Yes, sir.'

'You were saying?'

'His temper has made Mr. Roodle a figure of fun, sir, but I was going to say that he still has strong support. Some men laughed right along with Mr. Roodle's imitators and then said they'd vote for him anyhow.'

'That's to be expected, I suppose.'

'Yes, sir. Though your reputation in Stirrington is high, I fear that the voters you haven't met are still suspicious of your motives and character.'

'Then I shall have to be sure to try to meet them all.'

Indeed, over the next several days Lenox worked as hard as he ever had in his life. He slept no more than five or six hours a night, and aside from a hearty breakfast each morning, when he remembered to eat it was usually a hasty sandwich with a glass of beer. Heretofore he had stuck to the town of Stirrington, but now he and Sandy Smith visited the countryside around it, stopping at small farms, villages with a dozen houses in them, and the pubs and coach stations that served these places. More than once Lenox despaired of finding votes among such sparse populations, but Smith always assured him that these men would remember their five- and ten-minute visits with the candidate. Roodle had deemed it beneath his dignity to visit the thousand voters who might make a crucial difference. Smith and Lenox hoped it was a grave error.

As they rode over the countryside in a coach and four, Lenox read the news from London, devouring each dated article but especially those concerned with Inspector Exeter, who had knocked Hiram Smalls, Simon Pierce, and Winston Carruthers off of the front page. There were few details of his shooting, however, and each day the articles grew more restless and more speculative. The facts that they all confirmed were these:

• Exeter had been in Brick Lane, a poor part of East London where gangs ran riot and police kept their heads down.

• He had been shot in the back, just below the right shoulder.

• Despite the street's crowds, nobody had witnessed – or anyway admitted to witnessing – the assault.

• Officials from Scotland Yard confirmed that Exeter had been working on the Fleet Street murders.

The strangest part of all this to Lenox was, of course, that his investigations had taken him so far away from Fleet Street and the two houses in the West End where Pierce and Carruthers lived. Smalls had lived in the East End, too, but in Liverpool Street, twenty minutes' walk from Brick Lane. It was perplexing. He must have perceived something Lenox had not. Either that or he had been off on a wild-goose chase. Lenox hoped it hadn't been that.

Immediately after Exeter had gone into the hospital Jenkins had been reinstated, a fact that he relayed with much happiness in a telegram to Lenox. Unfortunately, he didn't have – or wouldn't offer, after his recent trouble – any more detail about the shooting of Exeter, other than to say that he felt sure it was tied into the Fleet Street murders. Lenox agreed and wrote back to say so, but he felt frustrated at his lack of access to the case's finer points.

Still, it was good to have his mind on Stirrington. Election day was drawing precariously near.

On the fourth evening after the debate, Lenox had dinner with Mrs. Reeve again, though an entirely new and more agreeable set of guests joined them. Her influence was tangible, he saw as he grew more intimate with the town, and he was grateful for her good opinion.

Afterward he sat in the empty bar of the Queen's Arms, drinking a companionable glass of port with Crook. He asked the bartender a question he had refrained from asking his entire time in

Stirrington. 'Am I going to win?'

Crook shrugged philosophically. 'You have a chance, anyway. It all depends on this town's feelings about Roodle, really. If they dislike him mildly, resent him mildly, then he'll be elected. There's a powerful instinct to stick together in your northern towns. If on the other hand there is deep resentment toward Roodle, you have a damn good chance.'

'That makes my time here seem rather futile,' said Lenox with a rueful smile. 'If it all depends on Roodle.'

'On the contrary – you've done it all perfectly. You have a light touch with people, Mr. Lenox. I'm sure it has helped in your first career, at times. You've introduced yourself to the people of Stirrington and within a week become familiar and acceptable to them. Without having done that, it wouldn't matter in the slightest what the opinion of Roodle was. A sluggish turnout and a victory of a few thousand votes for him, were you a different man.'

'I'm pleased to hear it.'

Crook, lighting a cigar, said, 'Mind, Mr. Graham has helped, and Sandy Smith and I long had a theory that if you visited the outlying farms and villages you would find undiscovered votes. It's all gone well, I must say. It never mattered when Stoke was in the seat, but Sandy and I are excited to see if the strategy works.'

'All things being equal – two wonderful candidates, neither of whom had ever traveled a foot outside of Stirrington – is this place Liberal or Conservative?'

Crook grimaced and puffed at his cigar. 'Cetainly we're conservative in our morals, here. There are those who recognize that Liberal policies favor our kind. Myself, for instance. In the end, though, yes – Conservative.'

'An uphill climb for us, then.'

'You've known that since Mr. Hilary left, haven't you?'

'Yes,' said Lenox. 'To be honest, I thought it was all lost then.'

'The party is fearful of looking as if it really tried for a seat it might lose. Better that the onus falls on you, a dilettante, or me and Smith, locals. Harsh, I know, but true.'

Lenox saw the verity in this. He took a sip of the amber port. 'I hope we can give them a surprise, then.'

'So do I, so do I. It's wonderful finally to get my hands dirty and play at real politics, I can tell you. Stoke never had any juice in him.' After taking a sip of port he added, 'May he rest in peace.'

Graham came in at that moment.

'A telegram, sir,' he said to Mr. Lenox.

'Who from?'

'Inspector Jenkins of Scotland Yard, sir.'

'Hand it over.'

'What an inundation of telegrams has come to my pub since your arrival!' said Crook with a belly laugh. 'We ought to send a wire straight to your room. It must cost a pretty penny to stay abreast of the London news.'

'Worth it to me, though,' said Lenox. He opened the telegram and read it.

He gasped.

'Sir?' said Graham.

'Just a moment, Graham.'

Lenox read it over. 'Gerald Poole has confessed. He killed Winston Carruthers.'

CHAPTER THIRTY

The news that followed the next day was scarce and overwrought. According to the papers Lenox could find, all of Lndon was in an uproar about Gerald Poole's confession. Each front page ran a long recapitulation of Jonathan Poole's treason, and the names of the few tradesmen and servants who had met Gerald popped up again and again, uniformly to say how surprised they were. The more febrile stories called the shooting of Exeter a second treason.

There was no confirmation that Poole had indeed employed Hiram Smalls as a mercenary, but given the two men's meeting at the Saracen's Head pub the evening before the murders of Simon Pierce and Winston Carruthers, there was little doubt in most minds about their complicity. With Lenox, however, the idea sat uneasily.

'The question is, why on earth would Poole have sent that letter to Smalls?' he asked Graham as he read that evening, another long day of campaigning behind them. 'Does it make any sense that he would meet Smalls in a public place, only to write a letter containing the same plan they had agreed to the night before?'

'No, sir.'

'Still, people get nervous when they mean to commit a crime.'

'Certainly, sir.'

'He may have been agitated and written the note to give himself some activity, I suppose. I hope Jenkins sends word of the contents of Poole's confession. I fear he's treading the line, however, after his suspension. Needless to say, I can't blame the man for it.'

Indeed, in the forty-eight hours after he received the initial telegram, there was no word from London except another letter from Lady Jane, which predated Poole's confession, and a stout and strongly worded telegram from Dallington.

IT SIMPLY CANNOT BE TRUE STOP I NEED YOUR HELP PLEASE RETURN STOP DALLINGTON

Lenox answered:

THERE ARE ONLY A FEW DAYS REMAINING UNTIL THE ELECTION STOP I SIMPLY CANNOT LEAVE STOP GATHER ALL THE INFORMATION YOU CAN AND THE MOMENT I CAN I WILL FLY TO LONDON STOP BEST LENOX

He felt guilty writing it but equally felt how impossible it was to write anything different.

Originally another debate had been set for that day, but Roodle had pulled out of it. With Crook and Sandy Smith satisfied that they had covered all the countryside there was to visit, Lenox turned his attention again to the local tradesmen and officials who would be influential among their peers. He heard a long soliloquy by Mayor Adlington about wool prices and another from a pig farmer about pork prices, all over one endless lunch at Stirrington's social club. He toured stockrooms and the fruit and vegetable market and commiserated with the fishmonger about rising costs.

For all this, the encounter that moved him most was with a small child, a boy of no more than nine or ten years, who was guiding a herd of cattle down a lane toward the public fields. It was at the very edge of the town of Stirrington, where a few buildings straggled out into empty meadows. Lenox and Sandy Smith were sitting on a wooden fence, eating roasted beef sandwiches, after attending a small gathering at the blacksmith's house. Lenox nodded politely to the boy, who stopped. The cattle did, too, after he made a *thock* with his cheek.

'You're the Parliament?' said the lad.

'I'm trying to become a Member of Parliament. A parliament is a whole group of men.'

'I thought you were the Parliament.'

'No,' said Lenox. 'Are these your cattle?'

The boy laughed, and Lenox realized that his own question had been just as preposterous as the one he had answered.

'They're my uncle's, my father's brother, as was.'

'What about your father?'

'Dead.'

'I'm very sorry to hear it.'

The boy shrugged and with a nod beckoned the

cattle again, and they moved onward down the lane.

'Shouldn't he be in school?' Lenox asked.

'I don't know that you've quite grasped the nature of people's lives here, Mr. Lenox. School is a luxury, in many of their cases.'

Now, Lenox was a gentleman of his age and thought himself enlightened, thought himself progressive; indeed, vowed to fight for the enlightened and progressive causes he had long believed in. Yet it was only now that he truly realized what life in Stirrington was like – and with a burst of insight realized that perhaps Roodle was correct, in some way. Perhaps he wasn't fit to represent these people. It was jarring. The slums of London he could comprehend, and he had grown up among rough men and women in Sussex, but for some reason the boy's utter abstraction from Pall Mall, from Grosvenor Square, from Bellamy's Restaurant and the House of Lords, gave Lenox a shock.

A shock for the good, though; for from that moment he had a deepened and more profound sense of the responsibility of his undertaking. For his entire adult life he had moved so easily among men who made large decisions, whether admirals or cabinet ministers or bishops, that he had forgotten to some extent what a privilege it was to stand for Parliament. The sense of honor overwhelmed him. He felt it keenly.

So the days passed, with every moment another hand to shake, another tale to listen to, until it was the day before election day.

In the late morning Crook appeared in the bar and announced that he was taking two days off, much to his patrons' surprise. He had found a replacement barman from a pub in the countryside, however, brought in for a little urban experience, and the grumblings in the Queen's Arms soon fell off.

Outside of the pub on the High Street there was a tremendous clatter. They were constructing a high hustings, and it was when Lenox saw this undertaking that he began to have butterflies in his stomach. He sent Graham to find a mug of tea and a piece of toast to settle himself, even though he had already eaten that morning.

'Nervous?' said Crook. He nodded in an approving, businesslike fashion. 'It's for the good. If you weren't nervous I'd think something had gone wrong.'

'What is it for?'

'For speaking, of course. We have a succession of gentlemen who will speak there this morning, and then around lunchtime, when people are on the streets, you'll give a speech. Another one this evening, and all day tomorrow we'll have a rotating group of people speaking from it.'

'Does Roodle have one?'

Crook nodded, 'Yes, a few streets down. Ours is in a better position, though. It may prove an advantage.'

'Good,' said Lenox. 'Good.'

Just then Nettie, Crook's niece, came out, dressed in a pretty muslin frock and with her hair in braids. Lenox saw the immediate softening of Crook's features, the unlining of his forehead, and began to walk away.

'Mr. Lenox!' said Nettie before he had gone

very far.

He turned. 'Yes?'

'I said a prayer for you at mass this morning.'

'Why, thank you, Miss Crook. I'm very honored.'

Crook colored, but Lenox pretended he hadn't noticed.

'I certainly hope you win.'

'So do I!'

Lenox bowed to Nettie Crook and walked inside.

So, Crook was a papist. It occurred to Lenox that this might be helpful, in a way, if it meant he had allies in the Catholic community of Stirrington. Then he cursed himself for the cynicism of the thought.

He stood at the door of the pub pondering all of this.

'How do, Mr. Lenox?' said a passing man. He wasn't past thirty, a wave of fair hair pushed off of his pink, sunburnt features.

'Very well, thank you,' said the candidate, looking up.

'I'm voting for you tomorrow.'

He felt a surge of affection for Stirrington. 'I don't know how to thank you,' he said.

'Lower the beer tax,' the man responded with a laugh, walking on. 'That should do. Good morning, now.'

So the day began, and as the sun slowly rose and slowly set there were speeches, emergency strategy sessions, and dozens of pints bought for potential voters, until at last at 1:00 A.M., exhausted, Lenox and Crook went to their respective beds.

At six the next morning Lenox was dressed and watching the day break – the day he hoped would change his life forever.

CHAPTER THIRTY-ONE

Lenox detested the fact, but it was simple enough: In elections for Parliament, bribery mattered. It was no surprise at all when Graham reported that in the Roodle pubs votes were worth two crowns a head.

'We must do the same,' Sandy Smith advised, nervously tying his tie as he prepared to get up on the hustings and deliver the first speech of the day, at seven o'clock.

Crook nodded.

'No,' Lenox said. 'Graham, here's money. If you see anybody accept Roodle's offer, match the sum and give the person the choice of the thing. Otherwise let's stick to buying drinks.'

Crook shrugged, as if to say that it was Lenox's money, and turned to consult with a growing line of men who had decided they wanted to vote for Lenox but needed assurance they would receive a pint later on. Crook set Nettie to handing out vouchers for the drinks.

At this Lenox felt ridiculously puritanical and changed his mind. 'A few shillings a head, then, over Roodle. If it's the done thing.'

Crook laughed. 'It is,' he said.

The day was a blur. A brace of carriages went

around the countryside, picking up all the voters Lenox had gone and spoken to and Roodle hadn't. Lenox and various of his supporters took turns on the stage, all giving rousing speeches that were generally of two varieties: one, that Charles Lenox was the greatest man of his age and would turn Stirrington into an Aztec-like City of Gold; two, that Robert Roodle was the most depraved, ill-mannered, and stupid man alive, the only mistake the otherwise wonderful town of Stirrington had ever produced, and a vote for him would be tantamount to treason – to a vote for the French – to a vote for more expensive beer – why, any number of things.

All of this was very pleasing to the growing number of Lenox supporters gathered around the hustings, who passed out handbills and pins to passersby. Every sighting of Lenox himself, who was making the rounds of the city when he wasn't speaking, was greeted with a high cheer. He noticed with satisfaction that at midmorning a small army of women led by Mrs. Reeve had appeared, holding homemade signs in support of the Liberal candidate and stopping to chat with the men and women who passed by on the street, every single one of whom they knew.

All of this was punctuated by an hourly event almost equally pleasing to the speeches, which was the arrival of a group of Roodleites who had a snare drum and beat on it to drown out Lenox's proxies, meanwhile passing out pamphlets in favor of Roodle in front of the Queen's Arms with, as Mrs. Reeve observed, the impudence of highwaymen. It was satisfying to Lenox's supporters to boo the small group until they left, and by noon or so their arrival was as highly anticipated as the candidate's himself.

A little after noon Crook returned from City Hall, where they were counting votes.

'No numbers yet,' he said, 'but I learned two things.'

'Yes?' asked Sandy Smith in an agitated voice. He was preparing to speak again, as soon as a corn merchant onstage finished his tribute to Lenox's impossibly various virtues.

'For one, there are about twice as many voters as the mayor remembers from the last election.'

'That only stands to reason, given that Stoke ran unopposed,' said Lenox.

'The more voters, the better it is for the Liberal candidate – there's a political truth for you, Mr. Lenox.'

'Second,' said Crook, 'when I was leaving, the carriages we hired to go to the countryside had picked up about twenty men, and the drivers said there were another twenty waiting to be picked up, and another twenty after that, and so on and so on. It's only a matter of getting them in before the polls close tonight.'

'That's wonderful!' said Lenox.

'There's my cue,' said Smith and ran off to mount the stage.

'Now, it's understood that each of them will receive a shilling or two to cover the missed hours of work.'

Doubtfully, Lenox said, 'I'm not sure I can approve–'

'It's absolutely understood,' said Crook gravely.

The candidate relented. 'Very well – but we must send another carriage, if we can find one.'

'I hoped you would say that. You have the money? Here, good. Lucy,' he shouted at the waitress, 'find Samuel Keller and tell him to follow the two carriages from Taylor's livery out to the country! He's to pick up voters!'

Lucy took the money and ran off to the livery company, and Crook shook Lenox's hand and with a look of determination on his fat, round, serious face said, 'I think we may win this election yet.'

Lenox scarcely hoped – and yet in the very few quiet moments of his day his whole mind was bent on an image of himself in Parliament. He pictured his first speech, the green baize benches of the chamber; he pictured himself shouting down an opponent; he pictured his familiarity with the doormen of that august body, with the secretaries and valets who ran their employers' lives. He yearned to be part of it all.

He recalled something his father had once said. Lenox had been four, perhaps five, and his father had been preparing to go into London for the start of the new session. Edmund, two years older and preoccupied with his schoolmates, had given his father a handshake and run off with a cricket bat. To Charles, though, it was a sorrowful occasion.

His father wore a pristine dark suit, and with a stroke of inspiration the young Lenox ran upstairs and found the old, tatty corduroy jacket, patched at the elbows and threadbare in the shoulders, that his father wore around the stables and out on his land. He handed it to his father wordlessly, and when the man realized Charles's purpose, a look of kindness came onto his often austere face.

'Oh, little one,' he said. 'Don't be sad.' He kneeled down and took Charles's hands and looked him in the eye. 'Remember,' he went on, 'that once a man's name is entered into the book of Members, nobody can ever take that achievement away from him. It is the highest honor one can receive, to enter Parliament. It may be a little sad for you and – I'll tell you a secret – for me, but it is for the thousands of men and boys we don't know that I must go, and serve my country.'

It seemed like an endless day, but slowly it began to fetch toward evening. Lenox spoke again at three and realized with a start that there were now hundreds of people around the hustings. By four o'clock all three carriages were running at full speed, bringing in thirty more people every thirty minutes, and when at four thirty Crook informed him that there were still far too many people willing to vote who might not make it into Stirrington, Lenox ordered a fourth carriage.

At five something novel happened, just when things had gotten a little bit sluggish: Roodle came to the Queen's Arms.

He had been expecting to find Lenox onstage, perhaps, and looked a little nonplussed when he found instead a grain merchant talking in a heavy northern accent of crop yields, but he went on with his plan anyway.

'Ask Mr. Lenox if he can take you to St. Mary's churchyard, where half of our ancestors are buried!' he said.

Boos.

'Ask Mr. Lenox if he can direct you to the Martyrs' Memorial – and not the one in Oxford!'

More boos, and then someone shouted, 'Ask Mr. Lenox if beer is too expensive!' which drew tremendous cheers and drowned out whatever Roodle, who looked furious, was going to say next. When the crowd finally quieted he said, 'Only a member of our town's community should be our town's Member!'

The clever little smirk he gave while he said this line infuriated Lenox's supporters, and they drove him and the small cordon of Roodleites with him down the street, catcalling them as they left, until they were gone.

At seven o'clock Lenox, hoarse and exhausted, mounted the hustings one last time. A harried cheer went up, but people had become a little weary – not of the man but of the day and its excitement.

'Ladies and gentlemen, whether I win or lose this by-election, today has been one of the most wonderful days of my life,' he said. 'Whether I win or lose, nothing I have done these past few weeks will be in vain, because I have discovered the best small town in England!'

He paused for another cheer. 'Thank you, thank you. Now I have one last favor to ask you. At eight o'clock the polls close, and I see many faces that were here at eight this morning. You all deserve to go home, but on your way please stop just one person and ask him if he's voted. Then, if he says no, tell him why you believe that Charles Lenox is the best man to serve Stirrington and why Robert Roodle isn't, for that matter.'

Another cheer. 'Thank you!' he said. 'I feel honored by your support.'

He came down from the stage but this time to the front, rather than escaping to the back and the pub, and allowed the people to engulf him. He shook hands until his forearm was sore and commiserated with the many people he had met. By eight only a dozen or so supporters remained, the rest spread out across the city, on their way home.

He went back into the Queen's Arms, where Crook gave him a broad smile and put a paternal arm around his shoulder. 'You did awfully well, Mr. Lenox,' he said. 'Really better than I expected.'

'Call me Charles,' said the candidate, who suddenly realized that he was not only falling-down tired but famished. 'I say, is there any food to be had?'

'Of course, of course.'

Ten minutes later, sitting at a table in a private room at the back of the building with Crook, Lenox fell upon a plate of battered cod and red potatoes. A new, more jovial side of Crook appeared as the two men sat and talked. He fetched a bottle of Bordeaux and regaled Lenox with stories of Stirrington's more eccentric history: Mr. Weathers, who went out to the middle of his fields every day and cast a fishing pole in the middle of his crops, then sat and dirt-fished all day; the mayor before Adlington, who had been fond of a rainbow-colored waistcoat that very nearly caused a revolt among his subordinates. It was as if he had finally shepherded Lenox through the campaign and could relax.

Then at ten o'clock, very suddenly – for Lenox was lulled into a gentle stupor by the wine, Crook's voice, the food, and the fire – it was time to see who had won the election. Sandy Smith stood in front of the pub and nodded gravely when they came out, and the three men walked over. At City Hall there was an agonizing half hour while the last few votes were counted and Mayor Adlington was roused from a nap to read the results. Just before they were ready, Roodle came storming in. Then, in a surreal tableau that Lenox felt more observer of than participant in, they went into a small room and heard the results.

It was over. He had lost.

CHAPTER THIRTY-TWO

It was a bitter, bitter thing to swallow. In the end only two hundred had separated the men. Pushing his pride to the side, Lenox reached out his hand to Roodle, but the brewer pushed past him with a sneer and went outside to announce the news to his waiting supporters. Lenox knew he had to do the same, though he scarcely felt equal to the task.

He was glad there were books in the world, at that moment; glad that there were maps and encyclopedias, and warm fires and comfortable armchairs. He wanted to retreat into his library for a year without leaving it and eat good lunches and take long naps. But he told himself that a

Lenox of Lenox Hall ought to have more mettle than to wish for something like that, and he went outside and delivered a brief, grateful encomium to his supporters before going back to the Queen's Arms.

'It should never have been so close,' was all Crook said. 'Roodle thought he'd win by a landslide. We did our side proud.'

'I can't help but think of that single day I wasn't here. Mightn't I have met another two hundred people that day and perhaps impressed upon half of them my suit? Mightn't I have won a hundred of them and drawn even with Roodle?'

Rather surprisingly, Crook said with a severe glance, 'That's no way to think at all – Charles. You did your level best. No other candidate short of Peel reincarnated could have done more or worked harder.'

They arrived back at the Queen's Arms, and in his weariness Lenox wrote two brief telegrams with the same message ('I lost. It's all right.') to Edmund and to Lady Jane. Then he took himself upstairs, had a few solitary moments of self-recrimination and sorrow, and fell into bed, exhausted.

When he woke in the morning it was to see Graham seated at the table by the window, a tray with coffee and sweet rolls before him.

'Is there something wrong, Graham?'

'Good morning, sir. I merely wished to see if you required anything.'

Lenox chuckled, 'Are you worried about me? I'm all right, I suppose. A bit of a setback, but these things happen.'

Graham stood, 'It was a pleasure to help you,' he said and then left.

Lenox went to the table and poured himself a cup of coffee. The rolls were good, chewy, soft, and sweet, and the dark warmth of the coffee complemented them well. Meditatively he chewed and looked out the window, trying to suppress even to himself the disappointment of the night before. He sighed deeply and swirled the last sip of coffee in the bottom of his cup before swallowing it. There was a telegram on the tray, which at last he opened with a sense of dread. It was from Jane (Nothing from Edmund? He worried he had let his brother down) and proved a very kind and thoughtful note, but at that particular moment Lenox detested the idea of pity, of consolation.

He was tired both in spirit and in body, aching all over from the exertions of the day before, but he was conscious that he had a duty to return to London and help Dallington. While he was glad that he had fought, how much more use might he have been in the capital, following the Fleet Street murderers? Then the depressing thought occurred to him that he was no closer to exposing George Barnard's criminality to the world than he had ever been – but he pushed that away. There were other priorities in the short term. It would have to wait.

He dressed and asked Graham to get tickets for the afternoon train. Given his preference, Lenox would have liked to hide out in his room until the train left, avoiding all of the people who knew his ignominy, but he keenly understood the cowardice of that and forced himself to descend the stairs to the main chamber of the Queen's Arms.

There he saw the most welcome sight he could imagine, perhaps even more than the sight of Lady Jane would have been.

It was his brother, Edmund, sitting with a cup of coffee and a morning newspaper.

'Edmund?'

'Hullo, Charles,' said Sir Edmund Lenox, the 11th Baronet of Markethouse. 'How are you going along?'

The two men shook hands. 'Not too badly,' said Charles, 'but what in heavens brings you here?'

Edmund shrugged. 'I had your telegram,' he said. 'I thought I would come visit you, and perhaps we might take the train back to London together.'

'That was kind of you indeed.'

Edmund smiled sadly. 'I'm only sorry that I encouraged you to run. It was always going to be a challenge after Stoke died.'

'Are Hilary and Brick very disappointed?'

'Yes, of course, but they understand how hard you worked. Still, I don't come here as a Member of Parliament but as your brother.'

Indeed, Charles felt like a little brother, grateful for his older brother's consideration.

'Well – it was a disappointment, that's all.'

'I'm awfully sorry, Charles.'

The two men sat down, and Lenox declined a cup of coffee but said he wouldn't mind a soft-boiled egg with a square of toast. Edmund said that sounded good, and soon enough they had their food and were talking companionably about Edmund's sons, about the old lands at Lenox

House, where they had both grown up but only Edmund lived now, and about Lenox's forthcoming marriage to Lady Jane.

'I was sorry to hear about Toto,' said Edmund.

Lenox nodded. 'What a terrible blow that was. Of course, she and Thomas were treading on thin ice already.'

'Any news?'

'Apparently they've reconciled. I certainly hope so.'

'How about' – Edmund tried to sound unconcerned – 'the Fleet Street murders? And Exeter?'

Lenox laughed. 'I'm sorry,' he said. 'You make a poor actor.'

For all the responsibilities of his position in Sussex and in Parliament, Edmund had a childlike enthusiasm for his brother's profession, often begging for details. Once he had been able to help with an investigation, and other than his wedding day it was the closest Charles had seen him to nirvana.

'Well?' said Edmund, now eagerly. 'What do you know?'

'Nothing very current, I'm afraid. I know that Hiram Smalls killed Simon Pierce, and another man – his accomplice – killed Winston Carruthers.'

'Do you? How?'

Lenox explained the note and indeed described his whole day of research into the mystery of Hiram Smalls's death.

'Who could have penetrated the prison?' Edmund asked.

Lenox sighed. 'Any number of people, unfortunately. Poole wasn't there yet, of course. Men making deliveries, other inmates. The gangs run riot in Newgate. Tell me, though, what do you hear of Exeter? Your knowledge is surely more current than mine.'

'Apparently he will make it through. The bullet perforated one of his organs, I forget which.'

'He was shot in the back?'

'Yes,' said Edmund. 'They're keeping him under wraps, however. There's very little information. The entire city is fascinated by the story, it goes without saying. Some poorer people are saying it's a good riddance.'

'Exeter was never tactful or gentle in his methods. Still, he deserved better than this. I shall take the matter in hand when I return to town this afternoon.'

'Will you?' said Edmund. 'Excellent! I really am delighted to hear it. May I help?'

'We'll see,' said Lenox. 'There's Dallington now.'

'You know, I've been asking for years if I could be your apprentice, Charles,' said Edmund with a frown.

'It would scarcely have suited,' said Lenox with a smile. He realized that for the moment he wasn't thinking of Roodle in Parliament.

'It will be a diversion, I hope, from your regret.'

'About the election?' Lenox shrugged. 'It stings a little, but I'm a grown man, after all. I can accommodate a little pain. My life hasn't been so hard.'

'No,' said Edmund. 'That's true, and you have a great deal to look forward to. Your marriage.'

'Yes.'

Edmund's eyes narrowed. 'Has something happened?'

'Because I'm not as effusive as you?' Lenox took a sip of coffee. The pub was filling up with early customers. One of the lessons of Stirrington for him had been that there was no hour at which a pint of beer was inappropriate. 'No, nothing has happened.'

Edmund stared hard at him. 'Really?'

Lenox sighed. 'Well – perhaps. It's so minor I shouldn't mention it, but she said – well, that she has doubts.'

'What sort of doubts?'

'I can't say, really. Perhaps that we've known each other too short a time,' he added rather lamely, wishing he hadn't said anything at all.

'You've known each other for hundreds of years.'

'So I told her. It *is* quick, I suppose, but I don't mind that.'

'It was a shock to her system,' said Edmund. 'Women and men alike are subject to these things. I was nervous – exceedingly nervous – before I married Molly.'

'I recall,' Lenox answered, smiling at the thought of his brother soused to the gills and alternately saying he wanted to marry Molly that instant or flee to the depths of the Orient.

'I know what you're thinking. Don't talk to me about China, there's a chap,' said Edmund with a grimace. 'Listen, shall we walk around town a bit before we get the train back? Put a good face on things?'

'Of course,' said Lenox. He hailed Lucy and gave her a few coins.

'Ah, Mr. Lenox – before I forget, it's another telegram for you. You'll wear the machine out, you know,' she said.

'Thanks, Lucy.'

He tore it open and read it quickly, then went completely white.

'My God, what is it, Charles?' said Edmund.

He looked up. 'It's from Jenkins. Exeter is dead.'

CHAPTER THIRTY-THREE

'Christ,' said Edmund, sitting forward in his chair. 'Can it be true? From all I had heard his wounds weren't that severe.'

Lenox shook his head, frowning, as he pored over the note. 'Apparently he worsened overnight. An infection reached his blood, and he died quickly.' He looked up. 'I hope not painfully.'

'What was he like, Inspector Exeter?'

'Did you never meet him? A bluff chap, proud – as a policeman he was determined and hard-working but never imaginative. He was a bully, I'm afraid. No use eulogizing him. Still, say this for Exeter,' said Lenox, thinking of the few times they had worked together, 'he was always on the side of the law. He wanted what was best for London. People forget that Scotland Yard is still a young institution, bound to make its own mistakes before it improves.'

'Yes,' said Edmund.

Lenox shifted uneasily. 'It's a selfish thing to

say, but I hope he wasn't shot because of the case. I feel a sense of foreboding about my return to London.'

'It hadn't even occurred to me,' said Edmund, a look of concern on his face. 'Good heavens. Well, it's simple enough – you mustn't do anything more about the murders.'

Lenox shook his head. 'No. I can't do that. If Poole is guilty, I have to confirm it; if Poole is innocent, I have to prove it. I've deferred Dallington's requests, but I cannot any longer. He saved my life, remember.'

'For which we're all in his debt – but surely he wouldn't want you to go about risking what he had saved, would he?'

'I'm afraid I must do what I think is right, Edmund.'

With a sigh, he answered, 'Yes, you must.'

'Come, let's go see Stirrington. The election doesn't seem such a serious thing any longer, somehow.'

The two brothers spent the midday walking around town. At first they were somber and discussed the implications of Exeter's death, but life is fluid in its nature, and it's a rare mind that cannot cope with death, however sudden, however sorrowful. Soon their congenial natures took over, and they conversed as they were wont to do. Something funny happened, too – all day long people walked up to Lenox and congratulated him, as if he had won. Almost nobody offered condolences. He remembered that it was something in itself to run, to push the democracy along, and felt slightly better.

217

Soon enough it was time for the train. Graham had packed Lenox's things, and all that remained left to do was say good-bye to Crook; he had already parted with Sandy Smith, promising to keep in touch and inviting Smith to visit him should he ever happen to be in the capital.

He ducked his head into the Queen's Arms while Edmund smoked a pipe in the sun, but Crook was absent from the bar. Lucy, ever helpful, told him that Crook had asked that Lenox be referred to his house next door. So the detective went to the small house and made his way again into Nettie's parlor. The maid went off to fetch Crook, and for the last time Lenox looked over Nettie's embroidery and her watercolors, and he felt strangely moved by it all. It was an honor to have been accepted by these people. He was glad he had done it, win or lose. There had been so much generosity toward him, where there might have been suspicion or indifference.

'Well, how do you do, Mr. Lenox?' said Crook, coming into the room. He settled his great heft into a deep armchair and set about lighting his pipe. 'Do you want a cup of tea or a cake?'

'We have to catch the train, unfortunately, and I can't linger. Thank you, though.'

'Do you regret having come to Stirrington?'

'On the contrary, I was only just thinking how glad I was that I had.'

Crook furrowed his brow. 'I'll never understand how we lost, Mr. Lenox.'

'However it was, it was despite your efforts, Mr. Smith's efforts, your friends' efforts.'

'And your own. I mean it, though – we ought to

have won. Really. It puzzles me more the more I think about it.'

'In any event.'

'I hope you take fond memories away, anyhow, and perhaps even visit again.'

'I shall,' said Lenox.

Crook stood up. 'Well, I suppose you had better be on your way.'

Lenox stood up and felt the queer consciousness that he would never lay eyes on Crook again, though for two weeks they had been in constant conference, even friends. He tried to treat the moment with the dignity it demanded.

'Good-bye,' he said, 'and thank you for everything you have done. I shall never forget it.'

'Thank you, Mr. Lenox. Next time, eh?'

On the train several hours later Lenox, Edmund, and Graham shared a medium-sized compartment and soon littered it with their newspapers and books. Edmund had read for an hour or so and then, because of his overnight train ride, had fallen asleep. Graham was taking a thorough inventory of the news (the train carried that morning's papers), and Lenox spent his time reading and glancing out the window.

He had said the election didn't seem as important after Exeter's death, but despite the nobility of that sentiment the vote kept sliding back onto the edges of Lenox's vision, a dark specter he hadn't wholly confronted, a decisive disappointment at the crescendo of his lifelong hopes.

They were nearing London, finally. It was dark and, he felt through the window, cold out, with the small houses and farms near the tracks bright orange with light, a thousand human lives contained in them, a thousand stories. As they drew up on the edge of the city, outside the old gate, each new geographic signpost recalled a past case, and he thought that whether it was dangerous or not, at least he had his work. He loved being a detective.

Naturally, his mind turned to what they were calling the Fleet Street murders, and he spent the last part of the trip in grim silence, going over the details of the thing in his head.

In the end the truly strange thing was the dichotomy that Pierce and Carruthers presented. The former was thin and gray, the latter fat and red; the former was religious and ascetic, the latter corruptible and drunken. Only two things united them: their profession, of course, and also – and then Lenox saw it all.

He looked up at Graham.

'Sir?'

'Gerald Poole is innocent,' said the detective with complete conviction.

'Sir?'

'I'm certain – but then, what desperate villain killed the journalists and Smalls, and perhaps Exeter?' he murmured, talking to himself. 'What stakes would be worth the risk? Not money, I would guess. Well, maybe money, but I really think it must be reputation – or livelihood – or family.'

'May I inquire, sir, how you have proved Mr. Poole's innocence to your satisfaction?'

'It's intuition, but I feel pretty confident, all right. The secret of the thing is that Carruthers was the true target. Pierce was only killed as a cover for the true motive, to falsely point Scotland Yard toward Gerald Poole.'

'I don't follow your line of thought, sir.'

'Because Carruthers and Pierce are so strongly linked by Jonathan Poole's treason, naturally an investigator would assume that their murders had something to do with that. Pierce is the perfect red herring.'

'Then you mean the murderer wanted to kill Mr. Carruthers and killed Mr. Pierce simply to place suspicion on Gerald Poole?'

'On Jonathan Poole's recently returned son, of course! In fact, the motive for the murders wasn't anything to do with Jonathan Poole's treason. The murderer merely wanted it to seem that way, and so in addition to killing his real target, Carruthers, he killed Pierce, who I'd wager wasn't involved in all this muddle.'

'It makes sense, sir.'

'Doesn't it follow, then, that Gerald Poole is innocent? He was set up!'

'Yes, sir, it seems plausible when you put it so.'

'Is there another way to put it that I haven't thought of?'

'I have one question, sir,' said Graham.

'Yes?'

'Why do you believe Carruthers was the real target? Is it not just as likely that Pierce was the real target and Carruthers the cover-up?'

'I don't think so. Pierce was incorruptible and untainted, and Carruthers was utterly corruptible, utterly tainted. There's something more important, though.'

'Yes?'

'The piece of paper missing from the desk in front of Carruthers. Do you remember I told you that he had ink all over his hands and a pen, but that there was no paper before him? I reckon Carruthers was blackmailing somebody, writing something incriminating – he was killed for that missing piece of paper.'

'Whereas Pierce died on his doorstep, and the killer never could have gone inside,' murmured Graham thoughtfully.

'Precisely. I feel sure we're right. Please go see Dallington when we get back and tell him that I think Poole is innocent. Fetch him to me then, would you? I haven't the patience to wait for a note to find him.'

'Very good, sir.'

'What's all this?' said Edmund, stirring.

'Gerald Poole is innocent,' said Lenox, eyes blazing.

Edmund blinked. 'How long was I asleep?'

CHAPTER THIRTY-FOUR

They arrived in London in late evening, and the station discharged the three men, a ragged procession laden with bags, into a thick, cold rain. Lenox grabbed the first newspaper he could lay his hands on and read the opening line of its lead article, on the subject of Exeter's death: 'A lion has vanished from the halls of Scotland Yard, and our nation's capital is inestimably poorer for it.' All of the news stories about Exeter ran in that way, and by the time his carriage had reached Berkeley Square Lenox was persuaded that the man might as well have been Alexander the Great, such was the tenor of the tributes to him. It gave him a queer feeling, to imagine poor Exeter dead; it can never be pleasant to mourn for someone that you've had equivocal feelings about.

When they reached Hampden Lane and Lenox's house, Graham handed the luggage to a footman and then was instantly off in a cab to find Dallington. The two brothers, meanwhile, dragged their tired bodies into the library.

'Welcome back,' said Mary in the hallway, curtsying. 'Coffee?'

'Wine,' said Edmund,

'Whisky,' said Lenox.

The fire was warm and made him drowsy, and Lenox felt a sluggish pleasure at being home after the dual calamities of Exeter and Stirrington.

'Thanks for coming up to Stirrington,' he said to Edmund. 'I was so awfully low. It saved me.'

'Of course,' murmured Edmund.

There were a few long minutes of silence, during which Lenox assumed they were both ruminating on the past day or two. It came as something of a surprise, then, when Edmund's head rolled back a little and he gave a great snore.

Lenox laughed quietly and pulled the wineglass from his brother's hand. Then he crept out to the hallway and said to Mary, 'Leave the library alone, would you, and have someone make up a fire in the Ugly Room.'

Now, in Lenox's house the Ugly Room was

223

rather an institution; it was situated toward the back of the first floor and had a few small windows overlooking the thin strip of garden behind the house. It took its name not from its situation, which was in fact rather pleasant, but from its contents. They were the debris of Lenox's life. There was a giant, hideous wardrobe that he had somehow convinced himself to buy when he came to London, a large oil painting that he had bought from a friend's exhibition and couldn't get rid of, a pair of ornate silver candlesticks that stood about two feet high and looked as if they had come from somebody's nightmare. Bad books lined the walls. Sooner or later every uncomfortable and creaky chair in the house found its way to the Ugly Room. Lenox went back there to wait for Dallington and surveyed it with some satisfaction. Most people had their terrible things spread throughout their house, but he liked to concentrate them all in one place, where he could make sure they never moved back into his life on the sly. He didn't come in here more than once a fortnight.

Soon Dallington and Graham had returned, and the former came in to sit with Lenox, who had been reading.

'How do you do?' said the detective when Graham was gone again.

'Why have we been evicted from the library?' He squirmed. 'I feel as though this chair bears a personal grudge against me.'

Lenox laughed. 'My brother fell asleep in there. Sorry.'

'What's all the cloak and dagger, then? Graham pulled me out of a decent game of whist.'

224

'That's probably for the best,' said Lenox. He couldn't help himself from lecturing his apprentice now and then.

'Yes, yes, and I should only drink barley water and meditate on the Sabbath. Still, it's damn hard to find a game of cards in this town!'

'I think Poole is innocent.'

Dallington furrowed his brow. 'Well, of course.'

'You say that despite his confession?'

With that the younger man looked uneasy. 'Well–'

'I have a theory that Poole is the victim of a plan to frame him for the murders of Pierce and Carruthers.'

'So do I – Hiram Smalls asked him for a meeting.'

'That relies on Poole's word, you know. Let me tell you what I think.'

Lenox repeated what he had said to Graham – that Carruthers was the murderer's real target and Pierce an unfortunate casualty, the murderer having known that the two men were connected by Poole and that Gerald Poole was in London again.

Dallington whistled, impressed. 'Could well be,' he said. 'So they may not be the Fleet Street murders after all, then.'

'Precisely – we can't quite say what sort of murders they may be, except that with Exeter and Smalls dead, too, they're for very high stakes.'

'Speaking of which – shall you be safe?'

'I hope so,' said Lenox. 'I don't speak to the papers, so I hope it's not widely known that I've interested myself in this business, Still, I mean to speak to Scotland Yard about it tomorrow. They may give me assistance.'

'There's such a public outcry over Exeter, I'm sure they'll be desperate to do anything to find his killer.'

'Yes,' said Lenox grimly. 'God, but it's an ugly thing.'

'What can I do?'

'Find out why Gerald Poole confessed.'

Dallington stared at Lenox for a moment and then nodded. 'All right,' he said. 'I'll see him first thing in the morning.'

'I'll see you tomorrow, then?'

'Yes – I'll come here when I'm done.'

'I may be out during the day, but wait, if you would.'

'Of course.'

Dallington left then, perhaps off for a few more rounds of whist to brace him for his morning task, and Lenox checked on his brother – still sound asleep. Molly and their sons were in the country, and he decided to let Edmund rest.

'Put him upstairs, would you, if he should stir?' he said to Graham. 'Tell him I won't hear of him going home.'

'Very good, sir.'

Then at last, blessedly, he could go see Jane.

He fairly bounded next door, hoping it wasn't too late to catch her. Her telegram had been brief but consoling, and he felt a powerful desire to see her, to remind himself that he had a wonderful life, well worth living, even without Parliament.

Her house, imperiously tall from across the street, seemed from their own sidewalk to be no more than a homely, silent thing, with one room dimly lit and all the others entirely dark. Before he could knock she opened the door and, without speaking, wrapped him in her arms. For a moment he remembered how it had been when his mother was alive, even into his thirties – that childlike comfort she was able to give him long past the age of scraped knees.

'Are you terribly disappointed?' she asked. Now she led him down the hall and into her rose-colored drawing room, from whence that solitary lamp had been visible from the street.

'It was more of a sharp, quick pain,' he said, 'than a long, dull one. I thought it would have been the other way around.'

'How unfair, though! Will you tell me about it?'

In such a way that he had barely noticed, she had maneuvered him into his favorite chair and then sat beside him. In a torrent, then, he told the entire thing to her – about Mayor Adlington and his long watch chain, about Roodle's squeal during the debate, about their impromptu exchange in Sawyer Park, about Sandy and Mrs. Reeve and Nettie and Crook and Lucy the waitress, about the awful dinner parties, the endless days out in the countryside, the hustings in front of the Queen's Arms and the speeches. The two old friends laughed at the funny bits and felt solemn together at the serious bits, and when he was through telling the story it felt as if he were finally through the experience. He had had his chance and lost. So it goes, he thought. Perhaps there will be another, but even if there isn't – if there isn't that's all right as well.

And here, he asked? What was the news?

'Thomas and Toto are doing the best they can,'

said Lady Jane.

'I'm glad to hear it, of course, but you know what I mean – London, the chatter, I've missed it all.'

'It's my turn to entertain you?' she said. 'Well, the Duchess is having her house redecorated, and the whole family is moving to the country for six months while it's done ... let me think ... Deborah Trice is going to marry Fordyce Pratt.'

'I haven't the faintest idea who either of them is.'

'He's a judge.'

'That ancient lump of flesh I see at the Devonshire? Surely he doesn't have it in him.'

She laughed. 'Yes, in fact,' she said, 'and you ought to know that Deborah is a very respectable widow, just returned from some part of India where her husband was posted.'

'A tiger ate him, I assume?'

'Fever,' she said, though still laughing. 'What else? George Barnard was to have a party, but he's gone to Geneva instead, some sort of conference, and people are terribly disappointed. You know he has that ballroom.'

'Humph,' said Lenox, or some grumpy noise approximating that.

'Yes, yes, I know you don't like him. Oh! Frederick Fleer was in a duel, you know, but neither man was hurt.'

Slowly, then, Lenox and Lady Jane resumed their lifelong conversation. An hour later, thoroughly exhausted, she led him to the door.

He gave her a chaste kiss on her red lips. 'Thank you for staying up,' he said.

A serious note returned to her voice after much

laughter, and she said, 'Oh, but of course.'

They agreed to see each other the next day, and as he walked back up the steps to his house Lenox thought happily of all the long hours he would sleep on his own soft bed. Tomorrow there was work to be done, but tonight he could truly rest. Maybe for a while in the morning, too.

The house was quiet. He hung up his coat and began to make his way upstairs, only to check himself and return to the door of the library, through which he peered to find Edmund sleeping still, and before Lenox traipsed up to his bedroom he stood and felt a deep swell of affection, of true kinship, for his brother.

CHAPTER THIRTY-FIVE

His first action the next morning, following his bath and his breakfast, was to go and see Thomas and Toto.

They were sitting in a drawing room when the butler led him in, Toto knitting something pink and McConnell reading the newspaper with a cup of tea close at hand, the strong green tea he preferred. They looked up at him, and both smiled. McConnell's great florid face looked battered, even wounded, but instantly Lenox saw that a resolute companionship had sprung up between him and his wife. It was easy to admire – and made it easy to forget the doctor coming up to Stirrington when he was barmy drunk and half mad with sorrow.

'I hear you lost, Charles,' said Toto. 'I'm so sorry.'

Lenox waved a hand. 'It's no great matter. I'm only happy to be back in London.'

'Have you seen Jane yet?'

'I saw her last night. Some man was in a duel, apparently–'

'Freddie Fleer,' said Toto, nodding.

'No doubt that's him. Two other people are going to be married. All that sort of thing.'

'Was it close, the by-election?' asked McConnell.

'Quite close, yes. I think it came down to the other man's local support. It's hard to win over a town full of northerners in two weeks.'

'I can't say I've ever tried,' said Toto with a laugh.

Lenox laughed, too. 'You'll have to take my word for it, anyway. Still, it was a close-run thing, and I'm happy I did it.' He wondered if he should ask after her health but decided against it. 'What about our little project?' he said instead, referring to his honeymoon with Jane. 'Have you been studying?'

'I have!' she said with some animation. 'When can we speak about it?'

'Very soon,' he promised. 'I have to look into these crimes at the moment, but then you'll have my full attention.'

'What in blazes are you two so mysterious about?' asked McConnell indignantly, having watched their exchange.

'Oh, nothing,' said Toto, acting perhaps a bit more cryptic than was necessary.

Lenox laughed. 'Toto's helping me with something,' he said. 'I'm sure she'll tell you all about it after I leave. Look, though, Thomas, I thought I might put you in the way of a bit of work. Not medical, however.'

'Oh?'

'I was hoping you'd come to Carruthers's apartment and act as a second pair of eyes for me.'

'To be sure. When?'

'This afternoon, I hope, though I have Exeter's funeral to attend. We'll see when they let me in. I'll pick you up, at any rate?'

'As you like.'

'See you then.'

Lenox left soon thereafter and, after stopping at home to make sure that Dallington wasn't waiting for him, directed his driver to Fleet Street.

Printers and pamphlet makers had inhabited Fleet Street since 1500, but it was only in the spring of 1702 that it had gained its modern character – that was when the first daily newspaper in the world, the *Daily Courant*, opened its office and began publishing from the street.

In the subsequent century and a half it had become a collegial place, its pubs full of dueling journalists who put aside their differences at the bar to drink, to laugh, and to trade barbs, often with the equally drunken and witty solicitors who inhabited the close-by Inns of Court. It all savored even now of Dickens and Dr. Johnson and the grand tradition of literature – of a certain kind of literature. As Matthew Arnold said, 'Journalism is literature in a hurry.'

Lenox planned to visit the office of the *Daily*

Telegraph, where Carruthers had worked, and then if he could the man's apartment. If Pierce had been the distraction from the real crime, as he suspected, then this was where he would have to begin his investigation over again.

The *Telegraph*'s building was a busy place, with young men running in and out and the tremendous whine, drumbeat, and squeal of the printing press audible from the street. On the fourth floor, however, where he knew from the newspapers that Carruthers had worked, it was quieter.

Lenox greeted a young woman, a typist, who was hurrying toward a closed door across the floor's large foyer. 'Excuse me,' he said, 'but who's in charge here?'

'Mr. Moon, of course,' she said.

'And where is–'

'Third door on your second right,' she said and was off again.

Mr. Jeremy Moon, when Lenox knocked on the door of his office and pushed it open, was a gray-haired man with big round glasses and the beginnings of a paunch. He had discarded his jacket and rolled up his sleeves, and his hands were covered with ink. He was hard at work reading proofs.

'Who are you?' he asked rather rudely.

'Charles Lenox.'

Moon scowled. 'I know that name. The detective, the Oxford murder. You appeared in our news section three consecutive days in September ... let me recall ... was it the ninth, tenth, and eleventh?'

Lenox shrugged. 'I'm not sure.'

'Of course, you may not read the *Telegraph* as attentively as I do,' said Moon with a short laugh.

'How can I help you, then? I should mention that I'm rather short on time today. Are you any relation to the chap by your name who lost the election up north two days ago?'

'I'm him.'

'Are you! Blimey, you put yourself about. At any rate, as I say, I'm quite busy. How may I help you?'

'Are you doing the duties for which Winston Carruthers was generally responsible?'

'It's about that, is it? I am, some of them. Others have fallen to our writers. He had a wide-ranging brief here, did Win.'

'I had taken a passive interest in the case before Inspector Exeter died, but now I find myself in a more active role and hoped to discover from you what I might about your colleague.'

'Well – what sort of thing?'

'Was he a genial man?'

Moon laid the proofs he had been reading down on his desk and pushed the big, round glasses from the bridge of his nose thoughtfully. 'Yes,' he said. 'After his fashion. He lived for his postwork drink, and here in Fleet Street he had a wide circle of friends. Carruthers was the sort of chap who could tell you at a moment's notice all the particularities of some obscure government matter to do with – well, say one of the colonies, and break it down so it made perfect sense. He could write an article on a subject he knew nothing about in half an hour. Save for those rather remarkable qualities, he would have been fired long before his death.'

'Why?'

'He was indolent and, as I say, overfond of drink. Had a bad temper.'

'Did he have enemies, then?'

'Perhaps, but I don't really think so – that sounds very sinister and all, but we lead pretty mild lives here, the pub aside, I promise you.'

'What was he working on before he died?'

'I'm not entirely sure, though I know in a general way. Because of his talent he was the only writer or editor we had who didn't quite answer to me. He was a pet of our publisher, Lord Chance. I reserved space for his articles and ran an eye over them but never asked much beyond that.'

'What was he working on in a general way, then?'

'He had a story he had been working on for months about Gladstone – a profile of the rising man in the other party, you know.' Moon smiled. 'We're Conservative here, as you may know. Pleased to see Roodle get in, though you seem a decent chap.'

'What else?'

'Let me see – he had a story about the Royal Mint – one about Ascot – one about the new railroads – and probably half a dozen others whose premises he scribbled down somewhere.'

'Was he writing about crime, in any way? The gangs?'

'He may have been. I didn't know about it.'

'Did he ever mention' – Lenox tried to think of a delicate way to say it – 'any testimony he had given?'

Moon laughed. 'The Poole thing? Only every day of his life. Which is how I happen to know that Gerald Poole killed him, Mr. Lenox. It's our first lead tomorrow morning. I can promise you we're taking Win's death pretty seriously around here, and Poole's involvement, too. He should swing for what he did.'

'Then who killed Inspector Exeter?'

'That's why you're here, I presume. To discover who Gerald Poole's allies were, no?'

'Well,' Lenox murmured, unsure of what to say.

Moon nodded. 'Take it as read, yes, that's fine.'

'Did Carruthers ever mention Poole's son to you?'

The answer to this question Lenox was destined never to get, for just then a bright-looking young man came in without knocking.

'Who's he?' he asked Moon, pointing at Lenox.

'Nobody you can't speak in front of why?'

'It's the Carruthers thing.'

'What is it?'

'Winston Carruthers's maid is back, Martha Claes. She says she assisted Poole every step of the way.'

CHAPTER THIRTY-SIX

The funeral of Police Inspector William Exeter took place in a small church near his home named St. Mary Abbots, a peaceful ground of ancient provenance that was perhaps to be rebuilt, according to someone Lenox overheard. Exeter had lived with his family in the Portobello Road, off of Notting Hill, and although it was in Kensington

Lenox scarcely knew the area, which was spotted by hayfields and untouched meadows.

As soon as his carriage stopped, Lenox had a lump in his throat. He felt for his colleague some unlooked-for affinity that they had never shared in life. Perhaps it was because, whatever their two views of it had been, they did the same work, and it was work for which Exeter had died.

The inspector's death was the great story of the day in the newspapers and the neighborhoods of London, and the trappings of his funeral combined what might have been normal for a man of his station and what might have been normal for a man of a much higher one. A long procession of empty carriages, sent by their illustrious owners, was passing the church, and from a respectfully gentle clatter nearby Lenox saw that the funeral line was to be quite grand. He himself was standing on a small patch of green earth near the front of the church, watching people amble in, generally of two types – Exeter's relatives and his fellow officers of Scotland Yard – and occasionally of a third, more exalted type, whom Lenox could recognize by the black velvet breeches they wore, or the silver-headed cane they carried. These would be Members of Parliament and London officials. He saw the Lord Mayor arrive and make his way breathlessly up the steps of the church.

It was intensely sad to Lenox.

The service was short. There were two hymns and a eulogy from Exeter's direct superior at the Yard before a speech by the church's vicar. Lenox found himself sitting with Jenkins, somewhere in the back third of the pews, listening with half his mind and speculating about Exeter's death with the other half.

Soon it was time for the standard procession between the church and the cemetery. On this no expense had been spared. First there were men on foot, an assortment of pallbearers in black, a series of young pages, and three mutes wearing black cloaks and carrying wands. All of these men, from the youngest lad to the oldest mute, were very certainly pickled to the gills on gin – a license of their profession, since they had to stand outside in the cold continually – but they did their duty solemnly.

Next came the funeral hearse, a grand black and silver object with gold trim everywhere, and following it a line of carriages full of Exeter's friends and relatives. His widow, a handsome, dark-haired woman, had held up admirably well, and their young son was well dressed and well behaved.

'I have my carriage if you need a ride to the cemetery,' said Lenox to Jenkins.

'I must be getting back to town, in fact.'

'Look – do you think I could see Carruthers's rooms, either today or tomorrow?'

Lenox had expected a difficult argument, but he got none. 'Yes. Certainly.'

'Thanks.'

'Not at all. You've the unofficial license of the entire Yard behind you now; in fact, I was instructed to tell you as much. I was only just going to do so.'

'How can I get in?'

'There's a constable there – constables everywhere, since Exeter died and this all became so famous.'

'You'll send him word–'

'Yes, go over any time.'

'Are you officially at work on this case?' Lenox asked.

'Now, yes.'

'Who do you think killed Exeter?'

'Honestly? I think it was unrelated to all this. A fluke. His job made him enemies all over the East End.'

Lenox nodded. 'Perhaps.'

'See you soon, Charles.'

Exeter was interred in a small cemetery not a mile from the church, and the procession made its increasingly ragged way back to Exeter's house. It was a modest, handsomely kept two-story building, white with a thatched roof and blue shutters.

Inside it was warm and comfortable, and Lenox had a vision of Exeter after hours, sitting by his hearth with his family around him. By now they had sloughed off the Lord Mayor and the majority of his ilk, and it was Exeter's cousins, his uncles, his subordinates at the Yard who ate ham and drank ale. Lenox found himself with nobody quite to talk to and soon wandered outside to the side of the house for a smoke.

It was here that he saw Exeter's son, John.

They had met once before. After a case that Lenox had been instrumental in solving, Exeter had taken the credit for himself and received a commendation from Scotland Yard. Lenox, used to it, offered no objection but was surprised when Exeter had invited him to the ceremony. There, by way perhaps of apology or explanation, he had introduced the eight-year-old John Exeter to Lenox with a sort of rough pride. Lenox had understood the inspector better in that moment than ever before.

The lad was playing near a chicken coop, among the rows of a small, productive-looking garden. He had on a black suit that was dirtied at the knees because he had been kneeling between two tomato vines.

Suddenly Lenox felt the pain of it all: Exeter had been alive, and now he was dead. The industry and hominess and practicality of the little rows of vegetables seemed somehow to summarize it all, more than the gloomy, garish funeral ever could, and it touched him profoundly.

'Hello, John,' said Lenox.

'Hello, Mr. Lenox,' said the boy, his face serious and handsome.

'You remember me?'

'Of course. My fa talks about you all the time, sir.'

Lenox absorbed this uncertainly. 'What have you got there?' he said.

John held out his dirty hand, which clutched a toy train. 'It's the best one I've got,' he said.

'Do you like trains, then?'

'Oh, yes.'

'I do, too.'

'I want to ride one.'

'Haven't you?'

'Not yet, sir.'

'You will, someday soon. When is your birthday?'

'March eighth, Mr. Lenox.'

'Well, we'll see,' said Lenox. 'Perhaps someone will send you an even better train set on March

239

eighth. I feel sure of it, in fact, John – just wait. Will you shake hands?'

The boy stood up and with grave concentration put his small, sweaty brown hand into Lenox's. 'Good-bye, Mr. Lenox.'

His pipe done, Lenox went inside to say good-bye to the widow. On the way home to Mayfair he looked out through the window of his carriage at the clear, cold day and felt the melancholy that veiled the city to his eyes.

Dallington was waiting for him in Hampden Lane.

'How are you?' Lenox asked.

'Bloody awful.'

'Gracious, what is it?'

'He really did it, by God. It was the worst twenty minutes of my life, listening to him. He had a reason, and he – he knew exactly how it had been done.'

'Forgive me, but – Poole?'

'Yes, Gerry Poole. He was a different creature today than he had ever been before. He talked about plunging a knife in a man's back as if it were the most natural thing in the world.'

It was the most upset Lenox had ever seen the younger man, who was always so quick with a joke and a smile.

'Did he give you any details?'

'Not really.'

'Anything about Martha Claes?'

'Not a thing.'

The return of the Belgian maid (who had apparently been moving along the Norfolk coast, unsuccessfully trying to find a way out of the country) had offered very few details about the murder of Winston Carruthers. She was in police custody now, but according to Jenkins she had only said she had acted as Poole's assistant, helping him gain access to Carruthers and standing by as he murdered him. She had returned seeking immunity to prosecution for providing evidence and refused to speak another word until she got it.

Dallington stayed for a few minutes longer, then left, still disconsolate. Lenox had felt that sort of anguish before, in his early days as an amateur detective.

Despite the confession, he had work to do still, he felt. Who had killed Inspector Exeter and Hiram Smalls? Not Gerald Poole, certainly; and if his proxies had done it, why and who were they? Almost at the same hour as Exeter was lying on his deathbed, Poole had been giving his confession. It made no sense.

So Lenox decided to persevere – and to begin with Winston Carruthers's rooms, a few streets away.

It was dark by now and cold outside. He waited for his carriage on the curb, stamping his feet to stay warm. Eventually it came and he stepped in.

Just as he was going to close the door, a voice called from behind him, 'You dropped a penny, sir.'

It was one of the footmen who had brought the horses around.

'Cheers,' said Lenox.

He took the penny in his hand – and as he sat down his mind started racing.

A penny.

What had he found under Hiram Smalls's bed? *A farthing, a halfpenny, a penny, threepence, six-pence, and a shilling*, he had told the warden of Newgate. *All the coins of the realm...*

Smalls had been sending a message, Lenox realized with a thud in his chest, a message pointing to the man who made those coins – at the Mint.

Then Lenox remembered: *He had a story about the Royal Mint*, Moon had said of Carruthers. A story about the Mint – had he discovered some-thing about the Mint? Corruption there? Was he trying to blackmail Barnard?

Just like that, Lenox remembered something funny – Barnard had called Carruthers 'Win,' his common nickname, at Lady Nevin's party but claimed he hadn't known the man the press called Winston.

A last thought flitted into his mind about what Jane had said, *George Barnard was to have a party, but he's gone to Geneva instead.*

It appeared that these murders led back, as half the crimes in London did, to one man: George Barnard. Who now had fled to Geneva.

CHAPTER THIRTY-SEVEN

It hung together in his head, the whole thing, but only tenuously – a number of disparate facts that couldn't bear much weight, that only hinted at the truth, but that together seemed definite. For instance, as he worked it through in his mind he remembered that Smalls's mother had mysteriously been relieved of a hundred-pound debt. Mightn't Barnard have paid that? If he had, then Smalls would have only felt comfortable leaving a veiled clue (the coins) rather than an outright declaration.

Then there was Carruthers's article about the Mint, of which Barnard had been head! He must find that. Could it be the motive – that Carruthers, a corrupt and corruptible soul, was trying to blackmail Barnard because he had discovered the man's theft from the Mint?

'Poole is innocent,' muttered Lenox under his breath. Then in a louder voice he said, 'Stop the carriage!'

He ran inside and took from a locked door in his desk the one-page file on Barnard he had compiled from his hundreds of pages of facts collecting and speculation and read it, searching for a clue to Winston Carruthers's murder – and to Hiram Smalls's murder.

The file distilled all of the crimes in which he had discovered Barnard's involvement – or thought he had – and combined notes on them with a biographical sketch. The most elusive part of his research for the latter concerned Barnard's recent time at the head of the Royal Mint, which was a well-guarded place both physically and informationally – a yellowing building on Little Tower Hill, near the Tower of London, which stood behind a tall wrought-iron fence, regal and, in a busy street, silent. Inside, delicate machinery converted bars of pure gold and silver into exactly weighted coins.

Digging further into the past Lenox had found, however, that Barnard's tracks were everywhere. Lenox kept a file of London's unsolved crimes, including both ones he had worked on and others, and so far he had attached roughly one in every nineteen to Barnard. It didn't sound like much until one took in the immense variety and size of that file. There was the Astor Grange fire, not five miles from the city, when thousands of pounds' worth of rare letters from Isaac Newton to his puritanical father were thought to have burned; Barnard had been staying with the private collector of the letters at the time and was well known to be fascinated by the history of Newton, who had himself once been Master of – yes, the Royal Mint. That was the higher end of things. There were also gin drunks found dead in alleyways, illegal casinos raided and their monies confiscated by people almost certainly impersonating officers of Scotland Yard, a thousand minor crimes and a hundred major ones all leading back to one man.

Lenox had for years known Barnard differently, as a politician and businessman with an ostentatious but also genuinely beautiful house off of Grosvenor Square, a place large enough to host one of London's most famous balls. That annual event aside, however, his commonplace birth in Manchester had prevented his access to the highest tiers of society. Instead he lived in an aristocratic demimonde, the wives of his colleagues prejudiced against seeing him socially. His friends had been snobbishly chosen, men with titles and standing but also possessed of some fatal social flaw – no money, no intelligence, no scruples. He would drop their names, moving slightly higher with each new friendship, until he realized they were no good, when he would drop them instead.

When he had left Parliament for the Royal Mint, however, he had become difficult to ignore and had finally gained access to the best clubs and the best houses. There are many men who sit in Parliament, and some of them make soap; on the other hand the Mint has only one Master, and he is an exalted personage. It was at this time that Barnard had begun to court the unresponsive Lady Jane, whom Lenox had subsequently rescued from the fate of being one of the richest women in the city.

Even then, though, there had been one peculiarity about Barnard: It was a common parlor game across London to guess from which obscure source his wealth had come. At twenty-six he had been a shipping house's clerk. He quit that job and four years later bought the shipping house. His activities in the intervening time were utterly mysterious. At the age of thirty-three he had entered Parliament.

Then, just over a year ago, Lenox had been investigating the murder of a young maid who had been in Barnard's employ. The man himself had no involvement in the matter (Lenox had since had plenty of opportunities to observe and note how clean Barnard kept his own hands) but almost incidentally the detective had discovered that a sum of nineteen thousand pounds was missing from the Mint's new batch of currency. Such a small sum, in the context of the vast numbers involved, and yet such a large sum in the context of the world! Exeter and his family might have lived on it their whole lives! It was this nineteen thousand pounds that had changed Lenox's opinion of Barnard – before, he had seen him as a petty, vain, but tolerable man. Now Lenox recognized him to be perhaps the most powerful and dangerous man in London.

There was no doubt of it – Barnard was a fiendishly clever sod, and he had played his hand very carefully and very well over the years. Now Winston Carruthers and Simon Pierce were dead because of him, and perhaps Hiram Smalls and Inspector Exeter, too.

But why? He remembered Dallington's crucial bit of information – Carruthers was corruptible. Had Barnard for some reason bribed the man and then elected to silence him?

Lenox scanned the rest of the sheet, his private and carefully compiled dossier. For muscle Barnard used the Hammer Gang, a group of East Londoners each with a green tattoo of a hammer curled around one eyebrow. Though he had a large staff in his home and at the Mint, he didn't seem to have any particular trusted assistant.

Then something clicked into place – *No green*, the end of Hiram Smalls's letter had said. Could it have been a reference to the tattoo? In effect, 'Don't get your tattoo before you pass this final test and gain entry to the Hammer Gang'? If so, Smalls had evidently failed the last test – and paid a high price for his failure. It seemed like a plausible interpretation of that mysterious phrase *No green*, in particular because Barnard probably knew by now that his association with the

Hammers was no longer secret. He couldn't have the man who killed Simon Pierce bear a tattoo that would link them.

Geneva – what could be there? Since retiring from the Mint (doubtless much richer than when he had begun the job, thought Lenox bitterly) he had been consulting with the government on several minor issues but had in general been very quiet.

It was ominous.

All of this flurried through Lenox's mind in a matter of moments as he held the single sheet that defined George Barnard's misdeeds. Then he thought that the case needed more than he and Dallington could do and called for his carriage.

It was a long drive to his destination, perhaps thirty minutes. Oxley Crescent was a small neighborhood on the southern edge of London, full of closely spaced but pleasant houses, each with a small porch and garden in front. It was to a white house with dark shutters and a charmingly askew chimney that Lenox came when he needed Skaggs.

Skaggs's wife answered the door, an insistent and gregarious creature who first shed a tear over poor Inspector Exeter, then scolded Lenox for coming to take her husband away again, and finally insisted he kiss the baby slung low on her hip, all as a toll before he could get through to the house.

Rupert Skaggs, a man who had once been the best middleweight boxer for a two-mile radius, was fearsome looking, with a bald head, a fat, intelligent face, and a long scar across the left side of his neck, but in truth his wife and his three children had lent him some docility, and he was quite happy in his little home. His looks still often came in handy, however; he was the best private investigator in England, if you asked Lenox. Once Skaggs had found a job as a waiter in order to gather information for him, and since then Lenox had never doubted him. He was forced to pay for Skaggs out of his own pocket, but then, he always reasoned, what higher purpose than justice was money for? Besides, less loftily, Skaggs always saved him so much time and effort – much of the unrewarding work of detection belonged to him, under Lenox's supervision.

'Hello, Mr. Lenox,' said Skaggs with a pipe in one hand. He had come onto the porch at his wife's call.

'How do you do, Mr. Skaggs?'

'Passably well. I haven't seen you for some time.'

Now, this was true – and true because of Dallington. Lenox shifted slightly. 'No, and I'm very sorry to call on you so late in the evening. I hope I haven't interrupted supper?'

'No, not quite yet.'

'That's all right then.'

'Will you come in, Mr. Lenox? Business has been going well, but I always enjoyed our work together. Thank you for the silver rattle you sent after Emily was born.'

They walked inside and sat together in Skaggs's business room, a small square space at the very front of the house that just barely fit two chairs and a table.

'You're quite welcome, I'm sure – and in fact I come on work today, too.'

'What sort of work?'

'You've heard about Inspector Exeter?'

'Aye, I have. It's very sad,' said Skaggs solemnly.

'It is,' agreed Lenox.

'Are you trying to find out who killed him?'

'I think I know, in fact.'

'Do you!?'

'Perhaps – yes, I think so.'

'How may I help, Mr. Lenox?'

'I need you to go to Geneva, to follow a man.'

CHAPTER THIRTY-EIGHT

Lenox sat with Skaggs for some time, giving him all the details about Barnard's flight across the Channel (because Skaggs had helped Lenox track Barnard once before, he wasn't surprised to be spying on such an illustrious man), and then left Oxley Crescent. He was due to see Lady Jane that evening, but his mind was racing. Instead he had his carriage drop him at McConnell's house, sending it home with a message to Jane that he would be an hour or so later than he had promised.

'Hullo,' said the doctor with plain surprise when Lenox came into the drawing room.

'How are you? How is Toto?'

'She's sleeping at the moment.'

'I know it's late, but I wondered whether you might go see Carruthers's rooms with me now? There should still be a constable on duty, watching them.'

'Gladly,' said McConnell, standing up. 'I don't need my medical kit for any reason?'

'Well – perhaps. Just in case.'

'It's by the door. Let me fetch it.'

'Shall we walk? I sent my horses home.'

'To be sure.'

A little while later the two men had set out for the dead man's apartments and were talking seriously about Gerald Poole. Lenox still didn't want to tell anybody about his suspicions of George Barnard, a well-respected man, though he could scarcely hide his revulsion when the name came up in conversation. Now, however, he focused on Poole's innocence rather than Barnard's guilt. He explained to the doctor his theory that Pierce's murder was a cover-up for Carruthers's, a red herring.

'It strikes me as crucial that Carruthers's hands were inky and there was a pen on the table but no paper close at hand.'

'You think the person who stabbed him took the paper?'

'Yes, I do, and it seems beyond chance that Carruthers should have been writing a paper that the murderer wanted just when the man came in.'

'What about Pierce?'

'Nothing missing from his house, which Smalls couldn't have entered anyway, or he would have been discovered. Pierce had evidently been reading, after a week that was in fact rather less busy than usual at work.'

'I see.'

'Finally – could Smalls have been anything other than hired help? I have a difficult time believing that he would have any cause for revenge against Pierce, a mostly anonymous journalist.'

The house in which Carruthers had kept his rooms was a low-slung place, brown on the front, with three floors and perhaps five tenants, if anybody lived in the basement. The door was open when Lenox tried the handle, and he and McConnell followed a soft noise up two flights of stairs.

The noise turned out to be the sonorous snoring of a sleeping constable, a portly gentleman with a red face who was sitting on a chair in front of a closed door.

'Excuse me?' said Lenox in a soft voice.

The constable fairly jumped out of his seat. After a few furious shakes of his head he seemed to return to the world. 'Who are you?' he said.

Lenox stuck out his hand. 'My name is Charles Lenox, and this is my colleague Dr. Thomas McConnell.'

'Pleasure,' McConnell murmured.

'Inspector Jenkins sent word, I hope, that I might be coming by?'

The constable rubbed his eyes and blinked very fast, then gave his head a few more furious shakes, as if he were trying to teach it a lesson for falling asleep, and then said, 'Oh, quite, quite. The door is open. Shall I come in with you?'

'Only if you like,' said Lenox.

'Perhaps I'll just sit here and – and watch out

for everything?'

'All right.'

The apartment they entered was, Lenox assumed, as Carruthers had left it. There were three connected rooms, all decorated in the same rich, cloying style, with gilt everywhere, clothes lying at random on the floor and the tables, and expensive-looking liqueurs strewn among a vast number of books and newspapers. It looked to Lenox like an indulgent life, one perhaps made possible – or at any rate deepened in its luxury – by its inhabitant's corruption.

'He died here,' said Lenox, pointing to a large round table near the fireplace.

McConnell, his leather kit in his right hand, looked the area over. 'No blood.'

'He would have slumped forward, I suppose, and the blood would have fallen down the back of his shirt but no farther.'

Lenox went over all the rooms vary carefully, pulling out books and riffling through them, using a match to explore under tables and chairs, raking through the coals of the fireplace, and checking behind pictures for any bumps. McConnell meanwhile went through Carruthers's medicine chest.

'He had a touch of the gout,' said McConnell when they met at the door again. 'Nothing much else.'

'I'm not surprised, with all the champagne and rich food here.'

'Did you discover anything?'

'One thing – in the bedroom there's a square patch of floor where the wood is much darker than everywhere else in the room, as if the sun

252

had never hit it.'

'Oh?'

'He must have moved something recently. I just wonder…'

'What?'

'Perhaps he saw his enemy coming and moved his files as insurance. It's a bit surprising that none of these chests contains a single note about his work, isn't it? One sheet, yes, but the murderer would have had a difficult time escaping with a chest of files.'

'Of course.'

'Would you mind stopping by his office with me? It's just in Fleet Street.'

'Not in the slightest.'

They left the apartment and passed the constable, who was again peacefully asleep; in the street they hailed a cab. Rain had started to fall, the dark night illuminated only by smudges of bright yellow light from the blurred streetlamps.

Mr. Moon was working late, putting the paper to bed. He was far from happy to see Lenox but impatiently agreed that the two men could look into Carruthers's office.

'Where is it?' Lenox asked.

'You'll have to figure that out for yourself,' said Moon.

As they walked out Lenox and McConnell both started to chuckle, and as they went down the hall they were laughing heartily at Moon's rudeness.

Eventually they did find Carruthers's office, which had a pleasant view of Fleet Street. Unfortunately, the room was tidy and utterly bland, without so much as a stray sheet of paper blemishing the three clean desks. All of the drawers were empty, except for pens, ink, pencils, and pieces of string, and the bookshelf had only a dictionary on it.

'It's a marvel it's so clean,' said Lenox. 'After that apartment.'

'Perhaps he didn't spend much time here?'

'Or else he liked a Spartan office, whatever his home was like.'

'It's a shame.'

'Or else...' Lenox hailed a passing man. 'Excuse me, but did Winston Carruthers have another office?'

'Who are you?'

'Charles Lenox. I'm looking–'

The man grinned. 'The detective, yes. I don't know about another office, unless you mean the empty room that was technically his just there, but he had only one office – the Cheese.'

'The Cheese?' said McConnell,

'Ye Olde Cheshire Cheese.'

Lenox laughed. 'Thank you.'

He remembered Dallington's account of the pub, with its famous buck rabbit (toast drowned in beer and cheese) and its talkative tender, Ransom. 'One more stop?' he asked.

'To be sure.'

CHAPTER THIRTY-NINE

The pub was crowded and warm, with red-nosed, white-haired fellows lining the bar, trading bawdy jokes and laughing uproariously, as only men in their cups will. The front room, which contained the taps, was narrow and brightly lit, with a fire reflecting off of the brass above the bar and long time-scarred benches opposite, under a series of paintings of idyllic country scenes. A plaque under the paintings proudly declared that the Great Fire of 1666 had leveled the place. From the back emanated the unmistakable smell of the stables.

The bartender was a keen-eyed, sturdily built chap with sallow cheeks and dark hair.

'Ransom?' asked Lenox when he caught the man's attention.

'No, I'm Stevens. He's weekdays.'

'It's all the same – I came to ask a question.'

'Yes?'

'I understand that Winston Carruthers often worked here?'

'Aye, many a night. Who are you, may I ask?'

'Charles Lenox. I'm helping Scotland Yard. Could you show me where he worked?'

'It was a little room in back. Here, Billy!' He motioned to a lad passing by with a tray of glassware. 'Take these gents up to the burgundy room.'

Billy led them up a narrow flight of stairs and down a hallway. The burgundy room was a smallish, windowless place that fit four tables. Three of these were evidently open to patrons, though none of them was taken, but the fourth, in the back left corner of the room, boasted a scratched old brass sign that read RESERVED FOR W. CARRUTHERS.

It was apparent instantly that this corner of an old room at Fleet Street's traditional public house was in fact the dead man's office. There was a box full of pencils, India rubbers, and bits and bobs, and on a little ledge next to it there was a stack of clean paper. The table itself was covered in a thousand old wine stains and glass rings and was darkened with years of cigar smoke and splashes of tea.

'What's this?' said McConnell. He had gone around to the other side of the table before Lenox was finished looking at the room.

'What?'

'I think it matches your idea of the thing.'

The object McConnell was pointing to was a squat wooden box in two tiers, each with a drawer.

'Terrific,' said Lenox. 'The yard haven't been here, clearly.' He pulled open the top drawer and started flipping through the papers it held. 'Files on article subjects and public figures.'

'What are you looking for?'

Lenox paused. Of everyone in the world, only Graham knew Lenox's suspicions. 'I know I needn't ask, but can you keep a secret?'

'I hope I can, yes.'

'The file I want is about George Barnard.'

McConnell laughed incredulously. 'Why?'

'I think he may be behind all this.'

'He can't possibly be. He had nothing to do

with that dead girl in his house, did he?'

'No,' said Lenox. 'Theft is more in his line, on a grand scale. Murder is a new one, in particular if he had Exeter killed. I fear he may be desperate.'

'Good heavens, why?'

'I don't know yet.'

McConnell turned and scanned the room, as if to make sure it was still empty. 'Well, let's find it, then. Are the files alphabetical?'

'I don't know.'

They were. Winston Carruthers's physical life had been over, full of drink and food, his rooms messy and rich and abundant, but his files were at odds with that image of the man. They bespoke a different and more ascetic intellect. All of the papers were neatly filed and precisely written.

None among them pertained to George Barnard.

'Damn,' said Lenox softly.

'Perhaps he's in the G section?' said McConnell.

'I doubt it. Let's check.' A lengthy pause. 'No, nothing here. Perhaps Barnard has been here after all.'

McConnell laughed. 'That scarcely seems–'

'One does well not to underestimate him, I've learned,' said Lenox rather sharply. 'Let's go back to the *B*'s and make sure.'

McConnell sighed and seemed to look longingly out toward the stairs – and perhaps down to the bar.

'Here's something odd. A file marked G. FARMER.'

'In the *B* section? A middle name?'

Lenox frowned and opened the file. 'No, he

hasn't got a middle name.'

It was a thick file, and he began to leaf through a seemingly endless series of random articles, nearly all of them by Carruthers. One was about a broken church steeple in Cheapside and the plan to replace it. Another concerned a shipping accident, and a third was about crop yields in Northumberland. It was a bizarre miscellany.

'Farmer,' muttered McConnell. 'I wonder – Lenox, I wonder whether it's a pun?'

'What?'

'Barnard – it sounds just a bit like the word "barnyard." A farmer has a barnyard, after all.'

Lenox laughed. 'I think you've hit it.'

'That's why it's filed under *B*, too.'

'You're right.'

Confirmation came a moment later – one of the articles was about Barnard's tenure at the Royal Mint, a profile.

'I'll just borrow this, I think,' said Lenox. 'Let's go.'

McConnell asked whether they might have a tot of whisky, and Lenox, won over by the mood of the place, agreed to it. They fell into conversation with the men at the bar and stayed for half an hour, then shared a cab back to Mayfair and their respective homes.

Lenox entered his own exhausted and slightly on edge, the knowledge that Barnard was involved raising the stakes even higher. He thought briefly, as Graham greeted him, of Stirrington and then pushed the memory away, a painful one, something to be forgotten.

'It's Barnard,' said Lenox wearily.

'Sir?'

'The Fleet Street murders. It's Barnard.'

Graham, usually so imperturbable, inhaled sharply. 'I'm surprised, sir.'

'I'll need your help.'

'You shall have it, of course.'

'Thanks.'

Lenox spent a happy half hour with Lady Jane then, before returning to his library, where by low light he pored over the file on G. Farmer late into the night. At two he stood up exhausted and decided that he needed to sleep.

It was a disappointing haul. He had looked at every sheet of paper in the file, and only six of them mentioned Barnard by name. There were two articles that caught his eye because they were more recent: one about the history of the building that housed the Mint, which quoted Barnard, and another about a series of thefts from ships near the docks.

Ultimately, however, neither provided him with any insight into the case, and he fell asleep frustrated, puzzled, and certain that the elusive truth was closer than he realized.

CHAPTER FORTY

The next afternoon he was reading through the file again when there was a knock at the door. It was Dallington. He looked downcast and ill, wearing the same clothes he had been the day before.

'Hullo,' said Lenox.

'Before you ask, yes, I've been drinking.'

'Am I so draconian?'

'I can't get Poole out of my head.'

'I'm sorry, John.'

'What bothers me most is Smalls! If he had killed Carruthers in a fit of passion – well, I don't know, it would be somehow less appalling. Still appalling, of course, but less ... less cold-blooded.'

'It's the worst part of our profession, seeing all of this up close. I liked Poole.' Lenox hesitated. 'In addition, I'm not as certain as you are that he did the murder.'

'Oh, he did it.'

'How can you say?'

'He was persuasive.'

'He was also persuasive when he told us that he was innocent.'

'What makes you doubt his word, anyway? He's nothing to gain from confessing to murder.'

'There's another lead.'

'What is it?'

Lenox sighed. 'I don't know if I should say anything until I'm more sure of what I mean. I don't want to raise your hopes.'

'I see,' said Dallington.

It was an awkward moment. 'I have full faith in you, of course,' said Lenox, 'but I simply want to be sure.'

'What can I do to help?'

Lenox looked at the clock on the wall. 'Shall we go see him together? There are one or two questions I might ask him.'

'If you wish,' answered Dallington, looking miserable at the prospect.

'Or I could go alone,' Lenox said.

'No, I'll come.'

'Then let's have a spot of tea while they rub down the horses. Graham, are you out there?' he called into the hall. The valet came in. 'Will you bell for the carriage and bring in some tea, please?'

'Sandwiches, too,' said Dallington, in a voice so disconsolate that it was almost humorous to hear him ask for a sandwich with it.

Lenox laughed. 'Come, the world will turn again, you know.'

'Wait until you see him,' said Dallington.

It was true. They had their tea and sandwiches and soon enough were on their way again to Newgate Prison. It was a bitterly cold January day, of the kind that seems never quite to warm into afternoon before it falls again into night. A few flurries fell, vanishing as they hit the cobblestones, coating the stone buildings of London in a white stubble.

Poole, when he came into the visitors' room, was a different man. It was as though he had kept the facade up as long as he could and then collapsed under its weight.

'How do you do?' asked Lenox gently. 'Are you comfortable?'

'Yes, thanks.'

'Plenty of food? Warm enough?'

'Yes.'

'I thought we might have a word, since your confession took me by such surprise.'

'Every word of it is true,' said Poole sadly.

Yet Lenox had his doubts, even after seeing the lad. 'Will you describe it to me?'

261

'The maid, Martha, helped me slip into the building,' said Poole dully. 'Win – that man was sitting at a round table, writing. I stabbed him in the back, like a damned coward. I left as quickly as I came, sobbing the entire way. It was a despicable act, and I deserve to swing for it.'

'What was your motive?'

'Revenge.'

'On your father's behalf.'

'Yes.'

'Pray tell me – how did you learn of Carruthers's involvement in your father's trial?'

Poole shifted uncomfortably in his seat. 'It's – it's common knowledge.'

'On the contrary, I've lived here since before your birth, and I never heard of it. You only returned a few months ago.'

'Naturally I would take a greater interest in the matter than you, Mr. Lenox.'

'I concede that. Still, I insist that it wasn't common knowledge.'

'As you please.'

'Another thing, Mr. Poole. What about the paper Carruthers was writing on? Did you dispose of it? Burn it? Take it.'

Poole looked genuinely baffled at this. 'I didn't think twice about it, of course.'

'Yet it was missing from the table and hasn't been discovered anywhere among his personal effects.'

'I didn't know that.'

'Did you truly kill Winston Carruthers, Mr. Poole?'

'Yes, I did.'

There was such conviction in the lad's voice that Lenox believed–

Suddenly a possibility occurred to him.

'Your father was in Parliament, I believe?' said Lenox. 'Before the Crimean War began?'

'Yes,' said Poole cautiously. 'Why?'

There was a long pause. 'Did he ever know – or did you ever know – a man named George Barnard?'

Poole's face crumpled, but he managed to choke out the word 'Who?'

'George Barnard?' said Dallington with a disbelieving laugh. 'That codger.'

Lenox continued to stare at the prisoner, however. 'Barnard? You knew him?'

At length Poole nodded very slightly.

'Then you really did kill Winston Carruthers?'

'I told you, yes.' Poole began to cry softly.

'My God,' Lenox whispered.

CHAPTER FORTY-ONE

'George Barnard?' said Dallington again, uncertainly this time.

Poole spoke as if he hadn't heard his friend. 'For the last months he has been my only friend in London.'

'He knew your father?' said Lenox.

Poole nodded. 'Yes. He came to see me the moment I arrived here from the Continent. Soon we were together most afternoons, talking – first of generic subjects but then more specifically of the past. I had never been interested in what my father did or didn't do. It was too painful, and I tried never to be interested in the world – the world at large, I mean. Friends, a roll of the dice, books, all of those things occupied my time. Mr. Barnard told me every detail of my father's death, and the sudden exposure to something I had studiously ignored all of my life – it opened a wound. A deep wound. It changed me.'

'So you killed Carruthers?' asked Dallington doubtfully.

'I've a feeling there were many intermediate steps,' said Lenox, 'but tell me – why did you confess, after denying it at first?'

'The guilt became too much.'

'How could you have done it?' asked Dallington.

'I don't have any idea. It sounds funny, but truly I don't... I go over it in my mind and can't quite puzzle together how it happened. It seems like a dream.'

'Why have you been protecting Barnard?' said Lenox.

A stubborn look came onto his face, 'An informer killed my father. I never want to be a rat.'

'Is that what Barnard preached to you? The nobility of protecting a scoundrel?'

'A scoundrel?' said Poole. 'He's been a friend to me.'

'No,' said Lenox. 'He hasn't. Let's leave that aside and tell us how you went from a mild friendship with George Barnard to killing a man in cold blood.'

'In hot blood,' said Poole. 'I've never been drunker or angrier in my life.'

'Well? I want to help you with the police and the judge, Poole, but come now, why did you act as you did?'

'It's a secret, but George told me – he told me that this man Carruthers framed my father.'

'What?' said Dallington.

Poole sat back triumphantly, and a deep sadness, a pity, rose up in Lenox's breast. How eager we are to rewrite our fathers' stories, some of us; the delusions of the heart.

'I think your father was very probably guilty,' said the detective quietly.

'No,' said Poole, shaking his head confidently.

'Well, leave that aside, too. How did Barnard persuade you to kill Carruthers?'

'He didn't do a single damn thing, Mr. Lenox, except listen to me talk, and tell me how good a man my father was, and concur that he was undeserving of his terrible fate. I tremble to think of him, my poor father, knowing that he was innocent as he walked to the gallows.'

'Barnard never incited you to violence?'

'On the contrary, he advised against it.'

Clever fiend, thought Lenox. 'Then how did you find Carruthers? How did you come to kill him?'

'It was the strangest coincidence. One night I was drunk, and on the street I bumped into a woman – or perhaps she bumped into me.'

'The latter, I reckon,' said Lenox, who knew what would come next.

'It was a woman I knew from my years in Belgium, who had run a tavern near our house.'

'Martha Claes,' said Lenox.

'Yes,' answered Poole with some surprise. 'I never liked her all that well when I was a child, but we fell into talking about old times, and I asked her what she did now, and she said she kept house for six tenants. She described them all to me in detail.'

'Including Carruthers,' said Dallington. 'You were set up, Poole! He was set up, Lenox!'

Poole's confidence seemed to falter slightly. 'No, it was a coincidence.'

'Barnard found her somehow and installed her as Carruthers's landlady – money will do a great deal, and combined with a dangerous mind can do evil more quickly than anything else... So he put her in your path,' said Lenox. 'May I hazard a guess? She hated Carruthers. She thought he was the very devil. He beat his mistress and stole from the poor and threatened her children. Is that about the whole of it?'

'Yes,' said Poole, now less certain, 'and that he blackmailed people. She described all of the lives he ruined through the knowledge he acquired as a journalist. You think George – what, paid her to do that?'

'I'm certain of it, in fact,' said Lenox. 'So Martha Claes – what? What happened?'

'At last I let slip about my father.'

'She suggested revenge?'

'Not precisely – or I don't think so – I can't remember, Mr. Lenox.'

'What about Simon Pierce, though? Didn't that baffle you?' asked Dallington.

'Not especially,' said Poole, 'It was an odd coincidence, of course, but I never heard of the man, and I thought the newspapers had the wrong end of the stick, describing the two as linked. I knew they weren't, in fact.'

Lenox laughed bitterly, but all he said was, 'What about your meeting with Smalls?'

'That happened precisely as I described it, queerly enough.'

'You haven't put any of this together, Mr. Poole? You're an innocent indeed.'

'Listen – I'll never believe ill of George Barnard.'

'That's your business,' said Lenox. 'What happened on the day of the murder?'

'I was at George's, and somehow I got drunker than I usually did – got quite badly drunk, in fact.'

'Listen to yourself, you fool!' said Dallington. 'I haven't the slightest notion of how George Barnard is involved in all of this, but Lenox has it right!'

Poole ignored the outburst. 'He gave me a present that day – it was–' Suddenly true doubt dawned on his brow. 'It was the knife.'

'Did you pay Martha? When you went over that night?'

'I gave her a little something, as a token of old times.'

'Barnard must have, too,' said Lenox. 'He managed it terribly well. You were seen with Smalls, he had someone who matched your appearance buy the knife under your name, and best of all he must have had Martha burn the document Carruthers was writing and anything else she could find. Christ.'

The doubt in Poole's eyes had become full and

panicked. 'What an idiot I've been! What a drunken idiot! But then my father – he – he can't have been innocent, can he?'

These last words he said more to himself than to either visitor, and without another glance in their direction he went to the door and asked the guard to return him to his cell.

It was awful. Dallington looked shocked to the core of his being, and Lenox felt with something approaching fear the powerful mind that had orchestrated the journalist's death.

But why? Why?

There was one thing that pleased Lenox in a small way; Exeter had been right. Hiram Smalls and Gerald Poole had murdered Simon Pierce and Winston Carruthers. It was a vindication. Was it for this, though, that he had died? Or had he discovered something else?

He and Dallington had left Newgate Prison and were walking down the street. The younger man, plainly shaken, was silent.

At length Lenox said, 'There are times when this work destroys my affection for humanity. Look at this gang – the father a traitor to England, the son weak willed and impulsive and drunken, Barnard half a devil, even Carruthers a corruptible old toad.'

Dallington didn't respond, except to nod in a distracted way.

'I daresay that's the peril of choosing a job you think will do good, whether it's government or the military or the clergy. Neither a baker nor a banker ever sees the same ugliness.'

'Who is Barnard?' said Dallington. 'That is – I

know the man, but what have I missed?'

'What everyone else has missed, too,' said Lenox.

He explained at length his initial suspicions of Barnard and then his lengthening dossier of evidence against the man, explained the nature of his small crimes and his large ones, and how they intertwined; explained the mystery of Barnard's great wealth and the money that had gone missing after the murder of his maid. They walked through the bitter cold, impervious in their respective sorrow and anger, until they had reached Lenox's home again.

'How about a whisky?' said Lenox. 'It's early, I know, but nonetheless–'

'Are you mad?'

'Excuse me?'

'Did you not listen to Poole talking about his drunken fury? No, I scarcely think I need a drink at the moment.' Dallington muttered something about troubles coming home to roost and then said, 'Well? How do I help?'

'Do you wish to?'

'I take it as a given that I will.'

'It's not a pleasant matter.'

'You explained it to me when I first came to you – that it wasn't all heroic or happy work.'

They were in Lenox's library. 'Then find out what Barnard has been doing for the past few weeks, if you wish. I already have a man tracking him down in Geneva.'

'Geneva?'

Lenox explained.

With a determined scowl, Dallington nodded,

said good-bye, and went out.

Lenox stood for a moment and then poured himself that whisky.

CHAPTER FORTY-TWO

For a long time Lady Jane had known that Lenox felt a personal distaste for her old suitor, George Barnard, but hoping to protect her he had never *quite* confided in her his suspicions about the man, though she had seemed perhaps to perceive them.

Similarly, when he visited her that evening she could sense something was wrong. To make matters worse, now that the sheer relief of once again being together was gone, there remained the awkwardness of their London-Stirrington correspondence.

She was at his house now, where they were eating supper together.

'Shall you try for a different seat soon, Charles, do you think?'

'I don't know,' he said. 'It's still alluring to me, the idea of Parliament, but there are other men in line to try for open seats, I fear.'

'Clearly they should make you a lord and have done with it.'

Lenox laughed. 'Clearly.'

There was a pause, during which each took a sip of wine. He didn't know what she might be thinking, but in his own brain stirred the uneasy thought that in fact a lord or at least an MP would be more fitting for Jane, who was such a woman of the world, who knew so intimately all the mores of that little cadre in which politics and society mingled and became one.

Her thoughts were elsewhere, however. She looked at him rather strangely.

'Have I got sauce on my chin?' asked Lenox with a smile.

'No, no,' she said, smiling back. 'Only, I had an idea.'

'What?'

'Our houses – what do you think we should do after we're married?'

It pleased him that she spoke of their marriage so practically. 'I'm not sure,' he said. 'Mine is a bit bigger, but yours is warmer in the winter.'

'I should hate to give up my morning room, and you your library,' she said.

'Well – compromise is a necessity, I suppose,' he said, feeling uneasily that she was about to suggest they live separately. It was a very faint agony, love. He thought of that old line: *Ever till now/When men were fond, I smil'd, and wonder'd how.*

She put his mind at ease, however, with her proposition. 'What I thought was – well, that we might join our two houses together, Charles.'

'Physically? Knock down the walls?'

'Yes, exactly – or at least, one wall in each floor. We wouldn't want to knock down the wall between your library and that coatroom I have, but – for instance – we could make a very large bedroom on the second floor?'

Lenox smiled. 'I think it's a wonderful idea,' he said. 'It will be a union of minds and a union of houses, eh?'

Jane laughed, and they spent the rest of supper excitedly talking about their new plans.

It was a respite to see his betrothed, but by the next morning his mind was again fixed on George Barnard. He decided to go see Jenkins at Scotland Yard and have a talk with him about it all.

Jenkins would be the third person Lenox took into his confidence on the subject of George Barnard, after McConnell and Dallington, when previously only he and Graham had known. Part of him doubted the wisdom of this, but another part of him was glad that he could unburden himself of this obsession that had so weighed on his spirit.

He sent back word for Jenkins through the long corridors of Scotland Yard, and soon the young inspector came to fetch him.

'How is the mood here?' asked Lenox, 'About Exeter?'

'Nine parts frantic for every part sad. Everyone down to the lad selling newspapers is half mad trying to figure it out. It's an intolerable state of affairs – doing more harm than good, I reckon. Speaking of which, did you visit Carruthers's rooms, as we discussed?'

'Yes, I did, as a matter of fact. It's why I came to speak to you.'

'Oh?'

Lenox then explained the entire convoluted history of his suspicion of Barnard; he tried to be concise and complete but found himself rambling slightly. He could see the doubt on his interlocutor's face.

Jenkins sighed heavily when Lenox had finished. 'George Barnard?' he said at length, rather quizzically. 'Why are you telling me this theory?'

'At some moment, now or in the future, I may ask you to arrest him. I hope that you'll do so without hesitation and let the explanations come after. Our window of opportunity may be small indeed, when we find it.'

'He's a public figure, Lenox.'

'So was Attila the Hun.'

Jenkins laughed. 'You've rarely led me astray, of course, but – well, here's one thing – why Smalls? We've got such a plausible link between Smalls and Poole. Doesn't it seem more likely that it was a straight transaction between them than … well, than what?'

'After all, don't you see – it would have been so foolish for Poole to kill both Carruthers and Pierce, two men who were eternally linked by nothing except his father!'

'That does strike me as your most probable argument,' said Jenkins, 'but then why would Smalls willingly kill Simon Pierce?'

Here was a question that he could answer, thankfully. 'The Hammer Gang,' he said. 'As I said, they're linked to Barnard. It was to frame Poole.'

'Smalls hadn't a Hammer Gang tattoo, I'm sure of that. The hammer above the eyebrow – ugly thing.'

'I think Barnard may have recruited somebody new to the gang, in an effort to be particularly careful. Smalls didn't have a tattoo' – here Lenox paused to explain the words *No green* – 'and he was ultimately disposable.'

'Who do you think killed him?'

Lenox shrugged. 'At any time there are half a dozen of the Hammers floating in and out of New-gate – one of them would have done it, I imagine.'

'Very tidily, too,' said Jenkins skeptically.

'I'm sure the idea was Barnard's. If only we could find his liaison within the gang – for it's surely impossible that he knows more than one or two of them.'

'Smalls, then? Just did it for money? Or to be initiated?'

'Both, to be sure. There was something else as well.'

'Yes?'

'Mrs. Smalls told me that she was only months away from debtors' prison. A hundred-pound debt, which she could never have paid, and Hiram wiped it clear in one moment. That's what she said. Barnard must have used Smalls's mother as leverage over the man.'

'Yes,' said Jenkins thoughtfully.

'Hence the cryptic clues – the note, the stack of coins,' said Lenox. 'If he came right out and said anything that might save his skin, his mother would go straight to prison. The clues were a kind of insurance.'

'It hangs together, I suppose,' said Jenkins, 'but most importantly, Lenox, I don't understand what Barnard's motive for all this mayhem might have been.'

Lenox had been afraid of having to address this. 'I'm not entirely sure, to be honest. In general I believe it's because Barnard's whole criminal career was somehow in danger of being exposed. I think Carruthers may have been blackmailing Barnard. He wrote an article about the Mint, which I just read again – it doesn't contain any revelations, but Carruthers might have found something.'

Jenkins looked skeptical. 'That's all? What about Exeter? Pierce?'

'Pierce was cover, I told you, a red herring. Carruthers was the true target.'

'If only there was any proof beyond your word.'

Lenox pulled his valise onto his lap. 'Here are the newspaper articles Carruthers kept about G. Farmer. Read over them?'

'Certainly.'

'Look, more importantly,' he said, handing the younger man a sheet of paper, 'here's the dossier I put together.'

Jenkins studied it. Halfway down the page, he said in a quiet sort of yelp, 'My God! Half of the unsolved crimes in our files are on this sheet of paper!'

'I know.'

'He must be ungodly rich.'

'You were at his house, before Exeter replaced you on that case,' said Lenox.

Jenkins looked up sharply. 'There's the question, I suppose. Why did he kill Exeter?'

Ruefully Lenox shook his head. 'I wish I knew.'

CHAPTER FORTY-THREE

The case went slowly, very slowly indeed; for two days nothing happened. Lenox passed his hours not in any traditional pursuit of George Barnard but by sitting in the British Library's Reading Room and going back through old newspapers, reading every article he could find by Winston Carruthers. It was dry work indeed, and worse still it was unproductive. Eventually he gave up.

On the afternoon of the second day he was sitting in his library at home, having a cup of tea and a sandwich, when Dallington arrived at the front door. Graham showed him in.

'I've some news,' the young aristocrat said, his face lined with fatigue but also bright with excitement. 'It's about Barnard.'

The butler started for the door.

'Stay, Graham,' said Lenox. 'Do you mind?' he asked the lad.

'No – at least – no,' said Dallington, slightly puzzled.

'Graham is my oldest comrade in arms against George Barnard, as I mentioned to you once before.'

'Of course, then.'

'What have you discovered?' asked Lenox.

'Barnard has been emptying his bank accounts.'

There was a moment of silence. 'How could you possibly have discovered that?' Lenox asked.

'I went to the banks and looked at Barnard's accounts, of course.'

Lenox laughed. 'How?' he asked.

'I went in to look at my accounts and tipped the teller a few pounds to bring me Barnard's papers as well as my own. It seems he emptied the two accounts I saw of all his ready money – several hundred pounds – although his investments still deposit there.'

'The banker wasn't reluctant to do that, sir?' Graham asked with some astonishment.

'What? Oh, I see what you mean!' Dallington laughed heartily, still pacing the room. 'No, you don't understand, I'm afraid.'

'What don't we understand? It seems profoundly unlikely,' said Lenox. 'Banks aren't known for their accessibility.'

Dallington laughed again. 'You must understand – for years I've been poaching out of my parents' accounts. Since I was thirteen or so. I know all the most corrupt men at the bank.'

'You amaze me, John!'

Dallington waved a hand. 'Nothing too heavy – a quid here or there, you know.'

'I see.' Lenox couldn't help but smile. 'So, then, you knew which man to visit?'

'Yes! I only thought of it this morning. I told them it was fearfully important and acted very hushed and secretive, and you know they like to pal around with a duke's son.'

'I can't help but disapprove,' Lenox said, but still with a smile on his face. 'At any rate, it was well done.'

Quietly Graham said, 'That must mean Mr.

277

Barnard has fled to Geneva for good.'

'Yes, perhaps,' said Lenox, now furrowing his brow, 'and perhaps it means he felt some imminent danger. From Winston Carruthers, from Hiram Smalls, from Exeter. Graham, do something for me, would you?'

'Of course, sir.'

'Go to Barnard's house in Grosvenor Square and see what's happening there, whether the servants have remained, whether the upper floors are shut. It's such a massive place that if he's really left it for good they may still be in the middle of closing it.'

'Very good, sir. The usual method?'

Graham had a tenderly cultivated skill for quick friendship with fellow servants. Lenox had often asked him to employ it on a case's behalf. 'Yes, precisely,' said the detective.

Graham left, and Dallington and Lenox sat silent for some time, Lenox staring into the fire and contemplating Barnard's actions.

Suddenly Dallington burst into speech. 'Listen, Lenox – I want to apologize. I came to you in the absolute certainty that my friend – my acquaintance, whom if I acknowledge it I only knew briefly – was innocent, and I was wrong.'

Lenox waved a dismissive hand. 'You're young,' he said. 'There are many lessons before you, some harder than this one.'

'I doubt that.'

'Well, perhaps not. I think in our first case together you had such great success – in fact, saved my life – that it must have seemed easy to you. All too often things are blurry, though, John. It's the way of the world. Humans are blurry creatures,' said Lenox. 'Now – did you learn anything else at all about Barnard's last few weeks?'

With a scowl, Dallington shook his head. 'Not much. He was as upright as a parson the whole time. In his house, at his club, at his office–'

'Office?'

'In the Mint. He kept an office after he left – insisted on it, to smooth the transition to the next fellow, he said.'

'Did he see anybody?'

'Not to speak of. He had been to one or two parties.'

'He went to Geneva without any notice?'

'Yes, apparently – or on short notice. Announced he would go in the morning and left a few hours later.'

There was a noise at the door then, followed by footsteps in the hallway. Dallington and Lenox exchanged a look, then stared at the closed library door, waiting for it to open.

'Where is Mary?' said Lenox irritably after a moment had passed.

Dallington stood up and peeked out of the door.

'Good God, there's a chap in your hallway who looks as if he might eat glass for a lark,' said the young lord in an urgent whisper. 'Head like a walnut.'

Lenox laughed and stood up. 'That must be Skaggs.'

'Who the devil is Skaggs?'

'You'll see. Very useful chap, quite intelligent.' Lenox went to the door and called out, 'You must come into the library, Mr. Skaggs! Would you like a cup of tea? This is John Dallington, by the way.'

'Something stronger wouldn't go amiss,' said Skaggs, shaking hands with Dallington and Lenox. 'Been cold.'

'How about a glass of brandy?'

Skaggs nodded approvingly.

'Do you have any news?' Lenox asked, walking to the sideboard where he kept his liquor. 'It seems to us that Barnard has been acting strangely. John, I hired Mr. Skaggs to trail George Barnard to Geneva.'

'Nothing strange at all,' said Skaggs, accepting a glass of brandy and sitting. 'Well, except one thing.'

'Yes?'

'Mr. Barnard never went to Geneva.'

'What!' said Dallington.

'No. In fact, I very much doubt he left London,' said the investigator, a small, triumphant smile on his face.

'How did you draw these conclusions?' asked Lenox.

'It was simple enough to check on his travel out of the country. There's no doubt that he left by his own carriage for Felixstowe, from which he was to take a ferry south, but he wasn't on any of the company's passenger lists, and nobody who took a first class cabin answered to his description. He hadn't hired a boat privately, either, according to the local operators.'

'He might have done any of these things under a false name, however,' said Dallington.

Lenox shook his head. 'Why? He spread it far and wide that he was going to Geneva. No reason to cover his trail, was there?'

'Moreover, I wired to Geneva – I haven't had to go, because there was plenty of evidence on these shores – and he never arrived at the conference he was meant to attend,' Skaggs said.

'He might have gone anywhere on the Continent.'

'If he had left Felixstowe,' said Skaggs. 'He might have gone to another port, though again, why go to the trouble of doing that? No, I firmly believe he never left England. Or London, for that matter. I think he took his carriage to the edge of town, so that everyone could see he had left, turned around, and came home with the curtains drawn over the windows. Even at night, perhaps.'

'Surely he's in the countryside, then?' asked Dallington.

'London,' said Skaggs stubbornly.

'Why don't you believe he left the city?'

Skaggs smiled. 'Horseshoes.'

'What do you mean?' Lenox asked.

'I visited his stables. His horses' shoes haven't been changed for two weeks, I discovered in the course of an idle chat with the groom, and when I picked up one of their hooves there was practically no wear on the shoe. They haven't traveled more than a few miles, I'd reckon.'

'Wonderfully done,' said Lenox, smiling.

Rather dismally, Dallington said, 'I've much to learn, I see.'

'Why would he have pretended to leave town?' asked Lenox thoughtfully.

After half an hour or so in which the three men discussed the subject, Skaggs left, gracefully accepting Lenox's compliments, and shortly there-after Graham returned from Barnard's nearby house, flushed red with the cold.

'Well?' Lenox asked.

'It's completely dark, sir, the house. Only two maids are there, who will stay until the new tenant arrives.'

'New tenant?'

'Ah – the most consequential part of it, sir – Mr. Barnard has sold his house. The staff under-stood that he was retiring permanently to the country and have been telling all visitors as much. They have been packing his things for the past several days.'

The idea of Barnard living outside of London was laughable – it was his home and his solace, the center of his spiderweb, and he despised the northern life he had sloughed off when he came to the metropolis to make a success of himself.

Why, then, between Geneva and the country, was he trying so hard to persuade everybody that he was gone forever?

The three men sat and discussed it for some time before finally agreeing that they would reconvene in the morning. Lenox felt discouraged; it all seemed so opaque.

Then, in the middle of the night, long after Dallington's departure, Lenox woke out of a dream and sat bolt upright.

Suddenly he understood it all.

Barnard had insisted on keeping an office in the Mint, according to Dallingon, but why would he have wanted to, unless–

'Of course,' said the detective softly. 'It's the

only reason he took the job in the first place, I'd wager. The cunning fox.'

He stood up and hurriedly began to throw on clothes, in the absolute certainty that even at that moment, George Barnard was somewhere amid the wide corridors and large offices of the Royal Mint—

Robbing it.

CHAPTER FORTY-FOUR

Lenox was peering down the long, narrow stairs that led to the basement and the servants' quarters. He had rung a bell as soon as he woke and heard noises below.

'Graham? Graham?'

'Sir?'

'Come here!'

'Just a moment, sir.'

'Hurry!'

Poor Graham, who was a deep sleeper, struggled as quickly as he could to fit into a suit and appeared a moment later.

'Yes, sir?'

Lenox explained.

'What do you propose to do, sir?'

'Go there, of course! Don't be daft! I need you to go fetch Jenkins – there's not a moment to lose!'

'Yes, sir. Are you certain that you wouldn't prefer to wait for the inspector?'

'No,' said Lenox. 'It will be dawn in two hours,

and Barnard'll only feel comfortable working at night – probably he's been there every night since he supposedly left for Geneva. I only hope he isn't gone already.'

'Are you certain of all this, sir?'

'Of course I am – he wants to make one last fortune before he leaves London, Graham. And I was also thinking as you dressed, do you remember that I found all of the articles under Barnard's file in that pub?'

'Yes, sir.'

'One of them was about the history of the building, the layout and architecture! What if Barnard asked Carruthers to write that article, as a way of obtaining the information without asking for it himself?'

'Perhaps, sir,' said Graham doubtfully.

'Oh, bother – listen, I know it! I know his mind! He won't be easily able to extricate his investments if he disappears, which he's evidently chosen to do in a great hurry, and every fiber of his being will be yearning for more money! I know his mind, I tell you!'

'Yes, sir. I shall be close behind you.'

'Will you get my brown leather kit?'

'Of course, sir.'

It was a long ride east, just past Tower Bridge, to get to the Royal Mint Court in East Smithfield, and Lenox spent it contemplating the Thames through his window and slowly rubbing out the imperfections of his reasoning until it was satisfactory to him. His mind was roiling with possibilities.

At length he told his driver to stop, one street

short of his destination, and walked the rest of the way. He stopped when he saw the broad facade of the Mint; it was a long building made of limestone, with a high, stately arch at its center, a building that managed to seem at once distinguished and entirely uninteresting. A black wrought-iron gate, firmly clasped shut, stood between its courtyard and Lenox on the sidewalk. He began to walk the fence, looking for a point of access.

The Royal Mint held an exalted place in the history of England, and it had been a great pride of Barnard's to know its history inside and out. It was Alfred the Great who had first gathered in hand the muddled system of moneyers' workshops in Anglo-Saxon times and founded the London Mint, in 886. By 1279 the Mint was firmly entrenched in the safest single place in England – the Tower of London, where it remained for five centuries. In 1809 it had moved to a vast, golden-stoned building in East Smithfield, where it stood regal, imposing, and remarkably well guarded.

It had been a coup for George Barnard to attain the post of Master, which was traditionally held by a great scientist or an aristocrat – and occasionally, as in his case, by an important politician. (The leader of Lenox's party in the House of Commons now, William Gladstone, had been one of these, Master of the Mint from 1841 to 1845.) The greatest of these Masters had been Isaac Newton, who held the post for nearly thirty years, until his death.

Yet now what a threat it was under! Lenox had assumed even after he began to suspect Barnard's nefariousness that the Mint was the one sanctified aspect of his life, his own fortress of immortality.

It seemed, however, nothing was inviolable.

Lenox had some idea of what it was like inside; he had never entered it himself, but when he had asked Graham to do his research on Barnard, Lenox had conducted his own about the Mint's building and the Master's place in it. At the Devonshire Club he had asked old Baron Staunton, a distinguished Liberal politician who'd sat in Parliament for many years but had once been Master himself, about the place – all ostensibly in the guise of polite interest but in fact with keen attention to Staunton's rather rambling and sentimental reminiscences. Thus Lenox knew that the machines and the money they made were kept in the lower floors, under heavy guard, and that the upper levels of the building contained the Mint's offices. He'd also learned that the Master's office itself had a view of the Thames, which meant it'd be situated toward the western part of the building.

Then again, Staunton had been Master twenty years ago, and as he walked Lenox felt a twinge of anxiety; it could be that all of his information was out of date.

At last he concluded that there was nothing for it but to shimmy up and over the gate. He had in his right hand a doctor's kit bag, the one he had asked Graham for, a battered pebbled leather case with an ivory handle that unclasped in the middle. It was light but spacious, and he had had it since he was twenty-four.

He set this down beside him and pulled from it

a long, stout piece of string, which he tested by quickly jerking it in the middle with both hands. Satisfied, he made a loop at one end and after several attempts managed to hook it on one of the (unpleasantly sharp-looking) spikes that lined the top of the fence. He tossed his bag over the fence and with a deep breath pulled himself over.

It was sweaty work, and he slipped back to the ground twice, but eventually he just managed to make it to the other side. He quickly pulled the rope down (he had loosened it when he was coming over the fence) and packed it carefully away in his kit before stealing across the empty courtyard to the grand, dark building itself.

At the front of the building was a series of heavy black doors, but Lenox knew he stood a better chance of gaining access through a side door and, trying to minimize the clack of his shoes on the stones, began to look around the perimeter. About halfway around he found something promising – a white door marked CARETAKER that had a window at eye level. If worse came to worst, he could break the window, but he didn't want to make the noise.

Instead he opened his case again and took two small tools from it. Fortune was on his side; it was an old-fashioned lock, and within about a minute he had managed to jiggle it open. As he had expected, it wasn't impossibly hard to break into the building (and a good detective, as he had once said to Graham, always needs to be in some small part a good housebreaker, too).

He imagined the vaults would be a different story.

With slow, careful steps he walked up the stair-way in front of the door, ignoring the caretaker's closet to the left. At the top of the stairway was another door, and opening it he found himself in a wide, marble-floored corridor, which he saw in the dim moonlight was of regal bearing, with busts of past Mint officials and portraits of past monarchs along the walls.

He paused, suddenly slightly discouraged. He hadn't any clue how many night guards there were here, or what their beats were, and he hadn't any clue either where he would find George Barnard. Or *if* he would find George Barnard. Somehow in his own bed it had seemed so intuitive, so correct, that the man would return to the place he had been most comfortable. The illusion of fleeing London had seemed to dovetail so well with his insight – and the fact of his keeping an office here – his long history of thievery – his emptied bank accounts.

Now, however, it all seemed insubstantial, even implausible.

His nerves on edge, Lenox stepped into the hallway. He had worn his soft-soled boots, which were much quieter than his others, but he still made noise. Walking west down the corridor, toward where he knew the Master's office to be, he stopped to examine the brass nameplates on each of the doors of the nicest offices. None of them bore a name he knew, and he decided to turn left at the corner.

Suddenly, he heard a soft whistling.

He froze and then pressed himself tight up against the wall. The sound drew closer and closer, coming toward him, and soon he saw coming from the corner he had meant to turn a guard, clad in black.

Just as this guard was about to discover the Mint's intruder, however, he abruptly stopped. Lenox saw him check his watch and turn on his heel to walk in the other direction.

His heart blazing, the detective forced himself to gulp deep breaths of air and steady his frayed nerves. He let one minute pass, then two minutes, then three. Finally he decided to go.

Just as he stepped away from the wall, an arrogant, cultivated voice spoke.

'Charles Lenox!' said the voice with a smile in it. 'Now what on earth could you be doing here?'

Lenox turned, his hands raised.

The security guard stood there – and beside him the man who had spoken. George Barnard.

CHAPTER FORTY-FIVE

'Couldn't sleep,' said Lenox with the hint of a smile, his hands still raised. 'Thought I'd go for a walk.'

'I can't congratulate you on the place you chose for it,' said Barnard, hands clasped behind his back.

Lenox decided to speak to the guard directly. 'I'm here on behalf of the police,' he said. 'Mr. Barnard is wanted at Scotland Yard.'

The guard made no move, and Barnard laughed

hollowly. 'Who do you think hired this gentleman, Charles? Use your intelligence. Half of the people who work in this building owe their jobs to me.' He paused. 'It's disappointing that you've found me so soon. I thought I had several weeks.'

'You should have had your horseshoes changed after you pretended to go to Geneva,' said Lenox.

Barnard didn't respond to this. 'Well, we shall speak soon enough. Westlake, take this man up to my office. I'll be there in fifteen minutes. If you want any tea, Charles, let Westlake know.' He chuckled. 'Must maintain the civilities, eh?'

Barnard's office was small and graceful, with a beautiful view of the Thames, exactly the sort of office – second best in the building, perhaps third – that an emeritus director would have wanted. There were coinage charts on the walls, and a long bookcase was full of volumes on recondite subjects: a history of the shilling coin, the memoir of an old currency designer.

Lenox had time to examine all of this as he and the crooked guard sat in the office, which was lit only very dimly by a single, muted lamp. He wasn't tied up, and he still had his bag at his side. If he could get into it, then perhaps...

Barnard appeared in the doorway and dismissed Westlake to the hall. He sat in the chair behind his desk and poured himself a stiff Scotch. He offered Lenox a glass, which was declined.

Barnard was a bluff, large man, with pink coloring and a bristle of the straw-colored hair older men who have been blond in their youths develop. He had a strong chin and eyes that seemed slightly too small for his head but were

290

undeniably sharp and intelligent. His dress tended to be pompous, if not showy, and at the moment he had on an immaculately tailored suit, which managed nonetheless to look secondhand and lived-in, comfortable. He was usually the liveliest and loudest man in the room, with a blunt, bullying manner, but now he seemed suddenly sunken, diminished.

There was a long, long silence, during which the two men very frankly observed each other – rivals and enemies for more than a year, though only one of them had known it all that time, now finally face-to-face, both in full cognizance of the stakes. Their lives.

Finally, after a great, heaving sigh, Barnard asked Lenox, 'How did you know?'

Lenox didn't know what to say; he could play his cards close to the vest, or he could tell Barnard everything. Did it matter? If he did the latter, he might make time for Jenkins to come. For he felt certain Barnard planned to kill him.

'Poole confessed to me, in fact, the other–'

'No, no,' said Barnard. 'That's all immaterial. How did you know about – about all of it?'

'All of it?' said Lenox.

'Listen, Poole would never have implicated me. I beat it into him day and night that there was nothing worse than a rat. Think about his father! He confessed to the Yard – only to *you* did he admit that I was his friend, or that I was involved.'

'Why should there be anything else?' asked Lenox. 'The murders aren't enough?'

'Ever since that damn maid died in my house... I'm not stupid, Lenox. I could see in your eyes

291

the revulsion you felt, feel it in your handshake, after that. Still I figured I had time... I thought I had time. I covered my tracks so well.' Barnard took a sip and sighed again, the sigh of a man at a crucial moment of his life, who knows that nothing can be as it was. 'How did you know?'

'It's a difficult question to answer. I knew you stole that money, back then, and suddenly – well, nobody ever quite knew how you got your money, George, and I somehow doubted it was your first theft, especially because I knew you were connected to the Hammer Gang. I have since you set those two Hammers to thrash me, when you wanted me to stop looking into the maid's murder. Their tattoos gave them away.'

'You knew that?' asked Barnard, astonished. 'I thought you might have an inkling – I told them again and again they should never get those laughable tattoos. Why mark yourself for what you are?' It was a philosophy that encapsulated Barnard's rise through the world. 'You knew about the Hammers and me?' he repeated.

'Yes.'

'Then a man died in vain.'

Lenox felt his stomach plummet. 'Exeter found out?'

Barnard nodded. Almost casually, he pulled open a drawer of his desk and pulled a gun out of it.

'That's why he died in the East End near the gang's base.'

'Yes.'

Lenox felt sick. 'Then – why haven't you killed me? I knew worse than he did.'

'You're a gentleman,' said Barnard. 'I couldn't kill a gentleman. A journalist, a police officer, perhaps – if it were crucial.'

Lenox almost laughed. Saved at the last by Barnard's snobbishness; saved at the last by Barnard's insecurity about his own tenuous relations to the upper class of his nation. It was remarkable how a brilliant mind could in one aspect have been so blind.

'Yet you mean to now?'

Barnard seemed to sense Lenox's incredulousness and bridle against it. 'Then there was a practical side to it. If I killed you I felt sure that letters would be instantly dispatched to the proper authorities. That what proof you had against me would be laid out – that – well, any of the ruses a clever man would have devised to ensure either his own safety or his enemy's downfall.'

Lenox nodded. 'You were right there, but why not flee sooner, George?'

'I knew you weren't the precipitate sort. You would tease out whatever information you could until you were certain. I knew I had time. More time, if it weren't for Carruthers and Exeter. It was those two who ... hastened my plans, shall we say.'

Here they came to it. 'Why did they die?' asked Lenox in a carefully neutral voice, inviting the confidence of the man with the gun.

Barnard laughed. 'You're awfully good, you know. I quite forgot for a moment that we were anything other than old acquaintances. No, it's not important.' Suddenly he became business-like, 'Look, in' – he checked his pocket watch – 'in fifteen minutes this will be over. Here's some paper. Why not write a note to Jane?'

Lenox felt a wave of panic that almost prostrated him; he thought in sudden succession of his brother, of his childhood, of his little house on Hampden Lane, and above all of Jane – and suddenly life seemed so dear and so wonderful that he would have done anything to hold on to it.

'Simon Pierce – that was to mislead the Yard?'

Barnard laughed yet again and checked his watch. 'Yes, of course,' he said.

'How did you find out that Carruthers and Pierce had both been witnesses against Jonathan Poole?'

'Carruthers told me. He was a fearful talker, you know. Told me the first time we ever met, practically. Trying to impress me.'

'He was the real target, then? Carruthers?'

'Yes,' said Barnard. 'Of course.' He looked uneasy. 'I never heard much good of Pierce, either.'

'Hiram Smalls was trying to become a Hammer?'

'Yes.'

'His mother's debt?'

This unnerved Barnard. He had been speaking in a rather bored way, but now he looked at Lenox inquiringly. 'How much do you know?' he said.

'Some.'

'I didn't kill anyone, of course.'

'Of course. Only your proxies did.'

'Well – but that's important. Gerald Poole was a crazed young man.'

'Who happened to run into Martha Claes, a tavernkeeper from his adolescence.'

'Now, how in damnation do you know that?'

'From Poole,' said Lenox. He decided to be as honest as possible. It might unsettle Barnard; might buy time.

'Well, there's no use denying that I had a hand in all of it.'

'Why Carruthers, George? What did he suddenly discover?'

Barnard looked at Lenox, again with that smirk. 'He found out I was going to rob the Mint. Found out I was going to leave England.'

'How?'

Barnard laughed. 'It's funny, isn't it,' he said. 'Life, I mean. He found out because of an article I paid him to write. I needed some research on the architecture of this place and didn't dare ask for it myself. I must have overplayed my hand with him. Asked him about getting in and out of here unnoticed. He twigged to it and challenged me face-to-face with what he suspected.'

'He threatened to expose you?'

'Yes,' said Barnard. 'Unless I paid him.'

'Why didn't you?'

'I would have. He knew too much, though.'

Suddenly a man in a low black cloth cap came in. 'Ready,' he said, not sparing a glance for Lenox.

Barnard did, however, and grinned. 'Coins are awfully heavy things,' he said, almost as if he were showing off.

'Notes?' said Lenox.

'White notes are quite lovely. We meant to come back tomorrow night, too, but why be greedy?' He laughed loudly and then turned back to his man.

A dozen years ago, the pound and two-pound notes of England had been handwritten; now they were printed in black on the front, with a blank white back. They would be infinitely more portable, of course. With any concerted effort Barnard might make off with a hundred thousand pounds, enough to make his entire career of thievery irrelevant by comparison.

'Don't do this, George,' said Lenox.

Barnard ignored him. 'All loaded?' he said.

'Yes, sir.'

Then all of a sudden two things happened.

In the hallway a voice – Jenkins's voice – shouted, 'Lenox! Where are you? The building is surrounded, Mr. Barnard!'

Lenox, taking advantage of the surprise and consternation on the faces of Barnard and his compatriot, pulled from his leather kit bag a tiny, pearl-handled revolver, which held one bullet – and shot George Barnard, certain that it would have been the other way around if he waited a moment longer.

CHAPTER FORTY-SIX

Barnard shouted, 'Run!' and, clutching his stomach, turned and bolted before Lenox could reload.

The two men sprinted away, and Lenox got to his feet, reloaded the tiny gun, and started after them. Jenkins's loud footsteps were pounding toward the noise, and at the door to Barnard's office the two men met.

'That way!' said Lenox.

It was to no avail. They searched the building's every hall, and in two or three minutes police constables were swarming the place. They found nothing, other than a vault left half open.

Lenox and Jenkins went out to the courtyard, where Graham was waiting. A trio of constables rushed to Jenkins and reported that they had found nothing.

'Damn it!' said Jenkins, looking hopelessly in every direction. 'They've simply vanished! We had men on every block, at every exit! Where on earth did they go?'

'They must still be in the building,' said one of the constables.

Suddenly Lenox saw it. 'No,' he said. 'The river. They've gone by boat.'

'Are you sure?'

'I am. Carruthers's article about the Mint – all the hidden passageways. It's like the Tower of London. There must be a tunnel or a gate leading directly onto the water.'

'Christ,' muttered Jenkins. 'We must put in for a boat from the Yard.'

'There's no time for that,' said Lenox. 'Will you lend me two men?'

'Of course,' said Jenkins. 'What do you mean to do?'

'For a dozen reasons they can only be headed east, out of town, rather than west and back through the heart of London. We'll follow them.'

'Why are you so sure they're going east?'

Impatiently Lenox ticked off the reasons. 'The Thames is only a few hundred yards wide in London – they'd be far too conspicuous. They'll

297

want to unload somewhere quiet – again east. Barnard as much as admitted he's leaving England – the eastern coast.'

As if by confirmation of all this, a constable came sprinting toward Jenkins and breathlessly told him that Barnard and his men had been spotted on a makeshift barge but that it was already out of sight.

'Two men?' said Lenox.

'I'm coming, too,' said Jenkins. 'Althorp, you stay here and manage the men. Send a team down east in a carriage to look for the barge and track their progress. I'm coming, Lenox.'

'As am I,' said a voice behind them in the courtyard.

It was Dallington.

'How did you discover us?' asked Lenox.

Dallington laughed. 'I have to confess – I followed Jenkins. My man was watching the Yard. I couldn't stand being outside of things. Where are we going?'

There was no time to be upset with Dallington, and in a way Lenox admired his pluck. Soon they had organized a small party, and, running the short distance to the river, Lenox found the smallest, quickest skiff he could, cut it loose, and left Graham behind with money to pay its owner. He, Jenkins, Dallington, and two constables boarded the skiff and instantly started to push out into the wide, rippling Thames.

For twenty minutes there was nothing. They took turns poling the lively little bark down the river, sticking close to the side and peering keenly forward.

'Damned cheek,' said Dallington indignantly. 'To think of him stealing from the Mint!'

'It's the brazenest sainted thing I ever heared o',' said one of the constables, his voice almost tinged with admiration.

'He was the only man in the nation who could have pulled it off,' said Jenkins anxiously. 'Before this is all over you have to explain it to me, Charles.'

'Yes,' murmured Lenox. He was less full of chat than the others; he had not thirty minutes before shot a man with whom he had shared port, at whose table he had dined, with whom he had played cards. He hoped passionately that they might catch him, but also that Barnard might still be alive when they did.

Dawn began to glimmer and rise. It came first as a lightening above the horizon, and then the dark pulled back to reveal a pink and purple range of clouds. It was bitterly cold on the water.

Then they came around a bend in the river and saw it, as big as life.

It was a small red barge, which sat low in the water; it had pulled to the left side of the river now, where a sandy embankment threatened to ground it. The barge's virtue was readily apparent – four small but very heavy-looking crates stood at the edge of the deck, next to a ramp that extended from its side.

There were five men on deck. Barnard was sitting against the cabin's outer door, directing the others with his left hand, clutching his right to his stomach. The other four men were engaged in stopping the boat and readying the crates to be off-loaded.

It was a good location, lying as it did in the fields between two villages, only two miles east of London's outer limits; for all Lenox knew, Barnard might have bought these fields. There was a dray cart with two horses before it standing on the bank and a single man in black holding their reins.

'The devil,' said Dallington under his breath.

'I'll call to him,' said Jenkins.

'No,' Lenox quickly interjected. 'He hasn't seen us yet. Stop poling.'

It was true. Their skiff was floating along the opposite side of the river, and the men on the barge were so absorbed in their work that they hadn't noticed the only other boat in sight.

'Look,' Dallington offered, 'the hammer above that chap's eyebrow.'

'Indeed,' said Jenkins quietly. 'George Barnard and the Hammer Gang. It will make for a tidy arrest.'

Lenox nodded but had a grim feeling it might not be so simple. 'Pole along this bank, and then we'll run over there as quickly as we can, try to catch them by surprise.'

Soon they had done it, and the two constables were rowing as hard as they could where it was too deep to pole the skiff along. 'You have a pistol?' Lenox asked Jenkins.

'Yes, I brought–'

Then a cry went up on the barge. They had seen the skiff, and Barnard, his face both livid and shocked, began to shout at them. Twenty yards off, Lenox heard him yell, 'Leave the last crate! Get me off of here!'

This close Lenox saw the hammer tattooed above the eyes of the men on the barge, and very fleetingly he thought of Smalls and his unfortunate mother.

A bullet cracked him back to attention; it came from Barnard, from the gun he had trained on Lenox at the Mint, and it splintered off a great chunk of the skiff's hull.

'Get down!' cried Jenkins.

Lenox reached over and pulled on Dallington's arm – the young man had been standing agog, staring at the barge – and shouted, 'Leave off the rowing! Fire back!'

Another bullet flew by them, this time whistling over their heads. A third took out part of the skiff's starboard side, crackling and singeing the wood there. All of these came from Barnard. Jenkins fired back, but the bullet skittered harmlessly over the river.

'We're taking on water,' said one of the constables.

'Hold on,' said Lenox. 'We can make it to the bank. Try to pull us under the barge, where they can't shoot at us.'

'Look!' said Dallington softly.

A fourth bullet hit the boat, only narrowly missing one of the constables, but then Barnard turned to stare at what the men on the skiff were looking at.

The four Hammers were in utter disarray. One of them was fleeing west, back toward London, sprinting as fast as he could. One was trying to lug Barnard off the boat to where the three crates rested (the fourth still stood on the deck of the barge). But it was the other two who were of the most interest. One of them had punched the driver of the dray in the face, and the two men were loading one of the crates onto the cart.

'Stop!' shouted Jenkins.

'Stop!' shouted Barnard almost simultaneously.

These were both excellent pieces of advice, no doubt, but they went unheeded. One of the two men was in the back of the cart, lovingly bracing the crates of white notes against the bumps to come in the road, while the other was furiously whipping the aged, stultified horses, who hadn't been especially perturbed by the gunshots and were only now drafted into motion by the blows on their flanks.

Soon the fourth Hammer, the one who had been helping Barnard, gave that up as a bad job. The third crate had cracked and split upon hitting the bank, and he ran to it and stuffed great thick chunks of money into his pockets and then ran off westward, too.

'Get them!' said Jenkins to the constables. The skiff was pulling up alongside the barge.

The two constables waded into the shallow water and started to run after the criminals. Barnard, meanwhile, had staggered off the boat and was filling his own pockets with money. He started to run east, but Dallington, spry and youthful, caught him almost instantly, tackling him to the ground, and a moment later Lenox and Jenkins had joined him.

Barnard was bleeding profusely, sweat upon his brow, and the impotent gun was still clutched in his hand.

'You're under arrest,' said Jenkins.

Suddenly everything seemed very quiet. The dray had turned behind a distant row of barns and gone out of sight. Lenox looked up and around him: the barge floating gently at the bankside; the skiff splintered and slowly sinking; the brilliant gold glimmer of light just coming up over the deep green fields and the gray, glossy water. It was beautiful.

'Lenox, you bastard,' said Barnard and fainted.

CHAPTER FORTY-SEVEN

'Why did he have Smalls killed?' asked Dallington. He, Jenkins, Graham, and Lenox were sitting in Lenox's library, gulping cup after cup of hot tea with milk and chewing on sweet rolls. It was much later, just past ten in the morning. For the past several hours the wheels of justice had unhurriedly cranked. The two men who had fled on foot were soon run down by the two constables from the skiff, and George Barnard was receiving medical attention as the entire police force buzzed about his identity and potential crimes. Still missing, on the other hand, were the pair of Hammers who had escaped in the dray cart. They had dropped one box of notes by the side of the road but still bore with them thousands of pounds. All across Britain and the Continent police forces were looking for them.

'Panic and caution,' Lenox answered, 'Exeter was releasing all of those cryptic, confident statements to the press, and Barnard must have felt the stakes were too high for much to depend on an untested man with uncertain allegiances, who had probably only killed Simon Pierce to clear his mother's debt.'

'Perhaps to enter the Hammer Gang as well,' Dallington added.

'Exeter,' murmured Jenkins thoughtfully, his coffee cup paused just before he was going to sip it.

The three men pondered their late colleague together; going through all their minds, no doubt, even Graham's, was some amalgam of pity, sorrow, and reminiscence. He hadn't been a perfect man, but he had been at heart a decent one, in over his head.

'Walk us through it all one time,' said Dallington. 'Won't you, Charles?'

So Lenox again told the narrative, beginning with the dead maid in George Barnard's house, which seemed like decades ago, and then running through Gerald Poole, through Ye Olde Cheshire Cheese, through Mr. Moon, through his emergency trip from Stirrington to London, and ending with his confrontation at the Mint, loosening for his friends the delicate threads that tied the whole nasty business together.

'Well,' said Jenkins at length, 'it's all fearfully complicated. We'll need to speak again, no doubt, but at the moment I must be off.'

'I'm going, too,' said Dallington. 'I'm dead tired.'

'Off to sleep?' asked Lenox.

Dallington shifted from one foot to the other. 'Newgate, actually.' He picked up his hat. The white carnation, the eternal marker of his compact dapperness, stood in his breast. 'Bye, then.'

The two men left, and only Graham and Lenox remained. 'He's going to see Gerald Poole, poor lad,' said Lenox.

'What will become of him, sir?'

'Of Poole? I don't know. I hope he doesn't hang for it, with all my heart.'

'Indeed, sir. If I might ask' – Graham spoke gingerly, his quick intelligence looking for the most delicate words – 'what are your plans? At the moment?'

Lenox laughed. It was typical of Graham's tact to ask an ambiguous question, one that might have been about either whether he wanted another cup of coffee or whether he was pulling up roots to pan for gold in the wilds of California.

'We were going to go to Morocco, weren't we?'

Indeed, they had intended to, although as it so often did in his life his wild imaginings about the journey he wanted to take had been blocked off by reality.

'Yes, sir, we had discussed it,' said Graham. 'Although if–'

'No,' said Lenox firmly. 'We must go. Have you bought the tickets? Spring, I think.' Aside from greatly anticipating the fun of the trip, the symbolism of it meant something to Lenox – a final bachelor jaunt, a final trip that the two friends, who had for twenty years seen each other nearly every day, could make together.

'Yes, sir.' Graham smiled. 'If you'll excuse me, I must return to the East End, sir, to see about the skiff.'

'Why don't you sleep first?'

'With your permission, I would rather go now, sir. I left a note at the pier but fear it may not be sufficient to quiet the owner's worry.'

'As you please, of course. You have enough to offer him? I jolly well hope there wasn't anything of his on board,' said Lenox. 'Here, take a bit more money.'

So Graham left, and Lenox, though tired, wished as soon as he was alone to see Lady Jane. He straightened his admittedly disarrayed habiliment and walked next door.

Jane was in her drawing room, perched upon her famous rose-colored sofa, having a cup of tea.

'Hello, Charles!' she said, greeting him. 'I'm so happy to see you.'

'You, too – happier than you know!'

'Oh? I've just woken up from the most wonderful rest, you can't imagine,' said Lady Jane, yawning in a self-consciously demure fashion, then laughing at herself.

'I'm glad of it. I, on the other hand, was shot at more than once last night.'

Lenox hastened to ease her mind, promising her that he had never been in real danger – which was, of course, something of a fib – and then explaining the entire strange circumstance of his encounter with George Barnard.

'Imagine it,' she said wonderingly. The shock was written on her face. 'One saw him everywhere. I daresay I've known him for a decade!'

306

'Yes,' said Lenox grimly. 'It's a bad business.'

'Thank goodness I was never close to him. I didn't accept, of course, but you know he wanted to marry me!'

'I can't entirely fault him for that, I must say.'

Lady Jane laughed and kissed Lenox on the cheek. 'You're a dear,' she said, though she still looked baffled, even slightly haunted, by the revelation of Barnard's character. 'Although, were you really safe?'

Over the next few days, the history of Inspector Jenkins's pursuit of George Barnard became public, and Barnard exchanged the name of the man who had murdered Inspector Exeter for the promise that he wouldn't die for his crimes. The instant and total hatred of the Hammer Gang was his other prize, and rumors of a fabulously large bounty on Barnard's head grew. He lived in deep solitude in Newgate Prison, allowing his food to come only in the hands of a certain waitress at a fashionable restaurant, refusing all visitors, and by all accounts rejecting any other kind of cooperation with the Yard.

The case became remarkably famous in a very short time; Lenox was just able to manage his absence from the reports, and in not very much time at all, perhaps seventy-two hours, Jenkins had been promoted to chief inspector, at least partly as a memorial to Inspector Exeter.

If there was a fallout in Fleet Street, it was nothing to the swift and ceaseless chatter of the upper classes, who moved between dinner parties in Belgravia and Berkeley Square, propelled out in the terrible cold only by a desire to commiserate with their friends over the late, despised George Barnard – for he could not have been more dead to them if he were dead.

'I never had him in *my* house,' sniffed many great ladies, though it must be owned that the great majority of them had. Meanwhile the men in their clubs chomped fretfully on cigars and said things like, 'Damn country is going to hell, been saying it for years. I expect the French to invade by the hour, I tell you,' which was very consoling and pleasant to contemplate.

George Barnard had, in fact, eventually become part of London's highest society. His ball, an annual event of great significance, had hosted royalty, and his country house in Surrey had given shooting to any number of dukes, who had fairly lined up in past years to slaughter his game. Yet he went entirely unmourned, for he had never precisely been one of them. As Lady Jane put it so succinctly, it was hard to see whether he reflected worse on them or they on themselves. The few people who couldn't help but own up to acquaintance with Barnard, because in better days they had drunk gallons of his champagne and sworn lifelong friendship with him, insisted strenuously that it had all been financial – that they had simply been friends 'in the City' – which was some marginal exoneration.

None of this concerned Lenox very much. He was constantly closeted with Jenkins, and sometimes Dallington and McConnell as well, and soon the assizes met. They convicted George Barnard and Gerald Poole within forty-eight hours of each other. The former would never leave prison; the latter was told he had to go to the colonies for a period of not less than fifteen years. The only people who saw him off at the dock were Dallington and one very old woman, who kept calling him by his father's name, Jonathan.

Martha Claes disappeared. She had promised to testify against Poole but had fled in the dark of the night, past – well, past a sleeping constable, who was situated outside of Carruthers's rooms and didn't hear her drag her family and their things out of the door. There was a watch for her on the train lines and at the ferry ports of the south coast, but eventually everyone concluded that one of the country's vast cities, Leeds or Liverpool or Birmingham or Bristol, had swallowed her and her family up and wouldn't regurgitate them any time soon.

Finally, it emerged that the poor, splintered skiff had been the property of a chap named Frank Pottle, who lived on the river, a junk and trash collector who found stuff along the Thames and fixed it to sell. Far from being angry, he was ecstatic that his property had been part of such excitement, and according to Graham, Pottle was the hero of every bankside pub in London; he hadn't bought himself a drink in several days. He received the money to replace his skiff with good grace (and in frankness it was more than the skiff was worth, which improved his outlook on the matter) but vowed that it would be put toward a different use – he wanted to open a gin bar and mingle the satisfactions of his personal life with those of a public career.

And so, Frank Pottle was happy.

CHAPTER FORTY-EIGHT

Now it was a month later.

Early February, and while the days were short and gray, and while those who tramped through London's streets longed for home, there was a happy glow to Lenox's life. His hours were taken up with warm fires, long books, slow suppers, his brother, and Lady Jane. He went out very little, and even when he did never commented to a soul about the downfall of George Barnard, choosing instead to focus on clearing up all of Barnard's myriad crimes by tracing them diligently through the cunning and subtle ways in which the man had pushed Winston Carruthers's work. The newspaper report of a fracas in some neighborhood, for instance, might dovetail nicely with a robbery several days later in the same area. It was the kind of deep research Lenox had loved since Oxford.

This morning, however, he was more pleasantly disposed, sitting in his library with Toto.

She had insisted on coming to him, although he had had his misgivings. 'I need to get out of that poky house,' she said, conveniently forgetting about its ten bedrooms, and so she sat now in his library, bent daintily over a small notebook she had been keeping about Jane and Lenox's honeymoon, her effervescent laugh ringing more and more often through the room.

It emerged from their tête-à-tête that Toto was

a furious negotiator on Jane's behalf and loved every moment of research and discussion about the honeymoon. She and Lenox complemented each other well. Every time he started to talk about local cash crops or cave art she would roll her eyes and return as soon as she could to the waterfall they had to visit, the dressmaker who was meant to be so clever.

'What do you think of Ireland?' Lenox asked.

Toto made a face. 'All those potatoes,' she said. 'Ugh.'

'It's meant to be beautiful, Toto. All that green! And the beautiful Irish babies!' Lenox halted.

'It's all right, Charles,' she said.

'No – it's – that was awfully tactless of me.'

'Charles, it's all right!' He saw that she was smiling shyly.

'Toto?'

'What?' she said innocently. Under his gaze, however, she soon broke down. Quietly she admitted, 'We're having a baby.'

A great weight lifted from Lenox's spirit. 'I'm so happy,' he said.

'We're being awfully silent about it,' she said, but then, breaking into a grin, went on, 'I am, too, though! How happy I am!'

'Is Thomas?'

'Yes, very, very happy, and the doctors say' – here she ran into the strictures of her age and couldn't say quite what she wanted – 'they say how healthy I am, and indeed I feel it! But Charles, you mustn't tell anybody. I've barely said a word about it, except to Jane and Duch.' Duch was the Duchess of Marchmain, Toto and Jane's

311

great friend. 'Thomas will tell you in due time.'

Rather sadly, Lenox remembered what her mien had been when she was first with child and bursting with baby names and nursery ideas.

They sat closeted for another half hour, talking about the honeymoon – Toto liked the idea of Greece – until McConnell came to fetch her, smiling broadly at Lenox, his face less troubled than usual, and walking his wife very carefully out of the house and down to their carriage.

After they had gone Lenox stood just inside the door, thinking about life, about its passing strangeness. He went back to his library to read a tract about the Catiline conspiracy.

Not half an hour later there was a knock at the front door, and he laid the pamphlet down.

Graham appeared. 'You have two guests, sir,' he said.

'Bring them in.'

A moment later the butler reappeared, with James Hilary and – to Lenox's astonishment – Edward Crook in tow.

'Crook!' he exclaimed, rising to his feet. 'I'm honored to have you here. Graham, fetch something to eat, would you, and drink? How do you do, Hilary? But Crook! I scarcely expected to see you accept my invitation to London so soon – which is not to say I'm not pleased that you have!'

'It isn't a visit of pleasure, in fact, Mr. Lenox,' said Crook. Lenox noticed the small gleam of a smile in the corner of his mouth.

'How do you mean?' asked Lenox.

Hilary and Crook glanced at each other, and it was the London man who spoke. 'Late yesterday evening Mr. Crook called on me. I must confess I was as astonished as you appear to be to see him, but he told me some interesting information.'

'I couldn't let go of that election,' said Crook. 'It seemed so unjust, after you and I had both worked so hard.'

'Mr. Crook went back over the rolls of the vote–'

'As any person in Stirrington could, by law,' Crook interjected rather pompously.

'He noticed that about a thousand more people had voted in the by-election than had ever voted before. Not that surprising, given that Stoke regularly ran unopposed – but certainly surprising, given that the number comprised about 95 percent of Stirrington's population.'

'The number of people in town has been decreasing, and it seemed altogether suspicious that 95 percent of them would vote,' said Crook.

Lenox scarcely dared to hope but said, 'What does all this mean?'

Again his two visitors glanced at each other, and again it was Hilary who spoke. 'As it happened, Mr. Crook recognized some six hundred names–'

'More than that.'

'Excuse me – more than six hundred names that *should not have been on the voter rolls*.'

'You see, Mr. Lenox, all six hundred of these voters were – are – dead!'

Hilary smiled. 'Can you guess for whom they voted, by any chance?'

Lenox flushed. 'Not–'

'That's right. Roodle.'

'The devil,' said the detective softly.

'Mr. Crook instantly lodged a complaint–'

'Instantly. Didn't want to get your hopes up, but I had to.'

Hilary paused. 'In any event, the complaint is pending, but we had a private talk with Roodle, who means to step down and–'

'We did it!' cried Crook. 'You're to be the Member for Stirrington!'

Hilary gave the large barman a wry look, then turned back to Lenox and said, 'Welcome to the House, Charles. I can't think of a fitter man to enter it.'

CHAPTER FORTY-NINE

Two weeks later it was the momentous afternoon when Lenox was to take his seat in Parliament. He was in his library, and occasionally the smack of a hammer sounded above; they were joining his house to Lady Jane's in anticipation of a marriage three months hence. The muted sound pleased him every time he heard it – the symbol of the thing, the jointure, made him happy.

The library he stood in was transformed by the letters and telegrams that lay on every surface, jammed in books, and stacked unread on the floor, all of which offered advice and some congratulations as well. He was dressed very nattily, he thought. His brother had ventured down to the kitchen to scrounge himself a cup of tea (something not strictly done in the best society, and which would no doubt send the staff into an anxious bout of indignation, but which the Lenox boys had done all their lives), and Lady Jane was standing with Lenox, adjusting his attire, giving him proud, happy little smiles, and generally bustling about in her useful way.

'Now, before you go I have a present for you,' she said.

Lenox smiled. 'You needn't have,' he said.

'Ah, but it was such fun! Here, look.'

It was a flat, square parcel, plainly a book, wrapped in patterned paper and tied with a blue ribbon Lenox recognized as usually belonging to her hair.

'What can it be?' he asked, slowly unwrapping it.

He saw that it was a smallish book, not longer than a hundred pages, bound in very supple brown Morocco leather. There was no title on it, only CHARLES LENOX embossed in gold in the lower right corner of the cover, and he flicked it open with his brow furrowed, slightly puzzled, though the smile remained on his lips.

'It's your father's speeches,' said Lady Jane softly. 'I had them bound.'

Suddenly he recognized what she had done.

For years Edmund and Charles's father's speeches from the House of Commons had been floating around in loose manuscripts. Each brother had a copy, Lenox House had one, and a few of the political clubs did, too. He had been a respected orator, if never among the chief of his party; the certainty of his seat and the lineage of his family ensured him that respect despite what were considered his eccentricities – a startling advocacy for the poor and the foreign, an indifference to British military pride, and a confidence unmatched by his peers in the power of the vote, which now seemed ahead of its time.

Lenox flipped through the thick cream-colored pages very gingerly now, each one a treasure. He turned to the front and saw the beautifully laid out title page, and opposite it a tintype likeness of his father's wonderful, kind, wise face.

He wanted to describe everything he felt to Lady Jane – he wanted to compliment the type, the effort, the secrecy, the speed with which she had had it made – but he found there was a lump in his throat, and to his shame tears stood in his eyes. He tried not to think of how much he missed his father, how much he missed always having someone to reassure him that the world would be all right – the desolation of his absence–

Jane, who always understood everything, kissed him on the cheek and held him for a moment longer than she usually did, and then made a great show of clearing a pile of telegrams off his desk.

'Are you going to give a speech?' she asked gaily.

He gave a choked laugh. 'Of course not,' he said. 'Not for ages.'

'My cousin Davey gave one on his very first day!'

This was the present Earl of St. Pancras, who was, unlike Lenox's father, genuinely eccentric. 'In the Lords, I remember. It was about how he didn't like strawberry jam.'

'Be nice, Charles! It was a speech about fruit importation, which I admit devolved into something of a tirade.' She couldn't help but laugh. 'Still, you could talk about something more important.'

'Than jam? Impossible. We mustn't set the bar too high, Jane.'

So they bantered until he was quite himself again and was ready to leave. Edmund emerged from downstairs gulping a cup of tea.

'Look what Jane has made, Ed,' Charles said, holding up the book.

'What is it? Oh, Pa's speeches? Yes, it's marvelous.'

'I used Edmund's version of them to have it made,' Jane explained. 'I have a dozen copies.'

'We sent one to the British Library,' said Edmund, 'and the library at Parliament. Come along, come along, we mustn't be late.'

Clutching his book in one hand, Lenox rode silently through the streets of London while Jane and Edmund talked. He was watching all of the people and places he saw with new eyes and with a profound sense of the burden of looking after his fellow men, a profound sense of the gravity of his new work.

The Members' entrance to the House was through a beautiful arched corridor, which led into an open courtyard and then into the chambers of governance. Never had the golden buildings of Parliament and Big Ben looked so momentous to Lenox, so majestic, as they did now against the backdrop of the river.

The Members themselves were a different matter. The courtyard was crowded by a series of glum, combative-looking gentlemen in black cloaks and very proper top hats. Small groups were deep in discussion, and only a few people looked up to say hello to Edmund, Lenox, and Jane as they came through the arch.

'We must leave you here, Jane,' said Lenox, 'but shall I come to visit you afterward?'

'I wouldn't forgive you if you didn't!'

'Oh – ah – I – I see a man,' said Edmund. 'Meet me by the door, Charles, Good-bye, Jane!'

Edmund went off commending himself on the extreme cunning of the maneuver (and it was perhaps for the best that he didn't notice their indulgent smiles trailing behind him) and stood off in a corner, waiting.

It was a beautiful courtyard, Edmund always thought. The light was falling through the high, old windows, the vivid lavender of winter evening, and he thought with contentment of going back to the country the next morning to see Molly and his boys. There was nothing he liked better than being married, and as he stole a glance at his brother and his old friend, Lady Jane, his heart filled with joy for them, and he pondered the vagaries of the world, which for all of its fault lines and difficulties could offer so much happiness sometimes, and often – as for his brother, who had so long lived as a bachelor, had so long struggled with the prejudice against his profession – often when you weren't even looking for it at all.

The publishers hope that this book has given you enjoyable reading. Large Print Books are especially designed to be as easy to see and hold as possible. If you wish a complete list of our books please ask at your local library or write directly to:

Magna Large Print Books
Magna House, Long Preston,
Skipton, North Yorkshire.
BD23 4ND

This Large Print Book for the partially sighted, who cannot read normal print, is published under the auspices of

THE ULVERSCROFT FOUNDATION